THE ACID TEST

Also by Élmer Mendoza in English translation

Silver Bullets (2015)

Élmer Mendoza

THE ACID TEST

Translated from the Spanish by
Mark Fried

MACLEHOSE PRESS
QUERCUS · LONDON

First published in the Spanish language as *La prueba del ácido*
by Tusquets Editores, Barcelona, in 2011
First published in Great Britain in 2016 by

MacLehose Press
An imprint of Quercus Editions Ltd
Carmelite House
50 Victoria Embankment
London EC4Y 0DZ

An Hachette UK company

Esta publicación fue realizada con el estímulo del Programa de Apoyo a la Traducción
(PROTRAD) dependiente de instituciones culturales mexicanas.

This publication is supported by the Programa de Apoyo a la Traducción
(PROTRAD), an initiative of the Mexican cultural institutions.

A CIP catalogue record for this book is available
from the British Library

ISBN (TPB) 978 0 85705 261 2
ISBN (Ebook) 978 0 85705 366 4

2 4 6 8 10 9 7 5 3 1

Designed and typeset in Minion by Libanus Press
Printed and bound in Great Britain by Clays Ltd, St Ives plc

For Leonor

TRANSLATOR'S NOTE

The Acid Test is the second novel in a series set in Culiacán, a prosperous and sweltering Mexican city of nearly a million people, half an hour's drive from the Pacific and nine hundred kilometres south of the U.S. border. Culiacán, the Sinaloa state capital, lies far off the tourist track, surrounded by desert and irrigated fields. While the city's elite still thrives on commercial agriculture, the trafficking of marijuana, cocaine and heroin has long outdistanced the sale of cucumbers and chilli peppers. This story occurs at the beginning of 2007. Mexico's president has just launched a war on drug trafficking, and Culiacán, already one of the country's more violent cities, will see its alarming body count rise sharply.

There is a smattering of blood at the origin of everything human.

GUIDO CERONETTI, *The Silence of the Body*

Is it the writer's task to bring more fear into this world?

RUBEM FONSECA, *Romance Negro*

Fear is what arms the murderer.

PATRIZIA CAVALLI, *Yo casi siempre duermo*

CAST OF CHARACTERS

THE POLICE

Angelita, Homicide Department secretary

Omar Briseño, commander of the Sinaloa State Ministerial Police in Culiacán

The Camel, Homicide Department officer

Gorilla Hortigosa, known as Gori, specialist in extracting confessions

Edgar Mendieta, known as Lefty, Homicide Department detective

Dr Montaño, Homicide Department forensic doctor

Noriega, police detective in Mazatlán, friend of Lefty Mendieta

Guillermo Ortega, head of the crime lab

Moisés Pineda, head of the Anti-Narcotics Unit of the Federal Preventive Police

Robles, Headquarters duty officer

Sánchez, retired detective, former work partner of Lefty Mendieta

Terminator, Homicide Department officer

Zelda Toledo, Homicide Department detective, work partner of Lefty Mendieta

THE NARCOS

Richie Bernal, member of the Valdés family clan

Sergio Carrillo, also known as Muerto or Guasave, enforcer for Dioni de la Vega

Max Garcés, chief of security for the Valdés family

Grunt, gunslinger and bodyguard for Richie Bernal

Guacho, driver for Samantha Valdés

Eloy Quintana, drug lord from Sonora state, member of the Pacific Cartel

Rafa, gunslinger and bodyguard for Richie Bernal

Imelda Terán, also known as Vanessa, assistant to drug lord Dioni de la Vega

Devil Urquídez, former policeman, now a bodyguard and enforcer for the Valdés family, engaged to Shorty Abitia's daughter Begoña

Marcelo Valdés, godfather of Culiacán, leader of the Pacific Cartel, father of Samantha

Minerva de Valdés, wife of Marcelo Valdés

Samantha Valdés, also known as La Jefa, daughter of the godfather of Culiacán

Dioni de la Vega, drug lord from Culiacán

CLUB ALEXA PERSONNEL

Bernardo Almada, part owner, lives in the United States

Mayra Cabral de Melo, also known as Roxana, Brazilian exotic dancer whom Lefty Mendieta met in Mazatlán at the end of *Silver Bullets*

Rodrigo Cabrera, part owner, former district attorney for the State of Sinaloa

Elisa Calderón, assistant manager

Alonso Carvajal, manager

José Escamilla, waiter

Yolanda Estrada, also known as Yhajaira, exotic dancer, Roxana's housemate

Luis Ángel Meraz, part owner, former federal congressman, gubernatorial hopeful

Miroslava, exotic dancer

Camila Naranjo, exotic dancer

The Phantom (Óscar Olivas), bartender

Othoniel Ramírez, the club's legal representative, who runs the business

José Rivera, also known as Bigboy, bouncer

THE AMERICANS

Mister B., father of the U.S. president

David Barrymore, assistant director in charge of the Los Angeles F.B.I. office

Adán Carrasco, former U.S. army sharpshooter, owner of El Continente hunting camp

Special Agent William Ellroy, second-in-command of Secret Service personnel guarding Mister B.

Win Harrison, also known as Jean Pynchon, F.B.I. special agent

Master Special Officer Mitchell, commander of Secret Service personnel guarding Mister B.

Donald Simak, also known as Peter Connolly, F.B.I. special agent

OTHERS

Begoña Abitia, daughter of Shorty Abitia, engaged to gunslinger Devil Urquídez

Shorty Abitia, childhood friend of Lefty Mendieta, father of Begoña

Esteban Aguirrebere, owner of San Esteban farms, Club Alexa customer

Andrade, arms dealer for the Mexican Armed Forces

The Apache, police informer, sells candy, gum and cigarettes outside Club Alexa

Dulce Arredondo, collaborator of smuggler Leo McGiver

Father Bardominos, priest who abused Lefty Mendieta when he was eight years old

Miguel Camacho, father of former boxer Kid Yoreme

Miguel Ángel Canela, businessman, Club Alexa customer

Foreman Castelo, childhood friend of Lefty Mendieta, owner of a killer-for-hire agency, who owes Lefty for getting him out of a jam

Miguel de Cervantes, Club Alexa customer from Spain

Curlygirl, waiter at El Quijote bar, friend of Lefty Mendieta

Marcelino Freire, Brazilian football player for Dorados of Sinaloa

Silvio García, legendary Culiacán boxing trainer

Rudy Jiménez, owner of Café El Miró, Lefty Mendieta's favourite spot

Mariana Kelly, publicist, romantic partner of Samantha Valdés

José Antonio Lagarde, businessman and former husband of Anita Roy, father of Marcos

Marcos Lagarde, son of Anita Roy and José Antonio Lagarde, lives in Toronto, Canada, friend of Paty Olmedo

Lili Leyva, wife of Alexa manager Alonso Carvajal

L.H., retired master perfume maker in Tijuana, now consultant to police investigators in California and Mexico, friend of Lefty Mendieta

Fermín de Lima, wealthy businessman in Mazatlán

Joaquín Lizárraga, mayor of Mazatlán

Susana Luján, long-ago girlfriend of Lefty Mendieta, with whom he unknowingly fathered a child, lives in California

Leo McGiver, smuggler and gunrunner, also known as Steven Tyler, friend of Fabián Olmedo

Enrique Mendieta, brother of Lefty Mendieta, former guerrilla, lives in Oregon

Jason Mendieta, seventeen-year-old son of Lefty Mendieta and Susana Luján, lives in California

Felipe Montemayor, district attorney for the State of Sinaloa

Fabián Olmedo, known as Gandhi, owner of a luxury car dealership, friend of Leo McGiver, father of Paty

Patricia Olmedo, known as Paty, fashion designer, daughter of Fabián Olmedo

Dayana Ortiz, publicist and girlfriend of politician Luis Ángel Meraz

Juan Osuna Roth, owner of a Mazatlán modelling agency

Elena Palencia, mother of exotic dancer Mayra Cabral de Melo

Dr Parra, Lefty Mendieta's psychiatrist

Daniel Quiroz, star crime reporter for "Eyes on the Night" radio programme

Rodo (Rodolfo Uzeta), boyfriend of police detective Zelda Toledo

Anita Roy, friend of Mayra Cabral de Melo, former wife of José Antonio Lagarde, mother of Marcos

Sarita, wife of crime lab technician Guillermo Ortega

Teo (Teófilo), trucker, former guerrilla, best friend of Lefty Mendieta's brother Enrique

Trudis, woman who cooks and cleans for Lefty Mendieta and whose children were fathered by several Mexican musicians

Danilo Twain, arms smuggling partner of Leo McGiver

Vinicio de la Vega, federal congressman, brother of drug lord Dioni de la Vega

Kid Yoreme (José Ángel Camacho Arenas), former boxer, Club Alexa customer

MEXICAN DISHES AND DRINKS

Aguachile: fresh raw shrimp marinated in lime juice with cucumber, red onion, and crushed chillies in water

Barbacoa: cubed beef and beef marrow stewed in beer with potatoes, onions, tomatoes, olives, chillies, and spices

Campechana: seafood cocktail of oysters, baby octopus, mussels, shrimp, squid, and scallops

Carne asada: grilled roast beef

Ceviche: raw fish or shrimp marinated in lime juice with chillies and spices

Chorizo: sausage made from smoked, cured pork, *guajillo* and *ancho* chillies, and spices

Eggs montados: fried eggs on ham and tortillas

Filete culichi: fish baked with *poblano* chillies and cream

Guacamole: dip of avocados, lemon, onions, and *jalapeño* chillies

Levantamuertos ("raise the dead"): spicy seafood stew made with shrimp, octopus, fish, and manta ray

Machaca: marinated beef or pork rubbed with spices, pounded, shredded, and dried

Menudo: tripe and hominy stew

Michelada: beer, lime juice, and assorted spices served in a chilled, salt-rimmed glass

Pan de pulque: sweet bread made with fermented cactus water

Pozole: pork and hominy stew

Quesadillas: deep-fried corn dumplings with cheese or other fillings

Red snapper chicharrones: deep-fried chunks of fish

Red snapper zarandeado: grilled fish marinated in chillies, garlic, and spices

Salsa mexicana: condiment of chopped tomatoes, onions, *jalapeño* chillies, cilantro, and salt

Salsa ranchera: very spicy sauce made with onions, garlic, tomatoes, and *serrano* chillies

Salsa roja: spicy sauce made with onions, tomatoes, cilantro and assorted chillies

One

Faced with a dark night that was growing darker, Mayra Cabral de Melo gave in. She realised that the man who was opening the car door and hauling her out would be the last man in her life, that Almighty God would not alter her fate, and that she had been wrong about something, maybe about everything. She stumbled. What good is a man? Behind her the city formed an icy painted backdrop. Good for everything and nothing. The man, a lover for the past two months, though lately she had been avoiding him, steered her by the waist with the roughness of a soldier. Oh God, after so many extraordinary times. She remembered her dreams when she was small: to be a firefighter, police officer, nurse, doctor, football player, actress, singer, dancer. The best in the neighbourhood and the best in the country. The queen. Right. But she set fire to her youth as if it were a snake-infested boat: night after night, when flames burn deepest and cause the most damage. When you answer to any name. Now nothing made sense, not here, far from the domain of her dreams, behind some big warehouse, walking through stubby plants that did not hurt though she was wearing a short skirt and strapless blouse, marched by that tall man with whom she had had fun and entertained guests, and with whom she had slept so often, but not, despite his insistence, in the past week.

Minutes earlier, however, after he had lured her with the offer of an exorbitant amount, she had agreed and tried to caress him. He brushed her off with sarcasm: I never do it with dead girls. My love, relax, do you want me to do it the way you really like? Get it, I'm serious. What are you talking about? what do you mean you're serious? No answer. Did I do something wrong, my love, my teddy bear? if I did, won't you forgive me? He did not turn to look at her.

She had not finished the letter to her mother or sent her the money. She did manage to pay the electricity, the water, and the telephone. She had gone to the supermarket, booked appointments with the gynaecologist for Saturday and with the pedicurist for Monday, and what about the people from Mazatlán? She had forgotten her housemate Yhajaira's birthday, first time that ever happened. No-one makes a fool of me, especially a stupid whore. Several times she had thought about buying pepper spray, but what for? It was not such a dangerous city and, anyway, right then she did not have her handbag with her. Inside it were the eighteen thousand dollars her pimp had given her so she would not have to work as of Friday, the unfinished letter, her relaxing cream, her sleeping pills, and a lot more. It will all end up with this swine, who may have introduced her to important people, but so what? Why didn't I leave the money at home? because I was in a hurry. I didn't mean to offend you. Shut up! you're a millionaire thanks to me, what more did you want? The plants brushed against her legs, but she no longer felt them. I wanted you to stop threatening me, my king, to stop scaring me with that temper of yours. If only she had got around to speaking with. She heard the shot and that was it: the night suddenly got darker. She landed with her face to the sky, tilted towards the whitish moon. The murderer, tall, somewhat heavyset, short hair, took his time, not to close her eyes, but to pull down her blouse and cut off one dark nipple.

On the highway close by drove oblivion.

Two

Two in the morning. Edgar "Lefty" Mendieta reared up in bed gasping loudly. He felt he was in the dark cave of his stomach, searching, and he kept bumping into a diminished, frightened version of himself, devoid of past or future. That is what he felt. He thought: I'll die before Mick Jagger. On the television they were selling exercise machines. That bastard Jagger turned vegetarian and now he stuffs his face with omega six and fortified calcium. He got up and switched it off. Who am I? who says I'm doing what I should? that I'm worth anything? at what point in my life did I mess up? is living worth the effort? What a numbskull I am, a loveless idiot, pursuing a profession that earns nothing but scorn. A 43-year-old jerk living alone in his brother's house, no father and what's worse no mother. A scumbag who never even got fucking divorced because I never got married, and no godfather from baptism or first communion. A hack fated to die before that skunk Jagger who's now a Sir and won't leave Keith Richards in peace. Wearing the white T-shirt and boxer shorts he slept in, he sat back down on the bed and turned on the light. The air conditioner was quiet. On the dresser, *The House of the Fortunate Buddhas* by João Ubaldo Ribeiro with a bookmark in the middle. Outside, barking. I'm a failure, he went on, a loser whose only future is to be a worthless nobody, because to be a Mister Nobody would be beyond me. He thought of the pistol in the car, and he stood and left the bedroom. There are things that cannot be fixed. He went through the door to the garage, opened the Jetta, and took the Beretta out of the glove compartment. I don't understand how I've lived this long; does it really make sense for somebody like me to live longer than he should? whatever that is. This is what it is: years and years go by and everything you do is wrong; you turn eighteen and you don't have a clue why you were born, what you should do, and you spend your life spinning your wheels. Somebody like that does not deserve to live, a person like that has no right to consume oxygen. He looked and the bullet was chambered. From inside the car he took a cigarette and lit up. That was when the barking registered. Fucking louse, for sure he's chasing his tail. He went to the gate, then into the street. The moon was large and reddish and the dog was barking away at it. You're fucked, you stupid beast. He addressed him in a low voice. What are you doing barking at the moon? You're just like me, you're in another world; just like me, everything you do is ridiculous. There's no way out, little dog, are you going to kill yourself or am I going to kill myself? because frankly isn't that what I've been doing my whole life? yapping at the moon? with the damn Bible on the brain? Don't tell me barking at the moon is poetic, poetic's my balls and nobody barks at them. The dog in the little front garden across the street knew Lefty, he came to the fence wagging his tail. So, you want to go first? You sure turned out to be one tough fucking pooch. He saw his shadow and the shadow of the 92FS in his hand. Eyeing him, the dog growled. What kind of support is that, you fucking pest? ah, you don't want me muscling in on the first shot? His own shadow again caught his attention and he studied it, raised the gun, and watched his shadow follow suit; he aimed the weapon at his temple and held it there as he walked back into the garage. Seconds later, he emerged without the pistol and holding a fresh cigarette. Let's see, tough guy, you who knows everything and whatever you don't know you make up: why have I been thinking what I've been thinking? what piece of me came apart inside? what fucking amino acid, amphetamine, or brain cell got all riled up and made me delirious? He crossed the street, went up to the dog, and patted his head. What provokes a man who is not suicidal to think that ending it all would not be such a dreadful thing? The dog wagged his tail. He smiled. Alright, you animal, tomorrow I'll go see Dr Parra. I'll get an appointment for you too, but you have to promise me something: don't pay any attention to what he says; if you like barking at the moon, just do it, after all, what can you lose? He took a drag, the dog watched. You want a cigarette? you've gone too far, you fucking beast, you're a bagful of vices. He crushed the butt on the pavement. O.K., try to get some rest, tomorrow is another day, and he went back into his house without a glance at the moon, which had turned whitish.

Three

No-one knew who McGiver really was. Some said he was English, others thought he was German. No-one ever said he was Iranian or Argentinian. He was born in Culiacán in Colonia Popular, a neighbourhood known as the Col Pop, fifty-six years ago and he worked in contraband. Happen to need a shipment of A.K.-47s or Barrett 50s? How about a fleet of helicopters? Happen to crave a Dom Perignon '54, a confession penned by Nicole Kidman, or one of Elizabeth Taylor's diamonds? Leo McGiver was your man; he took orders from the good, the bad, and the worse, and he was not hard to find in Mexico City. He liked high-class bars, half-light, and a smiling, wordless woman. Bars today are designed for smiling, drinking, and performing the eternal gestures of wooing, not for conversation. If any girl tried to offer an opinion he would shut her right up. Smile, my lady, that's the only thing I ask of you. Sexually replete, he was enjoying himself at the Jazz bar in the Hotel San Luis in Culiacán; he was in the city, among other reasons, to win the backing of a gang of drug traffickers and to close an unusual deal after days of concentrated effort, something he took on because it was for an old acquaintance, perhaps the only hometown boy with whom he remained on friendly terms, and the only one who knew his history. The least he could do was fulfil his end of the bargain. I like my friend, he's the nut who invented the printing press with moveable type. The brown-skinned girl with green contacts kept smiling and occasionally sipped a White Russian. Do you know what a printing press with moveable type is? She shook her head. Well, he invented it; quite the guy, though he happens to be nuts. The girl nodded without making a sound; if there was one thing she had learned in her brief training it was that the client is boss, and if this idiot wanted her silent she would find another occasion to speak.

They had been together for all of two hours and McGiver had had one too many. Why do people drink vodka as if it were water? He's invented other gadgets, the fountain pen, for instance, have you ever written with a fountain pen? She shook her head again. He invented it one night when he had nothing else to do, just like that, without any preconceived notion, and he lives here in this city where everything is always changing. He was the kind who liked to look you in the eye when he talked, the girl had that figured out after three minutes in his company. To the health of my friend and his inventions. McGiver drained his glass, the young woman took a sip from hers and filled his. This time, however, he's gone too far, not some new invention, I have no idea what he's cooking up these days, I'm talking about the piece he asked me for, which I managed to get hold of thanks to my contacts in Europe, but what an unbelievable headache, the search took twists and turns that were utterly surreal. He drank his vodka. If I tell you he's nuts it's because he is. But not straitjacket insanity, no way, his craziness drives him to ask for nutty and absurd things, understand? The girl nodded. A man can't possibly want such ridiculous things, do you have any idea where humanity will end up with people like him? She shook her head. In the most implausible chaos, global pandemonium, something I don't ever want to see; his desires are simply inconceivable, if I were to tell you what he sent me to find, you'd be amazed, you wouldn't think it was worth anything, but he didn't care how much I spent, do you know who Jeff Beck is? The girl again shook her head. I figured, have you seen the movie *Blow-Up*? Another headshake. He gestured that he understood and bent to his drink. Too bad you can't smoke in here, I feel like a cigarette, it's the alcohol, oh, and as I was telling you, you need to be crazier than a goat to invest in things like that; tomorrow I'll deliver his precious treasure which I searched for like an idiot all over Brussels and Turin and finally I found it in Lisbon, on the second floor of a house in the neighbourhood of Santa Catarina, do you know where Lisbon is? She rolled her eyes.

Sir, I need to talk to you about something. Hey hey hey, none of that, we're doing fine, don't break the spell, that's all I ask. I'll be brief. No, no, no, your health. She was annoyed and bored. A few minutes later the smuggler asked for his waiter. The girl waved a young man over. The bill. They were the last customers and he had it ready. I don't usually carry cash, could you add in the girl's fee and give it to her? Three thousand, she said, and now she smiled again. Make it four thousand, you really are an enchanting companion, what's your name? She mouthed it without a sound. With two s's? She nodded. They smiled. McGiver signed the voucher with a flourish and stood up. Get me a taxi. There are taxis at the door, sir. Could I possibly put in words how much I enjoyed this evening? The smuggler wagged his finger and as he walked away his body drooped. The girl eyed him with a scowl. Out of a corner of the room came Muerto, a watchful young man who sat down beside her, in McGiver's chair to be precise. They exchanged gestures: she of disappointment, he of love. They stood and left.

Four

Mendieta was reading the newspaper at his desk. Zelda Toledo was filing her nails. They were sipping their drinks, she Diet Coke, he coffee. Officers disappeared down the hallways after receiving their orders. Lefty's cell phone rang out its familiar Seventh Cavalry song, which so inspires fans at horse-racing tracks around the world. Mendieta here. Why are you talking like that? Like what? Strange, as if you'd swallowed a syllable. I told you so much screwing was going to affect you, asshole, you're going deaf. Don't make up stories, Lefty, you really do sound different, besides, I'm the doctor. What's up? Nothing, just I'm going to be out of circulation for a little while. You don't say. When I'm free I'll give you a call. What are her eyes like? Big and shining, the prettiest I've ever seen in my miserable life. Don't end up deaf, eh? Deaf are moles and. Lefty hung up. It was Montaño, right? muttered Zelda. On his morning errand. What an appalling excuse for a man. Agent Toledo, since you are flour from another sack, it shouldn't mean shit to you. Of course not, if I catch him with an underage girl I'll throw the fucking satyr in the can, who does he think he is? Are you jealous? That's the last thing I need, boss, no kidding, that guy won't ever touch a strand of my hair even if he gets born all over again. Lefty smiled. It's not all his fault, a couple of times I've seen the babes going after him. Well, I'll say it again: if I find out he's screwing an underage girl, he'll never hear the end of it. Ortega came in with an open newspaper. Did you see the president's speech? That's what I'm reading now. Is he nuts, or what? he's declaring war on the narcos, do you know how many badges are going to die? All of us, Lefty said and he fell silent. The guy doesn't know what he's talking about. At least he's saying something, Zelda chimed in, can you imagine a mute president? Sort of like a vegetarian policeman, Ortega smiled. That'd be the last straw. I don't like the way this guy's talking. Take it easy, buddy, Lefty spoke up, they all do it and in the end nothing happens. Yeah, but this one needs to win some legitimacy, they're already saying that's what's behind it. Don't lose any sleep over that either, if they cheated in these elections they've cheated before; in this country it's originality that would be a miracle. I don't know, papa, something tells me this time will be different. May your tongue turn to pork rinds. Listen, how about the case of that girl with no tits, they're all drooling over her and I hadn't even heard about it, who is she? Let them frisk us, all we've heard is the gossip, I guess she's from a powerful family. More than powerful, said Zelda, from what I hear they gagged the media, if you noticed there's no mention of it anywhere. You think the media would go along with that? Not in our country, papa. Of course not, and certainly not nowadays.

Angelita, the lithe secretary, peeked in. Good morning, did you all fall out of bed? What kind of comment is that, Angelita? It's just that I rarely see you in so early. You came in late, that's not the same thing, and since it's Monday not even the hens are laying. She smiled. You're sharp today, aren't you, boss? the chief wants you, let's see if you're such a tough guy with him. Laughter.

What the hell would I do in Madrid? Mendieta and Briseño looked at each other without blinking. The chief had called him in to tell him the case of the girl with no tits would be suspended. It was never assigned to us, chief. I know, but I don't want any hallway chit-chat, we've got plenty to do given the daily body count, we're about to pass Tijuana and Ciudad Juárez in the national ranking. Not a bad idea to have a trophy, imagine a miniature A.K.-47 on a golden pedestal on your desk, I know a buddy who could get rich making those. This is no joking matter, Mendieta, and that comment makes me sick. Lefty smiled, raised his hand, and let the topic drop. And regarding that lady, nothing, do you understand? let everybody else know; oh, we've got another invitation, this one from the D.E.A. for a course on fighting organised crime. That must be for Pineda. The chief handed him the letter, it's for you, it says so right there: Mr Edgar Mendieta. He read the contents, then said they should stick their course where the sun never shines; as far as the gringos are concerned, chief, the further away the better, I wouldn't even play marbles with those guys from the D.E.A. Briseño gave him a disapproving look, Well, then think about the invitation from Madrid.

Before rejoining Zelda he made a call to Dr Parra. Eight o'clock in my office. Couldn't it be earlier? it's just I feel really weird, every desire gone, it's as if I had a big hole in my body; I woke up in the night thinking my life was a piece of shit, I even got out my pistol. Call me back in two hours, I'll see if I can squeeze you in.

He heard the cavalry charge and answered. It was Trudis. I know you don't like me to bother you at work, but this time I have to, are you coming home for lunch? I can't, we need to solve the murder of a girl who got her tits cut off. Holy God, are you serious? With my hand on my heart. My God, how cruel, where are we going to end up with all this violence? No idea, the only thing I know for sure is that we're in the middle of it and it sucks. I won't take any more of your time; listen, the gringo just phoned, he says he really needs to talk to you. Mendieta had refused to speak with Susana Luján's son, but the kid was tenacious and called every day. If he calls again, tell him I'm away on a trip, I'll get in touch as soon as I'm back. Oh, Lefty, I don't understand you, he always asks me how you look, what you like, how you dress, how tall you are; when I told him you like black T-shirts he was happy. Tell him I'll be back in ten days. He hung up. Just thinking that his brother Enrique might be right terrified him; if he looks like me it's not my fault, or is it? there are people who are not born to be fathers and I'm one of them.

Zelda found him: Boss, they called in an S-26 on the freeway to Mazatlán, Ortega's people are on their way.

Soon enough they arrived at the crime scene. Ortega was checking the area marked off by his technical team, and a forensic intern sent by Montaño was making notes in a little book. The body was covered, lying in a field of Swiss chard about eight metres from a seed warehouse. Mendieta strode up to it, uncovered the face, and froze. *Are you a policeman? You don't look like one. You look a little gloomy, do you feel lost? Are you Lefty?* Her eyes were open and the beauty of her face, even in rigor mortis, was disturbing. Lefty was speechless. *Police usually have an air of cruelty about them that speaks of who they are, but you look so normal, do you exercise much?* They found her just like that, Ortega told him, killed by one shot, we've got the casing, they sliced off a nipple; we found footprints from work boots and from her slip-on shoes. Paralysed: That case we're not supposed to touch, he managed to think, was it just the nipple or the whole tit? Are you alright, Lefty? you look a little green around the gills. He could not avoid her eyes: one green, the other the colour of honey. The forensic intern came over. *You're a lefty! Me too.* From the temperature of the body she's probably been dead six or seven hours and she's got ant bites, he reported, in the morgue we'll see if there's any semen.

The ants went to town, the intern added, though I don't see too many now; the bullet came out by her left ear and she was killed right here. Observing carefully, Zelda Toledo deployed her spatial intelligence: boots, a hiker? new ones, did a narco do her in? maybe, only they wear cowboy boots. Someone from the district attorney's office who was taking pictures answered Zelda's thoughts: The boots were big, like a soldier's. Would a woman use men's boots to throw us off? The stride is long. Lefty took a step back, Mayra Cabral de Melo's curls were a mess. The Roberto Carlos song went through his mind: "Beneath the curls of her hair, a story to be told." O.K., when you've got the reports ready send them to me; Zelda, I'll be in the car. Ortega came up to him. Lefty, you knew that babe, I can see it a mile away. Of course not, I only know she's so pretty it's a damn shame she's dead. Don't play the dummy, papa, even one of the guys on my team knows who she is. Lefty walked away without a word. I understand, my friend, if you need to talk about this, I'll be first in line. Ortega's cell phone rang out. What's up, Pineda? He listened. We'll head right over, you think the war's begun? two bodies on Obregón, gangsta-wraps, near the fork for La Primavera, more blankets for my collection.

Lefty got into the Jetta, turned the ignition, felt the air conditioning and then the soft rhythm of Peter Frampton's "Baby, I Love Your

Way". There are memories that build a future and others that shut it down. *Do you really like that music? You are the most romantic cop I've ever met.* He remembered her astonishing lips, her raspy voice, her Brazilian accent. *I think the Portuguese call it "pimba".* The passenger door opened, but it was not Zelda who slid in beside him. Daniel Quiroz, the cleverest reporter in the city, smiled. What are you doing here, my man Lefty? Sucking my thumb, I was missing you. I went to Pineda's first. I heard you two were in love, when is the wedding? Have they identified the chick? Yup. That's what the badges told me, too, she worked at the Alexa; have you got diarrhoea? because you're really pale. What do you mean pale, fucking Quiroz, I'm fine. Aha, were you one of her customers? that's a weakness I hadn't known about you, Lefty. Would you like to shut up? he turned towards the journalist, his face crumbling. For one fucking time, shut your trap, you bastard. Oooh, sorry, I must have touched a nerve. You know what? just get out, I don't want to end up beating the shit out of you. You don't want to see that one, Lefty: "Policeman attacks defenceless reporter", imagine that. Mendieta tried to blank him out by staring at the highway choked with trucks full of produce for the city, at the curious trying to cross the yellow tape. Zelda was interrogating two workers at the warehouse who kept shaking their heads.

I know she was Brazilian, she worked exclusively at the Alexa, and that to go to bed with her cost a testicle and a half; what do you know, my man Lefty? Nothing, and just this time, if you have any respect for me, don't ask me anything else and just get out. Quiroz looked at him and did not move. If it hurts so much, you'll never find the culprit. I'll find him, you'll see, even if he hides in the womb of his whore of a mother.

Boss, there isn't much; the boys say she was a dancer at the Alexa and Ortega thinks you knew her; I called the watchman there and he gave me the home address of the manager, shall we go to him or to the club? Zelda Toledo pulled the passenger door closed and held her other questions for later. Mendieta simply followed his partner's directions to the manager's house. Months earlier he had met Mayra Cabral de Melo in Mazatlán, and they had clicked: *Are you a cop? You don't look like one, you look so innocent, so sweet, like you wouldn't break a dish and all your dishes are broken; you do have pretty eyes, a bit sad, but expressive; from now on I'll feel protected by the law; you should come see my show at the Alexa, it's not just the pole or the lights or all that collective heat rising, it's the dance, the beauty of the body insinuating things; besides, there's a tradition I need to uphold, when have you seen a Brazilian woman who doesn't dance? our bodies are born dancing and we begin refining it when we're small, we find a spot and a movement for every emotion, as if it were a spell. You could say I express the joy of living; if some people come in for other reasons I hope they at least feel something before they leave. No, I don't like to drink, but we can talk, eat, take a stroll, a bit of wine maybe if I have to; we Brazilians like beer, but it makes me feel bloated and I prefer other things. I came to work, I can't tell you about it, but you're right, it was for a private party; you nearly guessed it, they were such celebrities and more than a few wanted me to go with them, I didn't dare, that's a delicate matter and sometimes it's better to leave things the way they were agreed; if somebody insists, you can meet them later on and so far no-one has come looking for me. I understand, don't think I'm naive, life is more than dancing. You really do have pretty eyes. Of course you can talk about mine, but you're going to be hard put to say something original.*

Alonso Carvajal, thirty-eight years old, received the news in shorts and a T-shirt at his home in the Culiacán neighbourhood known as Las Vegas. Sleepy. His wife at work, his children in school. Poor girl, she was our star. Mayra Cabral de Melo, was she Brazilian? Zelda Toledo, her tone hard. Mendieta looked on, the grieving widower. That's what she said. You doubt it? The girls are smart and they're from all over, if they lie it's none of our business. Of course, as long as they know how to wiggle their asses that's enough for you. Lefty looked at her. It's a job like any other. You don't say, anyhow, we won't talk about that now; how long has Mayra been dancing at the Alexa? Four months, more or less, as a matter of fact, she didn't turn up the past three nights. What do you do if they miss a day? We look into it, but we couldn't locate Mayra or her housemate, who didn't show up to work either, no sign of her until yesterday. What's the housemate's name? Yolanda Estrada, she dances as Yhajaira, they lived together. Where? Zaragoza 2516-B, near Casino de la Cultura. Lefty called Headquarters: Robles, find Terminator, send him and the Camel, and he read out the name and the address. Tell them to stay with the babe until we get there and keep me informed. Mayra liked to call herself Roxana. How many girls dance in your strip club? It depends, right now a dozen. Who besides you has a direct relationship with them? Elisa Calderón, my assistant, she makes sure they come in on time and if they go off with somebody she takes note, and she coordinates when they're all supposed to be on the catwalk; and there's Óscar Olivas, the bartender, who we call the Phantom, and the waiters, too, especially José Escamilla, who's in charge of renting out the private rooms. Alonso Carvajal told them he had been on the job for fourteen months, that at first he did not like it, but now he was used to the way things were done. It was the first time someone was murdered. How did you hire Mayra? She came with a group of them from Veracruz, there's a circuit the girls follow from city to city, they move every three or four months. In other words, she was about to leave. She wanted to stay, she had good clients and, like I say, she was the main attraction; I think she was about to have it her way. What do you mean? Well . . . he hesitated. One of her clients is a partner. And his name is? Luis Ángel Meraz. Zelda gave Lefty a sidelong glance. The politician? No less; if it isn't too much to ask, when you go see him don't mention my name. I want a list of her clients right this minute. That's something we can't do. He could say no more because Lefty had jumped him and put him in a headlock. The list, asshole, are you deaf? we want it now and add in the rest of the partners. Alright. Lefty eased off: *like you wouldn't break a dish and all your dishes are broken.* Zelda looked at him alarmed. So? At first she went out with a dozen guys, more or less; in the end we knew she was going with two or three. Who? That's going to cost me my job. If I stick you in the can it's going to cost you your virginity, asshole; bit by bit the widower was turning into the villain. Miguel de Cervantes. Lefty leapt at him like a wild animal, pulled the guy up to standing, though he was heavyset and normal height, and gave him a sharp knee to the groin. Ugh. You don't want to see what we're really like, you dickhead, that's the name of a writer. I swear that's what he told me his name was, he's an engineer who installs greenhouses, he lives in

La Primavera and he's Spanish. The one who wrote *Don Quixote*. Lefty threw him down on the easy chair. Please, you don't need to use those methods with me, I'm cooperating, I'm telling you what I know, and I know about Cervantes, in high school we had to read his story "The Glass Graduate". What about the others? Attorney Meraz who I already mentioned, who used to be president of the P.R.I. and a congressman, and Richie Bernal, who you people ought to know better than I do. Zelda wrote it all down. I don't know their addresses. What about the ones from the very beginning? Those names I can't remember, it was when I first started; I'll ask Elisa to call you and give them to you. We need her address and telephone, she'll have to make a statement. She lives in Las Quintas, near Sinaloa Boulevard. Zelda noted down the information. Those men, did they go to the club to pick Mayra up? No, they'd call and we'd send her, it's part of Elisa's job. Where? Usually to hotels, private homes, to the beach; for Cervantes it was always to his house, that's how we know where he lives. What about the rest? For Attorney Meraz it was to houses he would indicate ahead of time, and Bernal would pick her up at the club or we'd send her to some private party; the parties were a good deal for Mayra, she even had clients in Mazatlán; if I remember correctly she was supposed to go there on the weekend. The blood drained from Mendieta's face again, but no-one noticed. Did Elisa Calderón also coordinate that? That's right, lately she's been complaining that Mayra would set up her own appointments and take days off without permission. Who are the clients in Mazatlán? Only Elisa would know that. And the partners? Besides Meraz, Bernardo Almada who lives in the States, and Attorney Rodrigo Cabrera, who you must know. Of course, the former district attorney. Othoniel Ramírez is the legal representative for the partnership and he runs the business. Besides Meraz, did the others have a client relationship with the girls? I've never seen Almada, Cabrera a few times, but not with Roxana; the one who comes in regularly is Ramírez. Did he go with Mayra? Never, she was Meraz's turf. You said she missed three days' work, do you have any idea where she went? No, last night Elisa didn't know either and she was mad as hell; Yhajaira told us yesterday she'd come home for a few hours in the morning to rest.

Thirty-five minutes later they received a call from Terminator. What's up, my man Termi? Nothing, Lefty my man, we have the information you asked for, we're at the scene and there is a young woman here with a bullet in her heart. Oh-oh. Someone does not like the fact that women are in the majority, Lefty my pal, what do you make of it? First clue, Termi: the bastard knows statistics.

Five

McGiver turned off the television, took a shower, ordered breakfast, and started making calls: Hey, Twain, Green Arrow here. Middle name? Danilo; how's our timing? Clocks in the night, how did everything go? Number Two; alright, all it takes is punctuality. We'll do our part. Number One wants publicity, photos in the media, and statements; and well, we're facing some strong turbulence. That's for you to take care of, did they hand over the down payment? Only Number Two; take a look, they'll make the deposit today; I expect Number One to call any minute, and regarding the turbulence I'm in a pinch, how is my proposal coming for the new guy? We'll be ready in a few days. Click. It was his contact for smuggling weapons and he wanted to make sure the man had everything straight: what he had been celebrating the previous night was the closing of a deal that would leave him millions of dollars richer, and he had another one in sight.

He dialled the next number. Hello, a sensual voice. Good morning, any news? They want it all up front. How mistrustful can you get? That's their style, you know what Mexico City people are like, when it comes to business they don't even believe the Virgin of Guadalupe. Tomorrow night we'll give them eighty per cent, we need a margin in case the work is a fake. They won't agree; besides, it is the original. Tell them it's our style. Let's not play with them, get it into your head once and for all: they won't lift a finger until they're satisfied they have the money. Set it up, I'll call you tomorrow. Are you still in Yucatán? No, I've never been there, however in Saltillo they still make a delicious *pan de pulque*. He hung up. Although he would never go to bed with her, he found Dulce Arredondo enchanting.

Señor Olmedo, please. He's not in, would you like to leave a message? You may not remember me, I'm Leo McGiver, we've spoken before. Oh, yes, I gave him your message, he said he would see you at his house tonight at ten. Perfect, although I'd still like to speak with him, do you think that would be possible? Hmm . . . no, I don't think so, he called me from Altata and when he calls from there we usually don't see him all day. You understand him, don't you. In twelve years a woman gets to know her boss. Well, congratulate him for me, a good secretary is half a successful business. You tell him, maybe he'll give me a raise. I will, and if he doesn't you can come work for me. I'd rather have the raise. They said goodbye.

He opened the door and the smell of breakfast invaded the room. How long had it been since he had had eggs with chorizo for breakfast? The moment the waiter left he uncovered the plate and tasted a mouthful. If I hadn't gone away when I did, today I'd be a 130-kilo pig; how could anyone not eat this delight? He punched in Olmedo's cell number, but no-one answered.

He continued eating. My mother, may she rest in peace, made wonderful chorizo. Back then, being a mother also meant being a good cook. Now women bring children into the world and feed them nothing but ham sandwiches with mayonnaise and French fries with Coca-Cola. What garbage. What times those were. And when it was cold they never sent you to school without first having oatmeal or hot chocolate. Maybe that's why the world has changed: food isn't as healthy and nobody cooks the way they used to. Ring.

Nobody ever called McGiver. Ring ring. He felt his heart tighten. He did not use a cell phone and usually no-one knew where he stayed. Ring ring ring. He picked up the receiver. Why don't you answer, asshole, what, are you taking a shit? With whom do I have the pleasure of speaking? With your father, jerk-off. Now his stomach full of chorizo and eggs tightened too. Yesterday you didn't want to listen to my message, idiot, so in five minutes two people I sent will be in your room and you'd better behave yourself. But who are you? Your father, I already told you. Click. What was that about? McGiver was not a delicate man, no smuggler is, but he loved formalities and he did not like this intrusion one bit. All that about him being my father, what did that mean? Naturally, it did not sit well; he decided to make himself scarce, but as soon as he was on his feet there was a knock at the door. Shit, he muttered. Open up, the voice meant business. McGiver, in his shirtsleeves, slipped on his jacket, took the safety off his Smith & Wesson, and stuck it in his belt. May it be as God wills. Who is it? They just made an appointment for us, dick-head, now open this fucking door or we'll knock it down.

In came Vanessa, his companion from the night before, and Muerto, who couldn't be more than nineteen years old, pointing a Herstal Five-seven, better known as a cop-killer, right at him. Well, fuck me, the smuggler shook his head, the only reason I'm not any stupider is I'm not any older.

No prick keeps me waiting, snarled Muerto, pistol in hand, giving the door behind him a shove. But McGiver was paying more attention to Vanessa, dressed in tight jeans and a red blouse. Will you look at this beauty, he thought. So you had a message for me. You shut up, now I'm the one who'll do the talking, do you know which of my girlfriends invented the A.K.-47? What would he know, the hitman said, he can't even open a fucking door. The smuggler smiled. Keep your trap shut, the girl threatened him again, she was prettier in the daytime than at night. McGiver gave an amused shrug to indicate he wouldn't say a thing. In case no-one's told you yet, she said, you are insufferable. Say the word and I'll put a bullet in the son of his bitch of a mother; the guy was getting excited and wanted to impress the brown-skinned girl with the shining eyes. Vanessa turned slightly towards him and the gunman gave her an eager smile. She was like ice. But the smuggler took advantage of the distraction to put two slugs in the man and then cover the girl. Muerto, surprised, wanting to recount what he was seeing on his way to the great beyond, fell slowly without dropping his pistol. McGiver slid the cop-killer inside his belt and turned to face a pale Vanessa. No way around it, Vanessa with two s's, we are condemned to be alone; the one who called, is he your boss? She nodded. Is he a businessman? Yes. Why does he want to see me? He'll tell you, but it has to do with weapons. Fear made the girl stutter, her face blanched, lips dry. You've got wheels? She squeaked out a yes. You can talk, we aren't in one of those awful dives where you can't hear a thing. McGiver spread some lotion on his hands and worked it in, then quickly packed his clothes, including a pair of blue overalls, put the pistol and his friend's treasure in the suitcase, and they left the room.

On the way he recognised Hidalgo Bridge and Colonia Tierra Blanca, the legendary neighbourhood of 1960s glue-sniffers from whose cobblestoned streets he had hightailed it out more than once. Then he took a good look at Vanessa. She was lovely, strong, soft skin, black hair to her shoulders; he knew that more and more women were part of criminal enterprises, so he would not ask her any questions; and not for a moment did he doubt that since he could not remain at that hotel something had shifted; he would understand where things lay soon enough.

The girl pushed a button and a gate rolled silently open. They entered an immense yard where four Cheyennes and a B.M.W. sat waiting. Two men, weapons at the ready, came over. Where is Señor de la Vega? In his office and he's boiling harder than water for chocolate. Why? Don't know. Vanessa signalled for McGiver to follow. A few neglected plants on either side. On the porch they frisked him, took his Smith & Wesson and the cop-killer. We'll hold them for you here, little buddy. Then he followed the girl inside. They crossed a living room with black leather easy chairs, decorations everywhere, family photographs covering the walls; the smuggler thought he should hang a couple of works of art over there next to the pictures of grandma and his children's first communion. They looked so like the walls of his childhood home; the morning light filtered in through sheer curtains and beyond you could see the stadium where Dorados play. In front of a white door, they stopped. Come in, said a voice after Vanessa asked if they could.

Regular office layout: computer, furnishings, coffeemaker, boardroom. Leaning back in his leather executive chair, Dioni de la Vega watched them enter. A curious case. He was upper class, his reasons for becoming a narco a matter of myth. Several versions circulated, all of which made him smile. He must have been thirty-five, thin, with a beard clipped short. So you are Leo McGiver. Your home is delightful, Señor de la Vega, a couple of details and it could be a palace. Stop talking bullshit and sit down, he pointed to another big chair. Imelda, bring this jerk something, what'll you have? A Turkish coffee. Hey, you aren't in Paris, thank the saints we have Nescafé. Then a Diet 7 Up, please. Man, do you ever play the fucking loco. For you? Water no ice, and send your buddy out to the Miró for the coffee in case we take a while. He's dead. De la Vega turned to McGiver, who looked straight back at him. You're a fucking bastard, fucking McGiver, a real bastard, that kid was a rising star. I don't doubt it, but he was more interested in Imelda than in me. Dioni de la Vega made a gesture of regret. Well, I've brought you here because I need weapons, the president has declared war on us and I don't feel like getting caught with my pants down; I know you closed a deal with the Valdés family and whatever they ordered I want the same, what do you say? Yes, I thought you were a businessman and I was not mistaken. Take it easy, take it easy, I hate it when people butter me up, just tell me the next step. Transfer seven million dollars to this account in Lithuania and three million euros to this other account in Switzerland. The smuggler handed him two cards, in exchange you will have a hundred and twenty-five A.K.-47 automatic rifles, twenty-five 50-calibre Barretts, eight hundred hand grenades, sixty-six Beretta 92FSs, twenty-five Smith & Wessons, forty-seven Herstal submachine guns 5.7x28mm, five long-range bazookas and twenty thousand live bullets. De la Vega listened all smiles. Delivery will be twelve days after receiving the deposit, between Yameto and Nuevo Altata; it will arrive by air and land on the water at dawn; you'll make the local arrangements for it to arrive happily in your people's hands. It's a deal. They shook hands. What about my drink? There isn't any, this is a warehouse, McGiver, didn't you notice? there's no television and a home without a television is no home at all. McGiver smiled, I won't forget that; there is something I would like to take up with you. What's that? About your business, I want in. De la Vega studied him. We're going to revolutionise this shit, McGiver, you'll see, and yes, you could be useful to us; but we won't talk about it right now, I can't, there's an assembly at my kids' school and all three of them are going to sing, if I don't show up they'll kill me.

Six

It was after noon by the time they made it to Zaragoza Street. Terminator and the Camel gave a garbled report that Lefty could not follow, but neither did he feel like probing. Ortega, head of the crime lab, was scrutinising the piece of lead he held in a pair of watchmaker's pincers: You wanted work, papa, here it is; there are days when somebody decides to trim the size of the human race and nobody is going to stop him. There are days that never fully dawn, Mendieta murmured as he approached the cadaver. Dr Montaño, who had not lost hope of bedding Zelda, welcomed her: You're glowing, Agent Toledo, you look healthier every day, what do you eat for breakfast? To hear that from a doctor is encouraging, thank you. Even more if the doctor is a forensic one, don't you think? Montaño applying his charm. So, what have you found out, doctor? Maybe eight hours dead from a bullet to the heart, speaking of which, mine is broken over you. Zelda turned her attention to the sallow face of Yolanda Estrada, who was wearing a plain T-shirt and pink underwear, then she ran her eyes over every detail of the room. Montaño hit on her again: Do you think that together we might find a way to heal it? Dr Montaño, buzz off or I'll beat the shit out of you. He panted excitedly. What, you think I look like a whore? Don't get so steamed up, Agent Toledo, I merely want to make it clear how much I admire you. Zelda gave him her back. We found a torn-up picture of the Brazilian football team from the last World Cup, Ortega trying to dilute the tension in the air, they took it from over there, he pointed to a spot on the wall; we'll dust it for prints. You do that, Lefty said. A couple of insipid landscapes occupied the spaces on either side of the protruding nail. Shall we break the rules, papa? Totally. Ortega patted him on the back. Would this murder have anything to do with the other? That was the kind of stupid question that could loosen Lefty's tongue. Well, they were co-workers, they died the same day a few minutes apart, the forensic intern said the first died at three a.m. more or less and Montaño thinks it happened here at four; but you know how this stuff works: what's obvious is always wrong. *It's like wearing two G-strings, right? I take one off and everybody thinks I'm naked, or when the G-strings are flesh-coloured.* Judging by her clothes she probably had been asleep, Ortega said, and for sure she knew the murderer, you don't open your door to many people when you're in your undies. With these girls you can't be sure, and in any case, their take on life is pretty harsh; Lefty's hand grazed his throat. Is she all there? Yes, and Montaño doesn't think she was raped, you know which room was Mayra's, right? Mendieta did not hide his irritation. Look, asshole, I wasn't her customer, get that straight. Silence. Then why are you acting like a beaten dog? She's the girl I met in Mazatlán, remember? but I never saw her again. Got it, papa, that's the door. Zelda was making notes. Mendieta, visibly worked up, entered her room and stopped in his tracks, dumbfounded. The walls were papered with huge nude photographs of Mayra in all her tribal beauty. From the front, the back, in profile. Titillating poses. He felt himself start to tremble and tried to focus his eyes on nothing. What good is a bonehead like me? he swallowed, a jerk who never managed to figure out his own life? The tattoo on her belly, just above the pubic hair, leapt out at him. *Are you timid? I can't believe it, a policeman accustomed to blood and guts, have you never seen a tattoo like this? Come on, you're a superhero: my superhero, you're the one who'll save me from the bad guys.* Ashes in his mouth. Beauty is a good reason for living, or is it? One of Ortega's technicians was dusting for fingerprints while the other, smirking, picked up her admirers' letters and business cards: She must have been a high-class fuck, boss, about two months ago we went over to the Alexa and we took up a collection so that at least one of us could taste her delights, do you think we got even close to her price? it was a bitch, even putting all our paycheques together wouldn't have done it. Mendieta stood there, speechless, until his cell phone pulled him out of his stupor.

Where are you? Commander Briseño from the other side of the world. Downtown, another dead woman. Are Ortega and Montaño with you? We're here working. Who is the dead woman? A dancer. From one of the dance companies? She danced at the Alexa. Oh, a table dancer; leave Zelda there and the three of you go immediately to the Hotel San Luis, they just found a body. This is a body too. But this one is a gringo, he's got two bullets in his chest, get going already, Lefty, and take the whole team!

Sixth floor. Room with a view. The housemaid found him. The manager, an elegantly dressed young man, accompanied them. His name was Steven Tyler and he lived in Scottsdale, Arizona; American. Profession? Pianist. Mendieta examined the body up close, then checked around the room while Ortega and two helpers set up and Montaño took Muerto's temperature on the carpet where he lay. O.K., kiddo, don't move so much. Beneath the pungent smell of cadaver fluids, Lefty caught a sweet, feminine scent: He smells like a woman. Shows the guy wasn't a faggot. Why are you pretending, asshole, you use Sarita's perfume. Ortega smiled, put on his gloves, and went through the dead man's pockets, pulling out a thick cloth wallet, which he handed to Lefty. Forty dollars plus a hundred Mexican pesos, but no identification. He returned it to the technician, who said: We'll take along the sheet, it always has something. The bathroom smelled of Hugo Boss and looked clean. Mendieta's cell phone rang, but he did not feel like talking to Dr Parra: bearded fuck, let him wait. Instead he came out of the bathroom, looked in the empty closet, opened a drawer, also empty. From the doorway, the manager watched like a hawk. When did this guest arrive? Yesterday noon. Did you see him? No, he went through reception like everyone else. Call the clerk who registered him. He comes in at two, I'll call down in a minute. Is something wrong, Lefty? Ortega noticed his friend seemed back to his old self. There's no luggage, in the bathroom only one fragrance, which he didn't use, and in the wallet a few pesos, no I.D. or credit cards; I don't think this guy's the guest, he's someone who came looking for him; and he's really young, how old would you say? Maybe twenty, twenty-one. What do you think, Montaño? He might have American citizenship, but his features – nose, mouth, eyes, shape of the face, etc. – say he's as Mexican as they come. May I use this telephone? No, we have to dust it for fingerprints. The manager went to the next room to make the call.

A short while later the young man from reception came through the door. This isn't Señor Tyler; Señor Tyler is about fifty, he's white and tall. Mendieta and Ortega exchanged glances. I need the form

46

he signed, Ortega said, and I'll send over my artist to make a sketch from your description. Montaño gave his conclusion: He's been dead for about four hours and the bullets came out his back. Our house-keeper found him at a little past twelve and no-one heard shots or saw anything. Typical, Lefty said, the society of crime is deaf, blind, dumb, and accommodating; let them take him to the morgue and we'll see who comes to claim him; then he let his thoughts loop back: Why did they cut off a nipple? knife or teeth? teeth?

He called Briseño. Chief, the gringo looks Mexican; what we found is a young guy, maybe twenty years old, but he's not the one registered; he's got two bullets in his chest, one of them went through his heart; the guest, by that I mean the gringo, fled; Ortega found the shells, 9mm. Is there anything for the press? I don't recommend it. Wasn't he a pianist? If he's a pianist, I'm the captain of Apollo 13; his hands are small, rough, and full of scars. Then I'm going home, Lefty. What are you going to cook? Shrimp Rockefeller. Enjoy it. Listen, in the case of the dancers do we have any suspects? Two, Richie Bernal and a Spaniard, Miguel de Cervantes, but Attorney Luis Ángel Meraz visited her once in a while. I don't believe he'd have anything to do with it, he's a gentleman with a great future, let's not bother him. That's why I didn't mention him as a suspect. Mendieta intuited some link between his boss and Meraz, and thought he would keep him out of the picture for now. That Cervantes, isn't he the one who wrote *Don Quixote*? One and the same. Didn't he die a long time ago? It seems he didn't, you should see how good he looks. O.K., feed that neuron in your brain, Lefty, it may be the only one you have left; ask Pineda for help with Richie Bernal, that asshole owes us one; see you later.

The chief called home. My love, how about we cook shrimp in garlic sauce so we can eat as God wishes? Once in a while in a game of chess it works to castle. Honey, please, that garbage? make it Rockefeller, you know how delicious they are when you make them. Very well, my love, I'm on my way, can I pick anything up? If you bring some wholewheat zucchini bread, I'll give you what you really like. You mean you don't have a headache? Me? where did you get that idea? I'm on my way to the bakery.

Friends, this is living, don't you agree?

Lefty returned to Headquarters where he found Zelda interrogating the club's assistant manager, Elisa Calderón; they seemed so absorbed he decided not to interrupt them and instead took José Escamilla, the waiter, to another office and left the Phantom cooling his heels. The women were drinking Diet Cokes. She was truly gorgeous, men took one look at her and they were transfixed, they went all googly-eyed, and that seemed to turn the hussy's crank; the way she moved her body even the other girls came out to watch, they'd be dying of envy, but they couldn't take their eyes off her. Today in her apartment we saw some photographs of her with a very unusual tattoo. She was so vain, there's no other explanation, and she wasn't exactly nice; she was friendly, sure, but she was incapable of doing her co-workers a favour and some of them couldn't stand her, Camila Naranjo, for example, told me several times she wanted nothing more than to see her dead; Mayra poached her best client. Who was that? Attorney Meraz, who had been nuts about Camila and then went crazy for Mayra, you know how fickle men can be, are you married? No, though I am engaged. I don't see your ring. It's a promise. In other words, nothing, didn't I say men are fickle? get him to give you the ring so there won't be any surprises. What about you, are you married? I was years ago, from that relationship I've got a sixteen-year-old son in high school. The manager told us Mayra had been stepping out of line. God forgive me, but she was a skunk; the contract they sign stipulates that we control their comings and goings, especially anything that starts in the club; if they pick up something during their time off we look the other way and nobody is really watching them; at first, she did as she was told, and then she started making her own deals; like now, for example, we didn't know where she was, she'd been missing for two days, the truth is I still feel like yanking on her ears; if we had known who she was with, probably she'd still be alive. Who was your contact in Mazatlán? The mayor, Joaquín Lizárraga, his office is near La Casa del Caracol bookstore; he did the hiring and the girls put on a show. Did you notice anything unusual in Mayra lately? She's been really snooty, this week she was supposed to go work in Mexicali and she didn't want to go; of course, with the clients she had I wouldn't either; imagine the pile of bills Richie Bernal must have laid on her, that guy thinks money only exists for him to spend it. Who was her favourite? She liked money and all three of them gave it to her, what I can't believe is that any of them would kill her; Richie is really violent, but in her hands he was a silk stocking; the other two are well behaved, but, look at the way the world is; I read about murders in the newspapers and I can only wonder if I'd do the same, and my answer isn't always no. Did Mayra get along with Yolanda Estrada? There were days when they weren't speaking, they'd fight like cats and dogs, but the two of them were inseparable, as if they needed each other; are the crimes related? We don't know yet, was Yolanda respected by her co-workers? So-so, though a lot more than Mayra; that one nobody liked. Not even you? Me even less, she made my job as difficult as she could.

They talked about the day-to-day work in the club, about problematic customers, and about the manager, who had finally settled in. One of the partners hired Carvajal because his predecessor turned out to be a soft touch. Do you remember which partner? Rodrigo Cabrera, I think Carvajal worked for him in the D.A.'s office. Can you recall any of the first customers Mayra refused to continue seeing? That's hard because she was very clever, she knew how to chase them away bit by bit. Who was Camila Naranjo going with before Mayra came on the scene? They started at the same time, I think there was already bad blood between them; Meraz took Camila out a dozen times, that's all. How often did Mayra's clients come to the Alexa? Cervantes was stuck on her, he'd be there almost every day; Richie could turn up; Meraz never comes, the Phantom lets him know when there are new girls and he decides if he wants to take one out. Zelda asked her not to leave the city until everything was cleared up.

I hope the boss forgives me for not bringing him in on the interrogation, she mused, he's upset and I really ought to help him get over it. Let's see: we've got a girl who's tough, envied, and very attractive, with three clients who will deny everything, though any of them could have murdered her. She got up from her desk; I've got to talk things over with Rodo. She called out to Terminator and the Camel and asked them to interrogate the waiter and the bartender. She was surprised when they said Escamilla was with Mendieta.

O.K., tell him I went out to eat; what about the bartender? We sent him out to get us Cokes, but the boss wants to make him sing, too.

Your stats, doll. José Escamilla, twenty-four years old, from here, married, a two-year-old daughter, three years working at the Alexa. Do you know why we're interrogating you? Because somebody killed Yhajaira and Roxana. Tell us about Yhajaira. She and Roxana were in huge demand, bros of all kinds came in because of them and they paid whatever the girls asked, what a drag what happened to them; look, we're all in this gig for the money, forget pleasure or any of that shit, especially the babes who are only young and fresh for a few years. What are the names of their regular clients? It's hard to say, one day an army officer might come in, another day a businessman, a teacher, a politician, a construction worker; the Alexa is like the church, everybody goes at least once; Yhajaira might be out several times one week with a colonel and the next week it'd be a professor from Sinaloa University. What about Roxana? She was the star, the prettiest and the best, last week I saw two with her: the owner of San Esteban Farms, he'd been after her for two months like a rabid dog until she convinced him to leave her alone; and Marcelino Freire, a Brazilian who plays for Dorados, the one who missed that penalty when they could have got into first division; people say he was paid off, what do you think? Of course not, only honest people get involved in football; give me the names you can remember, first Roxana's regulars and then Yhajaira's. Ramón Ibarra used to write her poems that made her smile; a skinny guy with an afro would come in with him, he liked to make music clinking on glasses and bottles; another guy with a beard liked to put on a red clown's nose and spend hours making faces at her; the manager of the Multicinema was incredibly persistent. Who stood out? There was a blond journalist, a guy who used to be really fat, he gave me good tips, he'd drool from the corner of his mouth watching her dance. He paused to think. No-one else? No, I don't think so, except for that Spaniard, Miguel de Cervantes, and Richie Bernal, who everybody knows. Mendieta opened the door and shouted: Terminator, call Gori, I've got a witness who's lost his memory, I need him warmed up; in a minute somebody will be here who's found a cure for Alzheimer's. What's that supposed to mean? Nothing, just in case you forgot to mention anybody. Escamilla lowered his head and began to sweat. It's not easy working there, I've lasted three years because I don't look, I don't hear, and I don't speak. Well, Gori is like a Bic pen, he never fails. In the end Roxana only took care of three people: Attorney Luis Ángel Meraz plus the two I mentioned, Bernal and Cervantes. Which did she prefer? Lately, it was Richie, who must have spent a fortune on her, do you know Richie? God forbid. I thought all the badges knew him. What about the manager? He's easygoing, at least we don't hear about anything, he's been on the job for a year and a half and he's only got involved with Nadia, she used to be a gymnast in university, at the club we call her the queen of the pole, and also with Miroslava, who's stuck around for a while and now she's the oldest. Where's he from? Around here, he worked in government in the last term, I think in the D.A.'s office. What about the owner, what can you tell me about him? As far as I know, the club is a partnership made up of Meraz, former D.A. Barrera, and a gringo I've never met. There are several clubs in the city, did either of the girls branch out? Club Sinaloa; you know, they could have gone there on their own, but, go figure, they asked me to keep them company and, well, I pocketed some change. Those gentlemen must like pretty girls. I'll say, Yhajaira was a complex beauty and they'd drool all over her, but Roxana was a goddess; when she walked by no-one could look away, and don't think it was only the men, the women too; she was one incredible babe, plus her eyes, one green, the other the colour of honey, and she would never blink. *Of course you can talk about mine, but you're going to be hard put to say something original.* Who else they saw, I couldn't say, Attorney Ramírez would call the girls in and close the door, I'd hear laughing or some sound of agreement, but I never saw who was in there, they must have been powerful people because there were always bodyguards around and cars with logos from some government ministry or some company; I never got any warning, so I'd drive them wherever and that'd be it; Attorney Ramírez didn't want me in on it, but the girls stood up for me; they never told me anything about the people or the places I took them, in this business it's wise to be discreet; Ramírez runs the show and, yup, he's a person to be reckoned with. O.K., live your life as usual, if we need anything more you'd better be on hand. If you want a girl, say the word, I know where most of them live and they all owe me favours. Do you know how many years you'll get for pimping? No, but I know how much I have to fork over every month if I want to work in peace, he smiled. You can go. He stood up fast. Wait, you haven't told me the name of the owner of San Esteban Farms. Esteban Aguirrebere.

The Phantom then confirmed everything Escamilla had said. The bartender was totally at ease, smoking; he was one tough cookie, calm as could be. So that's what you do? asked Mendieta, you say, attorney, we've got a new hooker, and then he comes by for her? More or less. Why does he trust your judgment? No big deal, I know his taste, he likes a big ass and a pretty face, well put together. Tits? However, small, big, he usually doesn't care, what he notices is the ass. Uh-huh. The others did not turn up for their appointments. Who was this guy Ramírez?

Seven

Samantha Valdés was listening to McGiver from the plush back seat of the latest model Cadillac Escalade E.X.T. He was in the passenger seat beside a very alert driver. They were travelling slowly down Niños Héroes Parkway. Ahead and behind, two Lobo pickups were protecting her, the daughter of the godfather of the Pacific Cartel, his only heir. The waters of the river were choppy. McGiver was half-turned towards her. I've got everything, Señora Valdés, a team of sixteen men ready to flood the Phoenix area with merchandise; you will receive the usual, plus a fifteen per cent premium; just like with the weapons, we are professionals and we get the job done, place a shipment in our hands and you will not regret it. She had been listening to more or less the same spiel for seven minutes and she had heard enough. McGiver might be a sure bet for arms or other contraband, but her man in Phoenix was among the most loyal she had and she was not about to betray him. Enough, she cut him off, we can't; we are a closed organisation and there is no place for anyone new; you're a businessman and I'm sure you understand. Won't you give me a chance? if not Phoenix, it could be Dallas or San Francisco. Impossible; I could tell you we have nobody at the North Pole, but you are a serious man and there is no point kidding you. She was wearing a light blue pantsuit: That's why I recommend you think before you act, I wouldn't want to have to do without your services. That will certainly never be the case, however, I can't deny that I would have liked your support for this proposal. I've already spoken and I'm not going to repeat myself; Guacho, leave me at Mariana's and take this gentleman wherever he asks you, then come back, I don't want you off somewhere if something happens at home. Is your father any better? At times, then he gives us a scare.

McGiver got out when she did, to say goodbye; although he knew they would never have a fling he liked to feel the spell of her perfumed presence. In any case, I thank you, señora, and of course I remain at your service. They were in the parking lot of the building. Samantha eyeballed him for a few seconds: I know you saw Dioni de la Vega and I can imagine what you talked about; continue seeing him and be careful; I want to know every detail and what you expect to earn from him, I'll double it on the spot. Cold smiles. She had just hired him; McGiver didn't like it, but he said nothing, since in some ways it suited him. He asked to be taken to the Hotel Lucerna. That night, when he met up with Fabián Olmedo, he would know the next step. Guacho was listening to Daniel Quiroz from "Eyes on the Night", but McGiver, busy wondering what was up with those art thieves in Mexico City, paid no attention. He would call Dulce. Would she have followed his instructions? If there is any balance to be found in this world, like they say, he had achieved it. He crossed the threshold of the hotel and went straight to the bar.

Alcohol is not a bad adviser, it's just that you don't always give it a proper hearing.

Eight

Without intending to he drove over to Malverde's shrine and parked.

From across the street he watched people of all kinds arrive. On foot, in cars, in Hummers. The fearful and the fearsome. A group of *norteña* musicians were playing *corridos* nonstop. *Life is strange, Edgar, I think with you I could make a life, I mean a different life, the sort of life a woman dreams about.* I won't promise you a thing, Malverde, it's no fucking cakewalk, but if I catch this sonofabitch I'll be here with roses, which for sure were what she liked; I never asked, but all women like them. He saw a lovely bride chatting with her bridesmaids while they filmed her, and for an instant he thought he saw Mayra Cabral de Melo, incredible body and all, but no, it couldn't be, she was lying in the morgue waiting for the next step in the investigation, waiting for them to locate her next of kin and hand over the body. He breathed deeply. The emptiness he felt was putrid.

It would be hard to say how long he sat there without moving, trying to understand the abyss into which he had fallen. What's wrong with me? I wasn't even in love with her, I didn't see her for more than a few days; neither did she make love any differently. But she was the one who brought me back from the brink. That red bikini I will never forget.

He turned the ignition and Queen belted out "Who Wants to Live Forever". Not me, he said, and certainly not her. He drove off slowly. I'm ground to a powder, he admitted. But Ortega is right, there is only one truth behind her death and it must be found, and when that happens . . . The dude cut off her nipple, why? is that a message, a signature, or was it something to throw us off the track? Shit! how could anyone dare kill a woman like Mayra? We are so fucked. He opened the glove compartment, saw his Beretta and the last envelope Briseño had given him: Here, so you'll stop whining. Does this have anything to do with me? who might have known there was something between us? He lit a cigarette. If this is what modern life is like, we should have never left prehistory.

In fifteen minutes he arrived at El Quijote. The city was an oven and everyone was baking along with it.

Curlygirl, bring me a roast pork sandwich and a beer. The same as yesterday, Lefty? don't you want something else? that's not the food for you, you're an officer of the law, a badge, always dealing with heartless murderers; vary the menu a bit, baby, or you're going to end up nothing but skin and bones. O.K., instead of the beer bring me a whisky. I hate it when you pull my leg, if your blessed mother had left me in charge, I would have given you a few good spankings.

He came back with a plate of steak, potatoes, and Caesar salad, plus a *michelada* in a mug. And don't push me away. Mendieta contemplated the plate and the mug, then looked up at his friend. Did you ever meet Susana? Which Susana? Doña Mary's daughter. Ah, of course, the blonde with that pert little ass, I haven't seen her in years, I think she lives on the other side, what about her? The *michelada* reminded me. Don't tell me you were one of her studs. How could you think that, I've always been a serious boy. Because that one slept with half the world, she was always hot for it, if you only knew the things she told me, her entire nature was in her crotch; is Doña Mary still alive? And living in the same house. That daughter of hers was such a flirt, I'd run into her in the places I least expected, telling me she wanted love, not sex, can you believe it? Mendieta remembered her as beautiful, kind, and an expert at doing it in the back seat. Practice makes perfect, he thought, and he recalled the few times they had gone out for supper, she always had steak and potatoes along with her *michelada*. O.K., savour that while I take care of my old man who just came in; have you ever seen such beauty? Smiling from ear to ear, Curlygirl went to seat a young construction worker.

Enrique said Susana and her son were coming in the summer and summer is already here, hotter than last year. We always say that, and we wonder why we still live in this place, but nobody leaves. Jason Mendieta: why would Susana have given him that last name? Was he really his child? Don't be stupid, as if we were the only Mendietas in the world; for sure she met someone with that last name and . . .

A few minutes before six, he took a call from Ortega. Are you still having your period, papa? No problem now, I just bought a box of Kotex, the kind with little tabs. O.K., here's a bit of the report that might interest you: on the second cadaver they used a 9mm and there's no powder, which means somebody with good aim shot her from a distance; and look, if you really had something going with the first girl, it doesn't matter to me, you ought to thank her for chasing the fairy out of you and apply yourself to catching the culprit. Agreed, we're going to throw the faggot in the slammer.

They used a 9mm on her too. Anything on the gringo? You think I'm a machine? you must live on the fucking moon. He hung up. Lefty turned back to his thoughts: a serial killer targeting exotic dancers? That's all we need, a moralist here in the twenty-first century; why not? Let's hope no more turn up.

It was dark when he left El Quijote, the temperature must have been about 38°C and he was sweating. *I'd like to stay with you, mister policeman, we could fool around and maybe break the law, but I have to work in an hour and I've got to get ready.* Why do people hate each other so? Humans are demons. They spend their lives killing each other. Couldn't they find another way to express their animosity? The fact is many people deserve to die, the ones who represent the worst of the human race, but, tell me, who ought to knock them off? Usually one of those same idiots looks in the mirror and says "me". He shoots his little pistol and upsets the balance. Somebody calls the police and off we go, as if there weren't more important things to do. Me, for example, it's been a long time since I've properly scratched my balls.

He turned on the radio. Quiroz giving it his all: "Two bodies were found this morning, one on the Coast Highway, the other in a house on Zaragoza Street right downtown. The police have no clues, is someone out there murdering table dancers? Because today's victims were employed at a well-known nightclub on Zapata Boulevard. Commander Briseño, chief of the State Ministerial Police, declared to this station that they would give no quarter until they have the criminals behind bars. For 'Eyes on the Night', this is Daniel Quiroz reporting." The chief must have raised the payoff to this asshole, he's going so easy on us. He popped in a C.D., "The Way It Used to Be" by Engelbert Humperdinck.

At home, meditating over a double whisky on the rocks, he concluded that he had better light a fire under himself. Was he going to be a badge his whole life? run to fat till his T-shirts wouldn't fit? The mentality at Headquarters was dragging him down. He worked in a city where his profession got no respect and never achieved a thing. Most everybody had an unbelievable aptitude for crime. Was I born for this? I can't be bothered.

The telephone interrupted his second drink. What now? He remembered that Jason was going to call. He was hoping the guy would give up, but no. Jason Mendieta, don't bug me, buddy, what kind of a son are you that you're messing with my life even before we meet? Do you think I only have time for you? I've got work to do, I've got a case that hurts more than I ever imagined. Has a woman ever got to you? I won't tell you what you're going to learn when you grow up, because you can learn things at any age and it still makes no difference. He concentrated on his third drink, which left the bottle empty, then he went out. The telephone continued ringing. The Alexa was waiting for him; he'd go alone, since Zelda hadn't reported in. *A man, to be a man must be incredible, and you are.*

Nine

Fabián "Gandhi" Olmedo was sleeping deeply in the living room of his home. It was not just any living room. Although he could afford them, no paintings by Toledo or Picasso were on the walls. Not even a Frida, though he had been offered one on numerous occasions, or a Teresa Margolles bracelet, which he had nearly bought in Madrid. None of that. Do you know what was hanging there? Pieces of guitars. Gandhi collected bits of broken guitars destroyed by their owners. He had five from Jimi Hendrix, three from Pete Townshend, four from Ritchie Blackmore, and two from Kurt Cobain. They were elegantly framed and protected by security glass. It was a gallery complete with No Smoking signs that no-one obeyed, fire extinguishers not maintained in years, and locked emergency exits.

Being a powerful businessman, Gandhi had it all and knew how to give himself every luxury and every misery. He was the one who had organised a contest among Culiacán's elite to see who could last the longest living with a poor family and eating what they ate. He won by a wide margin and that was how he earned his nickname.

Tonight he nodded off while awaiting two art runners who were to bring him the instruments sacrificed by Townshend and Hendrix at Woodstock, pieces he had pursued doggedly and was about to possess at last; in addition, the runners would leave something with him for a few months, a fragment of a guitar that John Lennon supposedly smashed the day the Beatles broke up.

Do you expect me to believe that? who do you take me for? It is true, Señor Olmedo, there is no record of that occurring and neither Paul McCartney nor Ringo Starr want to say anything about it, but the owner insists she was present in the bedroom where Lennon blew his stack. Blew his stack? do you really believe John Lennon was so mad about the break-up that he would smash a Rickenbacker 325? you better not think I look that stupid. I would never dare, Señor Olmedo; as I understand it the matter was so private the only witness was a Mrs Thompson, who was there for an appointment with Yoko Ono for something related to an exhibition of her work. I'm not interested. Don't think of it as a commitment, Señor Olmedo, we'll leave it with you for a couple of months and if it doesn't captivate you we'll pick it up and that will be the end of it. I never do anything if it's not a commitment, so just bring the pieces we agreed on.

He had asked them to come at nine because at ten Leo McGiver would be there with a treasure: the guitar smashed by Jeff Beck, then playing with the Yardbirds, in Michelangelo Antonioni's *Blow-Up*. A genuine rarity that had cost him a fortune. That McGiver was an ace, truly.

Olmedo had wisely invested his family inheritance in the automotive sector, and although his competitors considered his business dealings to be hardly patriotic he turned a deaf ear; he was where he ought to be and that was what counted. However, he was a man of extreme caution. He had been kidnapped three times and twice escaped unharmed; the first time he barely got out alive.

Olmedo set out a bottle of Buchanan's Red Seal and a small bucket of ice, then put on a Tom Waits record and eased into his favourite chair. He lived alone. A woman cleaned house for him, but she was in Mexico City with her daughter who had just had a baby.

A tough character. Fifty-three years old and, despite having lived with four different women and having a daughter, he was a confirmed bachelor. At least that is what he told Dr Parra, with whom he had dinner now and again.

By 10.30 he had consumed half the bottle, listened to two records, and was sleeping with his legs outstretched. The bell rang several times. He didn't feel like getting up and it occurred to him he should hire a tactful butler to take care of such details. Dressed in baggy clothes, his favourite style, he swayed a path towards the door, yawning. Are these guys really English? They show up when they fucking feel like it, next time let their whore of a mother believe them. Businessmen? my balls, in business you never show up late, especially when the deal is in your favour. With McGiver you can never tell, he's never been on time in his entire bitch of a life. He said he was in a hurry, I should have everything ready, that he would present me with a problem, and now look, even he's late. Reminding himself that he had placed the five hundred thousand dollars on the record player, he thought he would get this over with quickly. After looking at the certificates of authenticity and the pieces, of course. The business with Leo was already paid for.

He opened without asking who it was and collapsed. Nobody survives a bullet in the heart.

Ten

Outside the Alexa a skinny man was selling candy, gum, and cigarettes. He displayed them in a wooden box set up next to a one-way mirror near the entrance. The site of Mayra Cabral de Melo's triumphs. *It isn't the best one I've worked in, but I love it.* Mendieta watched the guy staring at the mirror. He was known as the Apache and he had done time for killing his wife. Lefty knew of him because he had been an informant for Sánchez, his former partner, now retired on a farm, growing radishes and making carrot marmalade. What do you see, Apache? The man did not turn around. Everyone is in this glass, señor, the good and the bad, criminals and martyrs, politicians and athletes; some days God himself comes by dragging a leather bag, I feel like asking him, "What have you got there, sir?" but I get the willies. He took off his baseball cap, wiped the sweat from a forehead marked by a jagged scar where he had once been scalped. I just ask what's up and he disappears, the man doesn't want to speak to me, he's ashamed; sometimes she comes by making fun of me, that daughter of her bitch of a mother; other times she's crying and I never know what to think. Mendieta saw reflections in the mirror, but nothing out of the ordinary. Every night is different, señor, sometimes I only see buildings, the people are inside sitting cross-legged, they won't show their faces, they're afraid of something, they won't even raise the blinds; I see rivers where nobody swims, empty beaches, deserts without any scorpions, cockroaches in outer space. I'll have a Trident. Choose your flavour, though by

65

your face you must like spearmint, am I right? Do you remember Sánchez? A charitable soul, once in a while he comes by dressed as a cowboy, would you like the mint? Try to see your future in the glass, Apache. What I wouldn't give for that, señor, but there is something very powerful that says no, like I told you; with whom do I have the pleasure? Mendieta. He thought for a few seconds. Lefty Mendieta? What, is there another? Sánchez had a lot of faith in you, how's it going? Best I can. A friend of Sánchez is a friend of mine, so whatever I can do for you. I'll keep that in mind. And if I've never seen you here before it's because now you're looking for something: that's prison logic. Outside logic, too. Absolutely true and your something must be that business of the dead girls. Where did Richie Bernal pick up Roxana? Under my nose. How many noses have you got? Those girls cut a big swath, Lefty Mendieta, so you be careful poking around; the shadows have eyes and wear Ray-Bans. Lefty put the gum in his pocket. What have you heard? The devil never sleeps, and when he sleeps he keeps one eye open. I've got three suspects. You're lost, Lefty, all you need is one. A group of young people came up, looking to buy cigarettes.

He knew the bouncer, had arrested him twice for carrying weapons issued exclusively to the army. They eyed each other. The guy gave him a cold smile and stepped aside with a slight flourish. Welcome, commander. Are you behaving yourself, Bigboy? Like a seminarian. You'd better be; come by Headquarters early tomorrow, there's a test you've got to take. I already passed, he smiled. Lefty, who was showing the strain of the long day, frowned. Let's see what you're guarding with your life. Nothing you haven't already seen and enjoyed, my chief. As soon as Mendieta stepped inside, the bouncer punched a number on his cell phone.

Lights. Loud music. Smoke. Perfume. He detected multiple scents, but paid no attention. The girls were doing their first walk-about on the illuminated catwalk that went the width of the room. Patrons were shouting excitedly, a few howled. Mendieta felt a great emptiness in his body. *It's not just the pole or the lights or all that collective heat rising, it's the dance, the beauty of the body.* So this was the site of her success; incredible, a pigsty would have been better. José Escamilla offered him a seat where nothing would obstruct his view, then brought him up to date on the variety of caresses he could receive from any of those now parading in a line for the modest sum of 180 pesos, a special offer for payday. Lefty listened, then asked for a beer and a tequila. Alonso Carvajal, alerted by the bouncer, went over to greet him. Welcome, detective, I'm here for whatever you need, is there any news? Your people aren't giving us enough help, Alonso, we're going to have to slap them around and interrogate the girls. The girls are afraid. Nobody leaves Culiacán until they can say the rosary by heart. You can count on that; Elisa told me your partner wants to speak with Camila Naranjo, I'm trying to locate her, she didn't come in yesterday, let's hope there are no surprises. That would be best. It's great you're relaxing, detective. Carvajal rubbed his chin, Mendieta smiled. Where's Ramírez, the real boss? he doesn't seem to be around anywhere. Carvajal handed him a card. Here are his telephone numbers. Good. I hope you will excuse me, I must take care of a couple of things, but please make yourself at home, we are at your service. And he said goodbye. Lefty watched about thirty men in the process of decomposing. Hello, my chief, what's up, are you here to work or to have a good time? The police are always watching, Escamilla. Great, do you see that man tossing back rum there in the shadows? Lefty looked. That's Miguel de Cervantes, one of Roxana's dudes. They watched him take a slug straight from the bottle and it hit him like a hammer to the thumb. He wiped his forehead, put his elbows on the little table, and covered his face with his hands; then he took another drink. Shall I introduce you? Please, before he commits suicide.

Mendieta sat across from the Spaniard, whose eyes were glazed. Got any hash? Lefty shook his head. Fuck, but *coño*, you must have something, crack, crystal, anything. I've got coke. That's not my thing but, well, bring it on, a couple of lines and another bottle, what are you waiting for? Tell me, what's the suicide rate in Spain? I shit in the milk, why the fuck should I care? He gave Mendieta a hate-filled look. When was the last time you saw Roxana? That's something I'll tell the fuzz. And what do you think I am, the Virgin of Macarena? O.K., my friend, take it easy, it's just you don't look it, you come over with that face and all, and I'm no clairvoyant. So? Five days ago. Did she tell you anything, mention any fears, any threats? Nothing, that woman made the world disappear, only the two of you remained, nothing else; I shit on the whore of a mother who killed her. Mendieta poured himself a glass of rum and knocked it back. *Coño*, you aren't a policeman, you knew her too. Their welled-up eyes met. How long had you been seeing her? Since I got here, more or less two months ago, and I wouldn't kill her even if they offered me all the gold in the world, fuck, that's something you just don't do; but what am I telling you for, you must have your own sorrows. Where did you see each other? At my house, in La Primavera, you know, that yuppie neighbourhood full of strange people. Do you like guns? Not even toy ones, my parents were pacifists and I know nothing about guns. He poured for Mendieta and they said your health and drank it down. They cut off a nipple. *Coño*, she didn't like anyone to touch them, if there was one thing that woman held back it was her tits. *I know, but I don't want them to droop; besides, you want them more just looking, right? It's better if you look without touching, like the tattoos.* The bastard couldn't resist, he cut off the nipple she wouldn't let him suck; he couldn't be sane. What's your name? Edgar Mendieta. Miguel de Cervantes, and don't waste your time with me, uncle: before I would kill a woman like Roxana I'd kill my own mother, and look, for that hooker I'd give anything. Well, you really are in a bad way. I'm serious. How did you set up your dates? She would say when, I wanted her every night, you understand? every fucking night I wanted that cunt in my bed. When were you supposed to see her next? Today; imagine how I feel, that sonofabitch broke my heart. Where were you last night? At home. Can you prove it? Sure, I watched the repeat of the Madrid–Barça match on the terrace; the gardener who was watering the lawn said hello. What time? First about ten, then again about two-thirty in the morning when I was headed for bed and he was making his rounds; in fact, there was a full moon and it was red; do you believe in U.F.O.s? He remembered the dog barking at a red moon that a few minutes later turned white again, would a murderer notice such things? that could have been when they killed Mayra in that field. Don't leave the city until we give the green light. Don't worry, I'll be here for a while yet. Cervantes poured again and they said your health, one with a glass, the other with the bottle. Now, give me your telephone numbers and office address, we've already got the one for your house. It's all here. He handed over a business card and Mendieta took his picture with his cell phone. Did she ever tell you about the others? Cervantes smiled drily. You want to know if you impressed her? No, I want to know if she felt threatened or harassed by one of her clients. Nothing, she was very discreet and she even read novels, *coño*, did she ever kid me about my name, I don't know if you know, but I've got the same name as a Spanish writer. I had no idea. I figured, you're a cop. And I'll still bust your chops. You're in a bad way too, eh, uncle?

His table was occupied when he got back to it, so he sat where he could. The girls were still parading, now one by one. The waiter arrived with a beer and a tequila. Courtesy of the manager, chief, have you picked yours out yet? look, that girl dancing now is brand new. Send me somebody who started with Roxana, the best-looking, so I can sin without remorse. There's one you'll really like, and besides, she was a good friend of those girls. He went over to a woman who was astride the legs of an old man, riding him. All set, here or in a private room?

The private room was a cave, one metre by two, in semi-darkness, with a plastic chair in the corner. A smiling Miroslava straddled his groin and started gyrating. Wait, tell me about Roxana. You think that'll turn you on? I'm about to find out. What a day, I don't get why everybody wants to know about Roxana. Who? Well, everybody, you just have to die for the whole world to want to know how it happened. Lots of people? More than I'll ever have in my life, same story with Yhajaira, from the moment I came in they won't stop asking about them; do you want me to get you warmed up for when you get home or do you want to talk about the girls? if you want the special service, right now I can't. Why, not? Company rules. Let's talk about Roxana. She hadn't shown up for three nights, but she was like that, when she was here she would pack the place and when she wasn't here, she'd still pack it, that's why we loved her; she was going out with that Spaniard, poor guy, he's nuts about her, you're a badge, right? One of the worst. Miroslava stopped moving, relaxed her body, and raised her face to avoid looking at Mendieta: Well, everybody works at what they can, how did they die? They were shot. You're always afraid of what might happen, every customer might be a gentleman or an executioner, the one who'll give you your best moment or your worst. The doorman hurried them with a loud knock. I'm coming; but she did not move. You haven't told me who else she went out with. She went with all of them, she was the star, how many times a week would you come? Me? never, I never saw her dance, I met her in Mazatlán three months ago. I never liked those trips to Mazatlán. Do you know who took her there? Time's up, the doorman shouted. Why don't we meet up tomorrow? do you know the Café Miró, the one in Chapule? No, she said, but I'll ask. Let's meet there at eleven. Could we do it at five? at eleven I'll be asleep. Do you want to go to Headquarters? No, suppose we meet at my house? then I could make you something special. He was on the verge of giving in when a sudden silence descended, no music: O.K., five o'clock at the Miró, and he hurried out to the table area, what was going on?

It better not be true, assholes, screamed a young man without much beard, maybe twenty years old, wearing a loud shirt and blue jeans. Around his neck gleamed a thick gold chain with a cross.

Richie Bernal, murmured Miroslava at his back. The young man was carrying an A.K.-47 and right then and there he emptied the magazine into the catwalk, sending splinters flying. Everybody hit the floor, under the tables, behind the chairs, wherever they could. A few shrieks. She better be alive, you bastards, because if she isn't this place ain't gonna be worth shit. He slung the rifle across his chest in a nifty move, pulled out his pistol, and shot up the ceiling, putting out a couple of lights. Alive I want her, assholes, I'm going to a party and I'm not going to show up alone without a fucking fight. Mendieta spied the manager taking cover behind the bar and the Phantom standing there, calmly smoking. Richie, please, a whining voice. Shut your mouth, fucking Carvajal; you shut up and the rest of you shut up too, the girls can shut up, everybody better shut up or I'll blow you to kingdom fucking come. He signalled to one of his henchmen and they traded Kalashnikovs. A trembling Miroslava hung on to Lefty. She had big hard tits, but he was hardly aware of them. He hated getting involved with the narcos, yet he knew he had to do it, he was the only badge in the place, right? What a drag. He saw the Spaniard had not moved, but he was alert, observing the scene. Or maybe he was beginning to think about hiding like everyone else because he looked down at the parquet floor. With your mouths shut you look prettier, assholes, Bernal shouted, now Carvajal, face-like-my-balls, bring me Roxana because I've got a bash with one of the big boys. Richie, it's not my fault, the manager said, sticking up his head, Roxana . . . Bernal let loose a volley into the ceiling. Don't tell me she's dead because I'll fuck you, you big fat prick, call her right now, tell her her Richie has come for her, the one who does it like nobody ever did it to her before. Stop acting like a jerk, Bernal. Mendieta took two steps forward; Richie turned to him like lightning. She's dead and nobody can bring her back for you. You are going to get royally fucked, Bernal screamed as he pulled the trigger, but the rifle had no more bullets. What is this, you dickhead? he threw the gun at the man who had handed it to him, so you're protecting me with an unloaded gun? Stop being a jerk, I tell you. Lefty, now standing in front of Bernal, thought about asking him, "Where were you last night?" however he went on: Stop acting like a little snot-nose who shit his pants. Bernal snatched a pistol from one of the other thugs and put it between Lefty's eyes. Before I fuck you tell me who you are, you fucking queer, Richie Bernal never kills anybody without knowing his name. I'm the daddy of all the little chicks, Lefty said, alert as could be and ready to save his skin. Well, you are going to leave a pile of feathers behind, you sonofabitch. It's Lefty Mendieta, one of the gunslingers muttered. The dude eased up a little. Are you sure? Lefty turned to the hit man, it was Devil Urquídez, who in another epoch had been a police officer and soon would marry the daughter of one of Lefty's best friends. The outlaw handed his boss a cell phone. What's up? nothing, I'm just going to kill Lefty Mendieta and . . . he listened for ten seconds. He lowered his pistol, dropped the cell: It's the luck of assholes that there's always somebody who loves them. He headed quickly to the exit, followed by his men. Devil picked up the cell phone and smiled at Mendieta. Don't forget we're expecting you at the wedding, my man Lefty, then he joined his buddies. It's a commitment, Devil my man; it was her, right? Who else?

Escamilla arrived with a beer and a tequila, but Miguel de Cervantes got there first. You've got balls, detective, and if you are going to fuck me in the ass it will be a pleasure. He handed him a glass filled with rum and they drank. Miroslava gave him a kiss and rubbed her breasts against him without Mendieta noticing. Before the merriment became irresistible, he slipped out. It was too much. He felt exhausted, empty; he wanted to cry.

Eleven

A bullet in the heart nobody survives, except for Gandhi Olmedo, who owns another collection, this one of bulletproof vests, which he started the day he escaped his captors and nearly croaked when they put a .38 slug through him.

I asked myself, what good is a man who's been kidnapped? No good, better off dead. That night I'd had a beating for supper and I was mad as hell, what good is a cadaver? The answer was the same. We were in the countryside, in a shack out towards Sanalona, my hands and feet in chains. I got ready: as soon as these pricks fall asleep I'm out of here. I'd been in their hands for about twenty hours. They wanted half a million pesos, which in those days was a pile of money, I couldn't pull that together even asking my enemies for a loan. My guard stayed awake until midnight, then he nodded off like his buddies. I made my way slowly, dragging myself along and I managed to squeeze through a hole in one of the tin walls; then I rolled for about twenty metres; everything slow as could be because I was handcuffed and my ankles were chained together and my fucking heart was leaping out of my chest. When I tried to jump like a kangaroo, they put a bullet in me; they shot several times, but only hit me once. All I could think about right then was a bulletproof vest, I wouldn't be going to church or to Malverde, no fucking way; if I got out of this I would never be caught without a vest. I was skinny then, more than now, I couldn't have had much blood because as soon as the kidnappers left, thinking me dead, I continued down that hill as best I could until I reached the highway. That was where a few long-distance runners out early in the morning found me dying. One of them was studying psychiatry: the now practising Dr Parra.

Gandhi was so drunk when he took the bullet that he slept until dawn. He got to his feet with difficulty, saw the hole in his white shirt, and went in search of a cold beer. After a long guzzle he took off the shirt and vest, inspected the projectile and the small dint it had made. Twenty-five calibre: fucking hitmen. He studied the hunk of metal. They can't even afford a decent pistol. He finished his beer. Who could it be? Who would use such an old-fashioned gun? He switched off the lights and sat down, swivelled towards the record player to see if the bag of money was still there, that none of the pieces on the walls were missing. He went to the door, which was closed but not locked, then he put the money in the safe. That asshole came just to kill me, who could he be? who sent him? It could be any of my enemies and now it's so cheap to run that game; from the pistol it must be somebody just starting out, good thing, because if it had occurred to him to give me a *coup de grâce* I'd be lying there rotting; what could have happened to those people? no English and no fucking Leo; no surprise with that bastard, he's always in the middle of eighty thousand fights and he sounded apprehensive on the telephone, but what about the others with all their fucking formality? He opened another beer. And the bullet? Who would send this little message? Chuco Valenzuela might, the fucking faggot, he's desperate because his business won't take off; the Legged Beast might too, I'm not sure about Fray Antonio, he's a crafty one. He drank, put on a Cream record, and sat down again. The first rays of sun poured in the window. Should he tell the police? What a drag, I can see those idiots all over my house asking questions; a private detective? I don't think there are any in this city and if there are they'd be real losers. "Sunshine of Your Love" filled the air.

He thought again about the guys bringing the pieces. Did they come? Probably I didn't wake up. As soon as it's office hours, they'll call for sure. Suppose I bring in a gringo dick? Those guys get the job done, not like our bunch of trash who call themselves police.

He came out of the bathroom after nine, turned on his cell phones, but had no important calls. He turned them off. His landline showed a call from the Hummer distributor made ten minutes before and another from a luxury car distributor. He got into his Jeep and went to cure his hangover at Puye's: a cocktail of shrimp, octopus, clam, oyster, and conch with *piquín* chillies would save his life. If the English wanted to do business let them wait and, yes, he would call the gringos, the same people that found his kidnappers who, by the way, did not live to tell the tale. If it was Chuco he wouldn't rub the faggot out, although it also could have been Sultan Camacho, or . . . who do I owe so much money to that he'd want me dead? Well, the gringos will figure it out, but just in case before I call them I'm going to ask Carrasco; all kinds of characters turn up at his place and he always knows what's going to happen before it does. They ought to hire him to predict earthquakes; besides he owes me a bundle. It better not have been Chuco; if I call the gringos now they'll be here the day after tomorrow. Puye, he shouted before parking the car, the Gandhi cocktail, and put chillies in that mother, I'm wounded. It's all ready and waiting for you, Don Fabián.

At that moment, Leo McGiver was lovingly oiling his Smith & Wesson in the Hotel Lucerna. He was whistling Mozart's Fortieth.

Twelve

Four in the morning. Mendieta had cleaned his pistol, watched two movies with Reese Witherspoon as a blonde, ingested a double dose of tranquillisers, and he was still awake. He would nod off in his chair every few minutes and then there he would be again, eyes wide. Lazily, he thought about the angel who had saved him from Richie: I hope it doesn't cost me too much. His glance came to rest on the book by João Ubaldo Ribeiro, but he did not pick it up. Mayra Cabral, eyes green and honey, what a way to look at the world. *I don't believe you're a badge, you've got that charm nice guys have that makes them look ridiculous; up to now you are the only person I've met who ever heard of João Ubaldo Ribeiro, even if you haven't read him.* And bro, she would clap those incredible eyes on me: one from a virgin jungle, the other from a Chinese restaurant. He stood up. Maybe if I go look for her she'll be there. They spend three months in each place and it's already been four since I met her. Maybe they'll tell me where she went. Hey, I'm looking for Mayra Cabral de Melo, they call her Roxana. Well, boss, she left about a month ago, they say she's driving the fuckers nuts in Mexicali. He slumped back down in his chair, discouraged. Why do I kid myself? Good things never last. He looked at his hands and wished one of them was like what Ruy Sánchez wrote, hot for desire. And I can't get hold of that bastard Parra, let me try spreading the fucking tranquilliser on my balls and see if that does any good. He thought about the dead kid in the hotel. Who killed him? That Steve Tyler is a heavy. Gringos come to

Mexico looking for what? drugs, gigolos, places to retire, scenery, a few for business; what is this guy sniffing around Culiacán for? There aren't any gigolos or ruins here, maybe he wants drugs or a place to retire; if he's here for business is he a grower? who are his contacts? is he looking for partners in something legitimate? does he have them? why did he knock the dude off? He left nothing in his room to go on. Suppose he was being mugged and he resisted? It would end up a lot cheaper for him if he'd come to us. He fled because he killed somebody. If it was self-defence and he took off, then the dude is Mexican for sure, most gringos would go to the police and tell all, but a Mexican would never trust the police. Steve Tyler, the singer for Aerosmith, is Mexican, Mexican? that would be news. Another impossible case? He put on "April Come She Will" by Simon & Garfunkel and he hung on, convinced that the dawn redeems.

Is sadness a human right? If not, it ought to be. I don't understand this emptiness, this lack of ambition, this orphan feeling of not having anyone to blame for what happens.

What was Mayra's routine? did she go to the gym, have cereal for breakfast, eat fish, watch soap operas, listen to music, have girlfriends outside work, use drugs, go to the movies? I know she liked to read and she didn't eat bread; so who took those photographs? where was she when they picked her up and took her to die behind that warehouse? That fucking Spaniard is a shrewd one, would he dare? The guy who obviously doesn't fit is Richie, fucking loco, I nearly didn't make it; we'll see what I have to shell out when it's time to repay that favour; what I won't get out of is Begoña and Devil's wedding; why did he choose that place? why didn't he kill her first, wrap her in a blanket, and get rid of the body? is he sending us a message? why did he slice off her nipple? why kill Yolanda Estrada? was it the same guy? it was the same calibre. Maybe he's not a narco.

He was eating *machaca* with vegetables and flour tortillas for breakfast and trying to cheer himself up with the Byrds' version of "My Back Pages". I've got to get the one Dylan did at his thirtieth anniversary concert. He chewed slowly. Forty times, they used to tell me, whatever made those quacks think a little kid could count that high? Did you lose your appetite again, Lefty? Trudis reproached him as she served him a second cup of hot water for his Nescafé, look, if you keep this up you'll never make it to old age. Life is pointless, Trudis, of that I'm convinced. That's the kind of thing José Alfredo would say, Lefty, but he wasn't always right, he was a troubled man, an alcoholic, always falling in love, and he was weak. Did you have a fling with him? Oh no, he was really old and my tastes don't vary; is it ever hot, you ought to buy another air conditioner so you don't have to sweat all over your breakfast like that. It's not the heat, you put too much chilli in the *machaca*. But you aren't so delicate; guess who couldn't even sniff a chilli? you won't know, Fito de la Parra. The drummer for Canned Heat? I met him in Mexico City back when I was bumming around. And you got your claws into him too. Hey, where do you get this about claws; no woman needs to grab or tear or wound or even sweet-talk a man, they fall all on their own. Silence. Oh Lefty, I'm sorry; things haven't gone the way you deserve, I know, but it'll happen, you're young, good-looking, and from a good family; what bugs me is how you don't shave like you should, it's something I'll never understand, why do men today choose to go around looking like beggars? Don't start making demands, Trudis, all the guys you've mentioned so far were a bunch of longhairs, lucky for them I never met them, I would have taken them straight to the Big House. What? half the city's criminals are on the loose, making mischief, and they all keep their hair cut short; if you can't even handle them, why would you pick on important men like musicians? So somebody could take a pair of scissors to them. Oh no, they're decent, creative people and that means a lot. Alex Lora decent? That one maybe not, arrest him if you want, cut off his curls, and if you feel like cutting off something else, don't hold yourself back, you have my permission. I don't understand why you don't like him, what did he ever do to you? Maybe later, Lefty, I don't feel like getting into it now, I need to go to the super, we're out of everything and I want to make you shrimp cakes. I know a guy who would marry you just for those. Is he good-looking? Let's say yes, for his type. Introduce me, I promise to treat him so well he'll forget all about the shrimp cakes; listen, I couldn't stop thinking about that girl with no tits, did they find the culprit? We've got him surrounded. I hope they cut off what's hanging from him. The telephone rang. Trudis picked up: Just a moment, please; it's Zelda.

How are you, boss? Finishing breakfast, have you seen Ortega? He just gave us the ballistics report and a few other things, but he left for a case on the highway to Culiacancito; listen, I didn't call you about that, I have a woman here who claims she killed her father last night. Has she confessed? She's right here in front of me and she just admitted to it, she says she did him in at his house in Chapule, she even gave me the murder weapon. How does she look? Normal, I've got the address of the victim. O.K., put her under guard and we'll go see what's there, call Montaño and Ortega so they send along their minions.

Mendieta arrived at the residence, which was not far from the Café Miró. A one-storey house with a big, well-tended garden and large windows with white curtains, a white wooden fence about a metre high. Wide dark-brown door. He rang the bell several times, then worked his skeleton key with care, pulled it out, and stepped inside warily. Big living room. Light filtered in from a window that gave onto the back yard. Austere but tasteful black leather furniture and on the walls strange works of art, most of them long and thin. He moved cautiously. He saw that the frames contained irregular objects made of metal and wood. On the table in the middle of the room sat two bottles, one half-full of whisky, the other a beer bottle, empty. A tumbler. He strained to hear any sound. The place smelled of fine wood and alcohol. He wandered the empty rooms, among them three bedrooms. The fourth was a mess, with several changes of dirty clothes on a sofa before a large television set. He glanced at the yard: flowers, gerberas in pots, a bougainvillea, ferns, a carport where a green all-terrain Jeep was parked, a barbecue, and white metal chairs. The kitchen empty, clean, and with the light on.

He went back to the living room, where's the body?

He looked closely at the artwork and realised they were pieces of guitars. Whoa, what a good idea. He looked through the record collection: blues, jazz, reggae, and classic rock. In one corner, seven C.D.s by Los Tigres del Norte. So who is this guy, Fabián Olmedo? At the very least a cultured man and his daughter killed him, but where's the body? did she knock him off somewhere else? This record collection shouldn't be left unprotected, suppose it gets lost or is never listened to again, I'd rather have it go to the devil. The telephone rang. With a handkerchief he picked up. He waited. A voice: Señor Olmedo? He listened, Who's calling? Who's speaking? His secretary. Your whore of a mother, I don't have a secretary. Are you Fabián Olmedo? Who are you, asshole? and what are you doing in my house? I'm from the State Ministerial Police, we received a report that you were dead. The bastard capable of killing me has yet to be born. Congratulations, where are you? In the street, across from the house. Come over, I'll go out into the front garden.

Outside a Jeep pulled in.

Gandhi Olmedo, in jeans, white shirt, and loafers, got nimbly out. From the doorway Mendieta saw a face that could eat you alive and he understood the daughter's urges.

Edgar Mendieta from Homicide, this morning your daughter came to our office and confessed she sent you packing last night, we didn't want you to rot and stink up the neighbourhood. Gandhi smiled and nodded. Is anyone inside? No, but they'll be here soon. Since I'm alive, call them and tell them to work on something else, and as far as my daughter is concerned, do with her what you will. What happened? They were still standing in the doorway. I was waiting for some people, the doorbell rang, I thought it was them, I opened up, and they greeted me with a slug right here, he pointed to his chest; I only saw a shape so I can't accuse anyone. What brand is your vest? He was wearing a DuPont made of Kevlar. The best, I saw your record collection, it's great. You didn't filch anything, did you? How could you even suggest? of course not. Olmedo smiled sarcastically. And how did you like my guitar collection? Impressive, but you don't have them all, do you, I didn't see any from Kiss. Those faggots only do montages and smoke bombs, that kind of thing; I'm not interested unless musicians smash them on impulse. Savage impulse, nearly always. Let's call it a tribute to paroxysm.

At that moment Zelda pulled up along with two other cars. A pair of young men carrying yellow tape got out of one and a guy dressed in white out of the other. Agent Toledo, allow me to introduce Señor Fabián Olmedo. Zelda did a double-take, mouth agape. You can all leave, the dead man came back to life. What do we do with the girl? Set her free, Zelda, there's no crime to prosecute.

O.K. Señor Olmedo, excuse the infringement, but two questions, why would your daughter want to kill you? How do you know she's my daughter? She said so. Well, prove it before you come and break into my house. He turned to walk inside. Mendieta held him back, felt his solid, weightlifter's arm, I said two questions, Señor Olmedo. And I've already answered enough, shaking him off and slamming the door behind him.

They drove towards Headquarters and on the way Mendieta told Zelda what had happened at the Alexa. They fell silent for a moment. What do you think, boss? Both Cervantes and Bernal seem innocent, but you know what this is like, you can't trust first impressions; we'd better speak with Meraz, he's the one with all the connections, even the chief said we shouldn't bother him; what did you think of Elisa Calderón? Very cooperative, but I have the feeling there is something I didn't ask her. Like what? Well, I don't know, I just wasn't satisfied. Call her in again and don't let her go until you're ready; me, I'd like to speak with Olmedo's daughter, call Records, see if we have anything on him, I didn't like his arrogance. What about the hotel? It looks like robbery, I'm going to go back and see what I can find.

Paty Olmedo was wearing tight low-cut jeans and a strapless blouse. The upper edges of a tattoo on her pubis and another on her left shoulder were showing. Lovely. Perfect body. Mendieta felt what you might expect. He introduced himself. She, no make-up, responded with a smile. Why did you murder your father? Hatred, he was a misogynist, a jerk who didn't have the least respect for anything human, he loved knocking people down, making them suffer; ask any of his employees, ask my mother or his other women, he traumatised them all, same story with me, his only daughter; do you have children? from your face I'd guess you're a great father; he was garbage, disgusting, a bum, that's why I killed him, he didn't deserve the oxygen he was consuming. Mendieta looked at her face all flushed, her breasts heaving, and he wanted to see her naked. *Women are at the centre of all things.* Do you know how many years you'll get for murder? However many, I don't care, what counts is I got rid of that vermin. They fell silent. Where did you get the pistol? A guy I met at a club gave it to me, he had two and he gave me one. What's his name? That I never found out, they called him Guasave, something like that, we chatted a bit, we kissed, we did it in his pickup, and he asked me what I wanted most, to kill my father, I answered, what do you need? a pistol; in the glove compartment he had a big one and a little one, he gave me the little one. What club was that? Studio Six, can I go to the bathroom? Not yet, did you tell anyone you were going to kill your father? No, my friends are easily swayed, pretty soon they'd all want to do the same thing and some of those men are really cool, I like them. You would have preferred any of them for a father. More or less. What did your father do? He sold cars, he was a dealer for several companies; he was what they call a success, but now he's gone. You're going to clean up with the inheritance. No way, he must have left his fortune to the devil. How often did he tell you that you might not be his daughter? Never, we barely spoke and I hadn't seen him in months, why do you ask? Just to ask. I wish I had Liv Tyler's luck, such a cool father, he loves her so much, they even look alike. Tyler, of course, Mendieta thought, Steve Tyler, like the one from the hotel. How old would you say the guy who gave you the piece was? About twenty. Hmm . . . do you work? Sure, I design clothing, how do you like this little number? She was referring to the blouse. You'll be a big hit in Aguaruto Prison. When will they take me away? gee, I can't wait to see my cell, decorate it, and wait for my friends to visit, and then there's the conjugal visit, my life will be so cool. Are you married? No, but I have at least twenty friends who could play that role. You may end up with a minder. Somebody tough? how exciting. Lefty saw no trace of her father, to him she looked identical to Scarlett Johansson. I have awful news for you. Paty grew serious. There's no cell for me? you know, I can pay for it, I've heard that's possible. Your father is alive and he does not wish to press charges; even though it's a crime we usually prosecute, you are free to go. She was surprised. So, who did I kill? he fell, I saw him. He was wearing a bulletproof vest. Her expression turned grave, then crumpled in misery. You didn't know he used a bulletproof vest? Tears rolled down her cheeks. I never remember. Pause. Señor Mendieta, look at me, it's awful to be utterly useless, you have no idea how horrible it is to feel you don't know how to get free, even of your worst enemy. Mendieta felt the same. Oh God, I'm useless, and she got up. Watching her walk out, Lefty considered her faint fragrance: Dolce & Gabbana? He followed her. He saw her get into a Murano and drive off at quite a clip on Zapata. Would it be worth testing her pistol? who would the dude have been? Fucking world, what other coincidences might there be?

Thirteen

I want to take cocaine into the United States, McGiver said, the war is going to disrupt the usual routes and the gangs will be thrown off their game; my Colombian contacts are all set and the gringos are too, I should take advantage of the opportunity while everyone regroups. You really are ambitious, you say your business is doing well, so why on earth would you get into such a complicated arena, which isn't even your own? Look who's talking. It's been nearly three years since I had anything to do with that. But you still launder money. I have never laundered money, I guard it, which is not the same thing; I'm just like the banks, the only difference is I don't give a penny to the government and I don't make loans. McGiver picked up a slice of octopus, they were in a private room at El Fara-llón, just the two of them, celebrating the incorporation of Jeff Beck into Gandhi Olmedo's collection. I want you to help me, you know everyone and you could open the doors I need opened. Gandhi smiled, I will not do it, Leo, I will not do you that bad turn. Why? The government doesn't know what it's saying and I don't believe it will have any effect on the real cartels; no-one is going to abandon such a lucrative business with a captive market. Especially the gringos. Of course, they're the ones who keep the lion's share. Day before yesterday I made a deal with Samantha Valdés, I'm going to arm forty or so men for her, and yesterday Dioni de la Vega wanted a platoon of his own; would they invest so much if they didn't expect some action? Olmedo picked up a scallop, squeezed lime onto it, shook on ground chillies, popped it in his mouth, and chewed, then he sipped his beer. So, even more reason you shouldn't get involved, if they're guarding their turf so jealously they'll do anything to keep new groups out, in that business the sun doesn't shine for everyone and the chosen are very few. McGiver tasted the *aguachile* and drank from his glass of wine, I can't get the idea that it would be worth a try out of my head. Don't get it out, just understand that nowadays dying for your ideas is no longer in fashion, and remember you aren't in your prime. They smiled. I'm not so old, you bastard. Nor are you so young. I can still shoot my load three times without even pulling it out. Come on, those must be sighs. They laughed. Will you give up smuggling? No way, being a smuggler is my destiny, is there anything I can get you? Before they kill you, find out if John Lennon smashed a guitar when the Beatles broke up, find a woman named Thompson who was talking to Yoko that day about an exhibit of her artwork. Her first name? That was all they gave me. O.K., that's something to keep me busy while I decide about this other business, which by the way is going places, you'll see. You mean, that's something to keep you alive; could I ask who your connections are on the other side? McGiver's eyes shone, he trusted Olmedo, but not that much; nevertheless, he decided to take a chance: my arms supplier. Forget it, Leo, it's like trading in a Mercedes for a Toyota. McGiver drained his glass of Muga and refilled it, You may be right, we are getting old, but I'm going to take a chance, what can I lose? Olmedo smiled and shook his head. Last night, while I was waiting for you, I kept downing whiskies until I fell asleep, I was dreaming sweet dreams when someone rang the bell, I opened the door and they put a bullet in my chest. No! Can you guess who it was? How could

I know? My daughter, you bastard, Paty Olmedo, the one who's going to inherit the entire fucking empire I've built in my bitch of a life; can you imagine how I felt? Like a bedbug, a disgusting germ. Worse, you bastard, worse, like the most abject being on the planet, a dumb fuck who worked himself to the bone in vain, who risked his life in vain, who shat on half the world in vain, do you know where that ditz studied? in London, I sent her to the best fashion design school in the world, for this? how could you not expect me to think I'm old? raising a daughter was beyond me, the only thing I made in my life was money and what good is it if it ends up in that retard's hands? probably I should have followed the advice of those nutty motivational speakers: wealth is selection not accumulation; then that fucking policeman shows up to scratch my balls, one Edgar Mendieta, wearing a face like don't blame me, a face like the worst bolero you've ever heard in your whole whore of a life, awful, dressed in black from head to toe; if I hadn't acted fast he would have robbed me, he said as much: what an interesting record collection; if I'd arrived a second later he would have walked off with it. Edgar Mendieta? he must be from the Col Pop, I had a buddy there, Enrique Mendieta, who was a guerrilla, I bet they're brothers. Who gives a shit, Leo: my daughter, you bastard, my own murderer, and all you can think about is making more money as a narco. He fell silent. Did you speak with her? Speak? what I want to do is beat the crap out of her. They looked at each other, Olmedo despairing, McGiver all smiles. From what you say, the honourable life is pointless, Gandhi, so I'm not going to suppress the urge tempting me. O.K. then, glads or mums? Roses, asshole, don't be cheap.

From the street they heard a blast from an A.K.: Richie Bernal was assuaging his grief. And at the Apostolis, a restaurant not too far away, a powerful competitor whom McGiver feared was managing to displace him as number one: he would arm two thousand troops of the Mexican army.

Fourteen

He called Dr Parra: Answer, you fucking shrink. His assistant picked up. Oh, Señor Mendieta, good that you called, I tried to reach you yesterday to let you know the doctor left for a conference in Austin, Texas, he'll be back in a week. Feeling like shit, he thought: That's what I like about him, what good is a doctor who's only around when you don't need him?

The reports from Ortega and Montaño were on his desk and they were the usual: 9mm bullet shot point-blank in Mayra's case, in Yolanda's from a bit further away; the former had her nipple sliced off with a fairly dull knife, and she died between two and four in the morning. You sonofabitch, why vent your fury on her breasts? They were so lovely, so *there*, so . . . They found no alcohol in her blood and they would hang on to the D.N.A. sample for whatever might come up. *Mexico called to me and I came just like that, I brought only my art, and look, I'm not complaining; soon I'll be able to retire and try my hand at other things, but I haven't killed anyone, mister police-man, I swear, though you might be the first: I'm going to kiss you to death.* It was like floating, to be there, to listen to her, see her, touch her, overcome all that horrible stuff. Fingerprints everywhere, in other words, Jack the Ripper up to his old tricks. I'm going to find you, whether you be man, woman, or beast, wherever you hide I'll smoke you out, in the name of God in vain I swear it; I don't know when or where, but I am not going to let this lie. Miguel de Cervantes doesn't seem like much, fucking Spaniard, but I'll be on his case; and

Richie Bernal, it's not his style, he would have peppered her with bullets; and the other girl, was it the same guy? for the same reason? but they didn't mutilate her. Two criminals acting at the same time? There are friendships that can cost you your life. The guy who murdered her deserves to get disembowelled too. They didn't find your purse, your cell phone, or anything: that implies what? The kid from the hotel is still nameless, he got plugged between nine and eleven in the morning, there were prints on the telephone, but they matched nothing in our files. He had before him a small metal box with Chinese-style decorations that held Mayra's papers and a few of her letters. On an envelope he read what might be her mother's return address in São Paulo. He dug further. Here was her passport: Mexican, born in Guadalajara in 1987. Huh? my, oh my. Lefty went still, he eyed Zelda looking thoughtfully at several papers on her desk and drinking her Coca-Cola. Then he took a sip of his coffee and opened the newspaper, which was playing up the war against the narcos. Mendieta thought: They can cut off one of my balls if it's true, that is, unless they've reached an agreement; who could possibly make war on those bastards? they've got it all: weapons, connections, strategy, spies, money, allies; what a fucking mess. His cell rang, he tossed the paper in the trash can. It was Daniel Quiroz: Why haven't they said anything about the girl with no tits, Lefty? What girl with no tits, you ink-shitter? Don't make like you're stupid, fucking Lefty. I don't know what you're talking about, asshole, what do you want me to do? Every source says the case got stopped cold, they didn't even let them write it up. Well, what I heard was that the ones who got stopped cold were you. And you tell me you don't know enough to shoot, eh, pistol? Mendieta smiled. If they open the case let me know. Forget it, Quiroz, it looks like it'll be a zero. Listen, what's up with the gringo? What gringo? Fucking Lefty, are we buddies or what? Hey, I'm serious. Here you go: this morning we received a call that there was a dead gringo in the Hotel San Luis; we went and they told us it happened yesterday; that Montaño has the body in the morgue, but nobody knows a thing; I saw Ortega a while ago, but he's busy with the gangsta-wraps. And so you thought, I'll call that jerk Mendieta and get a scoop; well, you fucked up, if anybody found a gringo it wasn't us. O.K., you bastard, we're on to it, and note that I did not ask about what's hurting you. He hung up, lit a cigarette. You'd better not, fucking Quiroz. He hadn't finished the smoke when he heard Angelita: Zelda, Rodo's on line one.

Face like stone: What do you want? Pause. No, I already told you no, not until you stop treating me like an idiot, I'm here playing by the rules and you are acting very fresh; what, don't I deserve to be taken seriously? how can you expect me to believe you if you haven't even thought about an engagement ring. She slammed the receiver down. Angelita, who had remained in the doorway, had her mouth open and even Lefty was astonished. Zelda turned back to her papers. Boss, the secretary muttered, the chief wants you.

Mendieta left the room without a word. He looked at the clock: 11.52, he remembered his date at five with Miroslava.

Briseño had a few notes on his desk. Sit down. Mendieta thought he looked preoccupied: something is bothering him, is it good for a chief to be so easy to read? this guy's transparent. Any news? Regarding the case of the girls, we need to interrogate Attorney Luis Ángel Meraz. I already told you to leave him alone; just call him and tell him what you've found so far. He's been in Mexico City for a week, but he's getting back tonight; that's regarding the case of the first girl, on the second we don't have a thing. Let that go, they're table dancers and we're not swimming in resources; you know Meraz can't be guilty since he's been away, what about the body in the San Luis? We only have the ballistics report and his fingerprints weren't in our files; the guest vanished, he paid his hotel bill with a coupon, his credit card is from a bank in Phoenix that refuses to give out any information, and we have no record on him either. Let's hope someone claims the body. Chief, what do you think about the president's declaration of war? One of these days I'm going to invite you over to eat, do you like pea soup? Only if it's made with black-eyed peas. Listen, the gringos are insisting you go, they think you're a catch. Yeah, they want me on a hook, like a fish. Is it true the table dancer who's making you suffer was gorgeous? *You really do have pretty eyes. Of course you can talk about mine, but you're going to be hard put to say something original.* The detective stood up. I know you met her in Mazatlán; he handed him his fortnightly envelope. A few drinks, Mendieta, that'll set you straight. You know that former D.A. Cabrera is a partner in the Alexa? Don't go there either, they'll pull the rug out from under you. As he left the office, he realised he was feeling even more desolate; he turned back: Chief, show me the invitation to Madrid.

Back at his own desk he searched on his cell phone. Zelda, send this photograph to this address and ask for a report on the guy, he's Miguel de Cervantes.

*

Mayra's apartment. In he went. He detected a faint aroma, distinct, manly. It's delicate, he thought, so the guy behind this, or related to it, or all over it, is someone who can afford an expensive fragrance. In perfume, delicate means expensive. He stood still in the living room for several minutes. There's no bell, he must have rapped with his knuckles: Who is it? Me, Yhajaira, I'm so glad you're here, let me in, would you? Oh, Roxana isn't here. I know, I've come to see you, the loveliest woman in the world. Are you serious? Have I ever lied to you? The girl lets him in. Have you been knocking for a while? you caught me sleeping. You look like a dream in pyjamas, my queen, no-one would guess you were up late. Thank you, sit down; what do you mean calling me the loveliest woman, Roxana is going to get mad, you know what she's like. Yes, she defends her turf like a wild animal, doesn't she? how did it go today? It was rough, I'm dead on my feet. Precisely. And he shot her in the heart with a 9mm, what brand? He imagined the murderer leaving, relaxed after sensing the quiet in the rest of the building. At what point did he tear up the picture of the Brazilian team for Germany 2006? He paused before the spot on the wall. It seemed bizarre and he pulled out his pad and made a note of it. The guy must have wanted to make sure Yhajaira would not mention him to the police; so it's possible the two crimes were committed by the same person. He focussed on the scents: diffuse, even the one that had struck him, Dolce & Gabbana? Hugo Boss? Polo by Ralph Lauren? He made a note of that too. The furnishings were simple and the technical team had only removed a few things. Small kitchen, full refrigerator: fresh fruit, dried fruit, vegetables, fish, eggs, condiments, a couple of beers. On the floor, an empty tomato box with the seal of San Esteban Farms. A door gave onto a small patio where they hung their clothes to dry. He heard the sound of the neighbours returning from picking up their children at school. They had told Zelda they knew nothing about the girls. Yolanda's bedroom was a mess and nothing in it spoke to him. He went into Mayra's trying to be objective, meaning he tried to ignore her body and her face smiling from every wall. I'm going to find you, you fucking murderer, he murmured. No-one is perfect and you will have left some clue or you will do something that puts you in my grasp. You will ask me or I will ask you the impossible question and you will not pass the acid test, you fucking faggot. He looked closely at her clothing, about thirty pairs of shoes with jewelled heels in all sorts of colours and designs. A drawer in the closet was stuffed with books in Portuguese, among them *The House of the Fortunate Buddhas*. Why Yhajaira? how would it have affected her executioner if he'd let her live? did she know that Roxana went out with him? He was concentrating fiercely when he heard a click at the door. As he turned he recalled that he had not closed the front door and that the carpet was thick and soft. Some luxury in this heat.

The Alexa's bouncer was pointing a gun at him. Mendieta ignored him and continued examining the room. A Mexican born in Guadalajara in 1987, he remembered. Who were you really, Mayra Cabral de Melo? Her maternal last name was Palencia. The passport was valid. At that moment his interest in the case became more professional. Why did you insist you were Brazilian? You talked like a Brazilian, you danced, as you said, like a Brazilian, you read Portuguese, this little library shows you weren't just pretending to be interested in books; like I said, you need to be Brazilian to read

The House of the Fortunate Buddhas, and you talked about Ribeiro as a great writer, and about Coelho and Fonseca. All the letters were from the same person, someone who urged you to be calm and patient. He remembered opening a manila envelope that contained a dozen business cards, reading the names, and putting aside two that he now had in his pocket.

On the carpet was an outline, forty by forty centimetres; a box heavy enough to leave a mark had recently been removed, by the murderer? If so, he must be strong. What do you want? he snarled at the bouncer, aren't you supposed to be at Headquarters? The guy lowered his pistol, I've got nothing to tell them. Well, start thinking about what you are going to say to my people, they're on their way here. The man pointed his gun again. I can see you're still using outlawed weapons, Rivera; you or your boss is going to have to answer for that. Stop fucking with me, Mendieta, you can't pitch and you can't catch. This isn't about me, you're the one who won't go straight.

His cell rang, it was Zelda. Boss, I looked through Mayra's box, read a couple of her letters. He let her go on. From what they say, her mother is from Guadalajara, her name is Elena Palencia. Look her up in the phonebook. I did already and found her number. I'll be back in half an hour, right now I'm with a detainee. He hung up.

What do you mean detainee? shit, I haven't been arrested. Of course you have, and what's more, you're carrying a weapon issued exclusively to the army. But I haven't committed any crime. That is something the judge will decide. Rivera gave him a good look at the mouth of the weapon. You're nuts if you think you can trap me like that, besides, what are you accusing me of? Of the murder of

Yolanda Estrada, alias Yhajaira. What? that's bullshit, how do you plan to prove that? Who cares about proving it? you've got a record and all over the world a record is forever, and people with records always make the same mistakes. On my saint of a mother, I swear I had nothing to do with it, I came here because she and I had something going; you don't know how hard her death hit me, I just wanted to see her place, her room, to relive her birthday last Sunday, we had such a good time here. Mendieta was going to tease him, but he fell silent instead, wasn't he in the same boat? What time was the party and who was here? Well, I arrived at five and left at eight, she was getting ready to go to the Alexa. Was she alone? Yes. So why don't I smell your cologne now? My wife, whenever I went to see Yolanda I'd put it on and my wife would fly off the handle. Which one do you use? All kinds, the girls give them to me. Did you meet all the men she went with? No way, that woman lived a very active life. What about Roxana? That'd be even more ridiculous, Roxana seduced half of Culiacán; you know what? take the pistol, but don't arrest me, I promised my mother I wouldn't get into trouble and the truth is I haven't. He tossed him the gun, Mendieta gave it a once-over, the bullet was chambered and the magazine was full; it was a Sig Sauer. He looked at José Rivera's face filled with remorse. O.K., he conceded, but you are going to help me out with everything I need for both these cases. He gave him back his pistol, Give it to your mother as proof you've reformed. You are strange, fucking Mendieta. Listen, bouncers always see more than they should, who was Roxana's stud? She had several. Among them, which do you think was her favourite? I couldn't pick out one, you saw the tango Richie danced last night; I should have already told you: congratulations. Was there somebody who was a client of both of them? For sure, several, that's common; the customers always want someone new. Think of one who knew where they lived and visited them here. I wouldn't know about that, neither of them mentioned it. Did you see the picture of the football team? Many times. Well, somebody tore it up. Roxana would have died, she was always talking about being a five-time champion. They fell silent. A few days ago you took Roxana to Mazatlán, on whose orders? Me? where did you get that? uh-uh, I never took her anywhere. Smarten up, I don't want any bullshit, and now get lost before the gang shows up.

He turned his attention to the bedroom: It's so hard to find the haystack that hid this needle.

Cavalry charge. It was Zelda: Boss, Elisa Calderón called, she says one of the girls saw Mayra go off with Luis Ángel Meraz last Sunday, her name is Camila Naranjo and she's on her way over. Wasn't Meraz in Mexico City? That's what the manager said, but I guess not, we'll see what Camila knows. Click. Another guy with a double.

Fifteen

Peter Connolly hated Mexico. It is no easy feat to hate an entire country but he found a way and he lived by it. After he became a member of the F.B.I.'s special advance team, it was his favourite place to visit. He would spit on the ground as soon as he got off the plane, and he claimed he even defecated in the gardens of his hotels. What a nauseating country, utterly incapable of dealing with its own mess; plus it's a fucking transit point for drugs from South America, pocketing a chunk of the profits and hungering for more. Somehow, no matter how, they all have to be done away with, same as that bunch of idiots who tried to block the war that's finally going ahead. They can scream all they want, pray to their saints, bawl their eyes out, it won't get them anywhere; what imbeciles. Besides, all those Spics swarming over fields and infesting restaurants and shopping malls will be the ruin of the most powerful country in the world, could we not exterminate them or at least enslave them? That would solve so many problems. I ought to get someone in Congress to propose it; if we don't, we'll end up speaking that awful gibberish they use to communicate.

He was a member of an influential group of hunters of undocumented immigrants operating in Texas, Arizona, and New Mexico. His goal: a killing a day, and he was proud of the fact that in twelve years he had never missed his quota. When he was on assignment, he enjoyed his daily execution even more. Early that morning, on a street in Westwood, California, near U.C.L.A., he had liquidated a woman who looked after children and a man who operated a steam shovel, each on their way to work. He knew from experience that the next day would be exhausting, so he'd wanted to get ahead of himself. Once he was back home, he would start in on a series of singers. Chakira, that splat of green vomit, would be first, then some folk singer named Ricky, and he would finish off with that guitar player, what was his name? Fucking race of perverts.

In his room he watched C.N.N. while he waited for the other gringos to finish breakfast and go off sightseeing, fishing, hunting. This hotel is a pigsty, he thought, but they're all the same. This country is disgusting, it can't be fixed, what else can we do but use it to our advantage? The agreement we signed last night was fabulous: two thousand troops is a good number. On the television the president of the United States was making a statement. His old man shouldn't travel to a country that's got nothing to be said for it, and certainly not to that camp that's so vulnerable; it's too risky. Somebody better listen to me. He was fully dressed, smoking, and now studying a map.

At 8.02 he decided it was time for breakfast. He made sure everything was in order, folded the map, and put it on the dresser. He turned up the volume on the television, then took the chain off the door, opened it, and received a bullet in the head. He managed to pull out his gun but not to shoot. Just what I always say. It was the last thing he thought. A fucking country of.

McGiver, dressed in blue plumber's overalls, had dropped to his haunches just in case. He verified the man was dead and stood up. Selling guns is more dangerous than selling information, he said to himself, while he dragged the body into the room and took

103

Connolly's pistol. He inspected his identification and from his overnight bag he pulled out the contract signed the night before; he noted the signature and smiled; he went over the map of the region without finding any marking and let it fall to the floor, open; he took the three cell phones and pocketed them, same with a few dollars. Money comes and money goes, he mumbled, this bit comes. On the television, something about nuclear weapons in Iran.

Stepping into the hallway, he took note of the number again: 522. He hung the "Do Not Disturb" sign and quietly closed the door.

Sixteen

At four in the afternoon he called Elena Palencia, but she was in São Paulo where she had been for four months and would not be back until the end of the summer. He wrote down her cell phone number and left for the Miró. "Honey" by Bobby Goldsboro. He resisted an urge to turn off the stereo and took Victoria Street, where an army roadblock searching for weapons held him up. Though he identified himself, it made no difference. I didn't think you had so little trust in us, he told the sergeant. Everybody gets the same treatment, but I'll let you keep your heater so you can do your job. Have you confiscated anything? Not even a jackknife. They finished checking the Jetta and he drove on.

Miroslava turned up at 5.30, looking older, eyes expressionless. She was dressed simply. Would you like something? the beef tapas are good. No, no, my cholesterol's up. Beef was taken off the list, you can eat it without fear. Can that happen? Of course, besides, it'll make your hair grow. That means soon we'll be able to eat pork, I love pork. Soon we'll be able to gobble up whatever we please. Rudy brought Mendieta his third coffee and the first for the girl, who refused it. I wouldn't be able to sleep later on. She wanted a beer.

She did not know Mayra well, Yolanda a bit better. She was from Cosoleacaque, Veracruz and she loved her work, even if she was getting past her prime. Mendieta mentioned the names of the principal suspects, but she did not think they were important. The only thing I could say about them is they were very good customers, have

105

you spoken with Kid Yoreme? Not yet. He was wild about Mayra, he's a bit of a creep and twice I heard him say he couldn't stand seeing her with anybody else, he'd rather see her dead. Tell me where he lives. I don't know, how would I know that? yesterday I didn't see him, but he shows up every day. Do you have any idea where he works? He's a boxer, or he used to be. Did you ever hear of anyone picking her up at her place? No-one admits to that; we all have those clients and we often earn more that way than at the club. The tapas arrived. Why did you envy Mayra? She thought a moment: Her youth, her allure, her luck, her beauty, will that do? And what about Yolanda? Oh, poor Yoli, she was a sweetheart; no, she never stirred up such strong feelings. Miroslava confided she wanted to get married and have a daughter who would be queen of the table dancers; she smiled: Better than Roxana. Wouldn't you rather she were a policewoman? Never, I can't understand how any woman could take on such dangerous work. Do you like the atmosphere at the Alexa? It's bearable, the manager is a good guy, he was a bit prickly at first but then he settled down, I was there when he started a bit more than a year ago, and the Phantom and Escamilla are good people; Elisa keeps us on a tight leash, watch your back if you try to strike out on your own because she'll reel you in; we girls are always competing, but not to the point of killing each other, that's what I think, right? Is Rivera going with anyone? I almost forgot, poor Bigboy, he was totally stuck on Yhajaira and I thought she was playing him like a yo-yo. Do the customers who pick the girls up at home also come into the Alexa? What for? lots of them don't like to be seen, and they can't take us out from the club anyway; she took a bite of her tapa. Let me guess what you think of Camila Naranjo, that she's a bitch, a snake, awful as a friend and horrible as a co-worker. Miroslava stopped chewing, her mouth fell open: How did you know that?

Conversation with Camila Naranjo held at 2.47 that afternoon at Headquarters: Tell us who sold you the pistol you used to murder Mayra Cabral de Melo and Yolanda Estrada. Her eyes filled with tears, blood rushed to her cheeks, and she began to sob. I wanted to kill them. Being a detective in the Homicide Department of the State Ministerial Police, Zelda Toledo observed such reactions all the time, but she was astounded. Shit. And she turned on both tape recorders. But it wasn't me, I swear; I thought about it more than once, I admit it, but I never had the guts, I suppose you're either born for that or you're not, and I.

Let's see, Mendieta broke in, the calm after the storm, you wanted to do them in, so? I did not murder them; I admit that's what I was thinking, they really got on my nerves, especially the Brazilian, but it wasn't me. What were you and Mayra doing in that field, planning to buy seeds? What field? How many people were with you? Listen, I didn't kill her because somebody else got there first, and I don't know anything about any fields; can you put me in jail for wanting to kill someone? because at the Alexa every single day we wish people would die, not one, but several. Mendieta signalled Zelda, who said, Let's see, you haven't told us the name of the guy who sold you the pistol. No-one sold me a pistol, Kid Yoreme promised to get me one, but he still hasn't done it; by the way he was crazy about Mayra. Where did you meet him? He's from the neighbourhood. What's his name again? Kid Yoreme. Do you know what he does? I think he's a night watchman, something like that. Why would you blow away your co-workers? I hated them. And you think that's enough to take someone's life? You don't think so? that fucking whore poached my best client, and I had just about won over Bernal when she came along; listen, I'm human and I'm building myself a house back home. What about Yolanda? Well, you can also hate the friend of the girl you hate, because you never know what she might do; besides, nobody likes me, she broke down; how I would have loved to skin that bitch alive! You told Elisa Calderón that Mayra went out with Luis Ángel Meraz on Sunday, do you know where they went? Señorita, please, where do we go with men? Did you see them leave the Alexa? No, I saw them come back, she got out of his truck, she looked angry, she said something I couldn't hear, but she was arguing with him, a few minutes went by and she got back in. Did you see Meraz? No, but it was his truck; he's the client she took from me, the lousy bitch. Maybe it was his driver? Only he drives that truck, I know that. Where does Yoreme work as a night watchman? How would I know? Mendieta left the room and let Zelda carry on. Camila was innocent, what was going on? As always, an endless line of innocent people turn up before the culprit makes a move. Fucking innocents, they just get in the way.

In the parking lot he said hello to Elisa Calderón, who was drinking a Coke. He was tempted to strike up a conversation, but he walked on, confused: Did he love Mayra more now that she was dead? That sonofabitch who cut off her nipple is going to pay big time, and I'm in this fucking hole, and there's Parra, drunk in Austin; I would never butt into his private life, but boy-oh-boy what he'll do for a beer.

Well, if you really want to know, Camila's the worst: a worm in a class of her own, mean, sneaky, vindictive, one night she might put on your best thong and not even let you know, she treats you like you were born to do her bidding; she and Mayra couldn't stand each other. Did Roxana ever tell you about her clients? That just isn't done, you think she would? Don't you girls ever feel sad? Sure, sometimes I'd like to be something else, but not Mayra, she was made for this business; the only time I saw her sad was a little while ago when a girlfriend of hers died, someone not in our line of work, she went to the wake and they wouldn't let her in. Did she tell you her name? Anita Roy. Do you know what Anita did for work? I don't think she worked, she was really rich, Mayra gave her dance lessons. Private lessons or to a group? Search me. After another three beers she was telling him she was a friend of Livi Leyva, the wife of the manager, who every so often would come around, to watch the girls she'd say, but the one she was watching was her husband. I don't know what she's watching for, he's ugly as sin. Lefty, who knew about Miroslava's relationship with Carvajal, just smiled.

She promised to point out Kid Yoreme that night, then she asked for a ride over to the Forum mall. Mendieta answered his cell. What's up? Boss, you aren't going to believe it, another body in the San Luis and this one really is a gringo. Let's see if the Americans declare war on us now, see you there.

At 6.45 in the evening he entered room 522. "Do not disturb." He was the first of his team to arrive. Television on. A murderer was here, did he knock? did he have a key? did he use a skeleton key? did he find it open? Hmm . . . The body lay on the carpet. He gazed down, sniffed, speculated. The murderer knocked, the dead man opened the door: Who are you looking for? he's not here; and he got the bullet. He knew him: robbery? So, in what situation would a gringo be that kind of victim? Are they mugging guests in this hotel? Of course Tyler, yesterday's gringo, was quicker on the trigger than the hoodlum, whose body by the way still hasn't been claimed. Was he armed? What's this map on the floor? He put on his gloves and picked it up: municipality of Culiacán. He looked it over, nothing circled or marked. The cologne is different from Tyler's, maybe Cartier Roadster and something else, I'm not sure what, maybe Hugo Boss? Everybody uses that fucking scent. He sniffed the bed, then nudged the body with one foot. Sorry, just trying to see if you fucked before dying. He sniffed again. Was it a man who shot you or a woman? women can be surprising. In what circumstances would someone who wanted to see the gringo have a key to his door? Someone from the hotel, a murderous housekeeper? Well, they're human, as Camila says, why not? The first condition for being a murderer is to be human; do hotel electricians have keys? I think so. If he had a skeleton key, there's no point thinking it through. I have the feeling this fellow opened up for him: Look, there's a leak in the bathroom and that lamp won't turn off, I can't sleep like that. You can't? well, sleep all you want now, asshole. The truth is a murderer gets in any which way. On the television, C.N.N. You were interested in the world, eh? in other words you weren't just anybody. In the bathroom he found a bottle of Cartier Roadster, deodorant, lotion, and an electric razor. Hmm . . .

He frisked the rigid body. Let's see, what do we have here? a holster without a weapon: Oh, you managed to take it out? But they got you first, plugged you before you could defend yourself, and then they pocketed your heater. You must have taken your leave at least ten hours ago, we'll see what Montaño says, that is if he isn't off somewhere getting laid. Let's have a look at the wallet, nice leather, two credit cards in different names, two driver's licences with the same names, hmm . . . The young manager arrived. Can I help you with anything, detective? Let me see the registry and the voucher he signed, and bring in the woman who found him. In the wastebasket an Aeroméxico ticket, Los Angeles to Culiacán, Name: Connolly/ Peter. Like I said, now they'll declare war on us for sure, they say the gringos aren't happy unless they're fighting and by now they must be bored with the Middle East; well, for a change they can wage a little war right on their doorstep. His cell phone rang out. Boss, where are you? It was Zelda. I'm with the body, why aren't you here? We ran into a demonstration of peasant farmers, we're almost past them now.

Peter Connolly. Profession: make-up artist. Home address: Westwood, Los Angeles County. Well, now. Mendieta looked at the rough hands and shook his head. The housekeeper who found him was trembling. He was lying there like that, he had the do-not-disturb sign up, I knocked and since no-one answered and it was really late, I opened the door and saw him. No, nobody else had seen or heard anything; neither the plumber nor the electrician had been called, in this hotel no-one bothers the guests. The manager looked on. What's happening to your customers? That's what I'd like to know, this place is turning into an elephant graveyard.

At that moment Zelda arrived talking on her cell: No, Rodo, understand me, dammit, I will be the mother of your children, but take this seriously, it's not that I want the ring, I want what the ring means, that much you ought to understand; only the ring can bring what the ring means, you aren't dumb, or are you? let me repeat myself, I am not going out with you until you fix this situation, it's embarrassing. She paused and shouted: I haven't said I don't want to marry you, I said a few details have to be taken care of. She jabbed the off button, inhaled deeply, and took in the people gaping at her. Ready, boss, she said firmly. All of you, wait outside, Mendieta chased them out. Where are the techies? They must be coming upstairs now, with the doctor.

We need to know who he is, you take care of that, here are a few of his basics. He handed her the papers the manager had given him. The main thing is the context, Lefty thought, curtains closed, lights out, watching C.N.N.; as far as I'm concerned, he didn't have company, whoever did it turned up, knocked, the victim opened the door and got plugged. He poked his head under the bed. Nothing. The technicians will examine the telephone. With a gloved hand he opened the dresser drawer. Only the Bible. I'm leaving, Zelda, tonight I have to go back to the Alexa to meet Kid Yoreme. Boss, I want to go with you. Lefty looked at her. To have you at my side is the best thing that could happen to me, but fix things up with Rodo first. He left before she could reply.

Chief, the second body in the San Luis really is a gringo, but I don't think he's who he says he is either. Tell me fast, I've got to go home and cook. Well, he claims to be a make-up artist, but his hands are covered in scars; I think you should call the consulate in Hermosillo and the D.A.'s office. Fine, I'll see you tomorrow.

He parked on one side of the darkened seed warehouse and sat there thinking. A bad time of day to find clues. He lit a cigarette. The guy planned it or the opportunity arose? Headlights from passing cars on the highway lit up the bushes. She didn't have her purse, in what circumstances would a woman leave that behind? Her purse is part of her story; which means the guy decided, if he brought her by car he didn't let her take it with her. So, he isn't a nobody, it's not Richie for example, but it could be Cervantes or Meraz. He pulled out the two business cards he'd taken from Mayra's box. Or these guys: Esteben Aguirrebere and Miguel Ángel Canela, or any of the dozens of others who desired her and dreamt about her, plus the ones who went to her house. The fucking sonofabitch must be rotting inside; you can't keep something so horrifying under wraps and you can't live with it, at least not for long. He stubbed out the cigarette in the ashtray and opened the door. If he cut off the nipple first, it must have hurt like hell; according to Montaño, who might be going deaf but not blind, the blade wasn't sharp, and no matter what some people are like, nobody gets over something like that. That bastard Montaño, maybe it's all the contact with stiffs that makes him want young live bodies all the time, or maybe you're just born for that. Me, what was I born for? The feeling that his life was simply not worth the effort suddenly swamped him. For being useless. The emptiness had appeared out of nowhere. For being a fucking shadow.

He walked across the deserted field and nothing made any sense. Too much stubble and the yellow tape was gone. About thirty metres beyond the warehouse a man was smoking at a construction site. Every so often he looked Mendieta's way as he blew out the smoke. Lefty went over.

Good evening. Are you a policeman? Like on television and I'm investigating the murder of the girl whose body was found here;

tell me what you saw. How do you know I saw anything? The devil sees more because he's old than because he's the devil, and you don't look the least bit stupid. Lefty tapped two cigarettes from his pack and offered one to the man. I heard the shot, I looked out; the guy was squatting down, then he stood up and left; he had a car parked behind the warehouse. What kind? All I could make out was the shape when he pulled on to the highway, he went off in that direction, away from the city. Pickup or car? Car. Was he wearing a hat? No, and his clothes were light-coloured, he looked tall, wasn't skinny, wasn't fat. Big car or small? More or less big, if he'd come this way I would have had a good look. Was it dark or light? Dark. Lefty paused. Did you see them together before the shot? No, when the guy left I went over and I saw the body. Did you call anyone? I don't have a cell phone, I called when I got home. What's your name? Buddy, I don't plan to tell you and neither will I go make a statement. You're right, it's a pain to go to the police. Are you a policeman or aren't you? What time would it have been when you heard the shot? Around three in the morning. Mendieta gave him another cigarette and lit his own. Did the guy leave slowly or did the car race off? He went calm as could be. Did he look young? Like you. Thank you, and don't go to the police; to get out of a jam they might decide to pin the blame on you. He left.

Tomorrow I'll get them to take pictures of the tyre marks.

Fuck, it's late and I haven't even had a beer. *We Brazilians like beer, but it makes me feel bloated and I prefer other things.* Of course, anything else, except for dying.

Seventeen

Heliport of El Continente hunting camp, at the northern end of a landing strip for small private planes located to one side of the owner's residence, which also houses the office. Nine o'clock at night.

A dark green U.S.-registered tandem-rotor helicopter touches down at the centre of a glowing ring of lights. A second chopper hovers above. Thirty metres away the owner of the property waits calmly with his foreman, a strapping man holding a rifle and a pistol. Several more of his employees, overseen by Secret Service experts, scrutinise every detail. The father of the president of the United States loves hunting and is here for the ducks at a nearby lake. Behind them the house is perfectly illuminated and secured, even though the distinguished guest only plans to drink a whisky on the rocks, have a light supper, then try to catch a few winks before getting up at dawn. On the other side of the heliport, a wire-mesh fence protects the area from intruders and animals. The fence is lined with bored men in uniform.

Before leaving Houston, Special Officer Mitchell, commander of the uniformed officers, was notified of the murder of the F.B.I.'s advance man Donald Simak, but he did not give it much attention beyond saying he didn't know him and no-one with that name had ever had any relationship with the Secret Service. Mister B. had forbidden him from ever cancelling a hunting expedition, under threat of demotion, so he was not inclined to tell him about it. Nothing spectacular had ever occurred while the father of the president of the most powerful country in the world shot ducks or rabbits. He was a skilled and very enthusiastic hunter. That is why Simak, who in his most recent reports had urged a heightening of precautions, did not even cross his mind when Mitchell heard the first shots and placed himself in front of the old man to protect him from sustained A.K.-47 fire.

While his agents repelled the attack with pistols and assault rifles, Mitchell buckled and collapsed on the old man, who was wearing a camouflage outfit.

The helicopter crew keeping watch from above used night-vision equipment to locate the four attackers; they shot them and continued hovering over the spot until they were certain nothing was breathing. Then they landed, confirmed all the intruders were dead, and piled the bodies next to the fence. Each intruder was wearing a T-shirt emblazoned with the slogan *Muro No*: "Stop the Wall".

Meanwhile, Mister B. was freed from the body of Special Officer Mitchell and put back in the helicopter, which took off immediately for the Culiacán airport; there he would board a plane that fifty-eight minutes later would deposit him back home.

Special Agent William Ellroy, second-in-command, took charge of the situation. He ordered the foreman disarmed and all of the camp's employees confined to a bedroom for interrogation. He took Adán Carrasco, the owner, with him into the office and closed the door. I hope you can explain this, you knucklehead, screamed Ellroy, a Southerner known for his crusty disposition; they nearly killed the father of the president, do you think this is a game? you damn fool, the hell you care what might have happened. You're the one who has some explaining to do, you and all those useless idiots you call agents, didn't they clear the area? Few things frightened Carrasco, certainly not that big oaf, 195 centimetres of insolence. They glared at each other. You take over my camp and you can't even spot a few stupid idiots hiding in the weeds. He added that in his youth he had been a sharpshooter in the American army. How do you know they were only a few? You think you're the only one with eyes? If you laid a trap, you're a dead man. You're the dead man, you and your whole team of bumblers. Ellroy stood up to punch him; who did this imbecile think he was to insult a member of the U.S. Secret Service? he was not about to take his lip just because he was a friend of the president and his father: You fucking bastard. He stopped short because they both heard the sound of a helicopter approaching. This is not over, Carrasco. Listen, asshole, you insist on blaming me and I'll call in the Mexican police. They went outside, as did most of the agents. What good are these guys? all they do is get in the way. Carrasco had promised not to involve any Mexican forces or police; no matter what happened, he and those already involved would have to deal with it. The helicopter was the one that had rescued Mister B., and as soon as it touched down the man himself disembarked surrounded by bodyguards. Carrasco went up to greet him: Mister B., you look great! Don't you dare try to serve me any of that Scottish shit, Carrasco, you better have something from Kentucky, and only two ice cubes. The old man strode over as if nothing had happened, while the second helicopter hovered above and every agent watched his movements. No doubt about it, danger rejuvenates you. We're going to be fine, Carrasco, I've never heard of two attacks in the same place on the same person and I know there are a hundred ducks out there just waiting for me. And they are damn impatient. Agent, the old man called to Ellroy, it's back to Plan A., I spoke to my son and there's nothing wrong; send Special Officer Mitchell home and let us know about the funeral. Yes, sir. Listen, Carrasco, I hope you have a surprise waiting for me like last time. Well, I worry about you having a heart attack, so I made sure it's not too surprising or exotic. He gave the old man a slap on the back. Just surprising and exotic enough. They laughed heartily.

Eighteen

He went straight to the Apache. How's the mirror doing? all better? It's not sending signals, my man Lefty, the last thing I caught was that everything is falling apart and we'd better keep our eyes peeled for death. What for? there's no beating it. The one-way mirror gleamed as usual. Look, you can see something in there. Those are reflections, Lefty Mendieta, they're always there, the signals I'm talking about are different and they're so clear you can't miss them. Did you know Yhajaira? So well that once I went with her. I'm envious, tell me about it. Men don't talk about those things, my buddy, what are you thinking? Sorry, I'm pretty out of it tonight, when did you two cook the stew? Last week, before the show. How did you manage that? What do you mean how? money makes the dog dance, Lefty, here as in China. So? Two out of three; after that other one, may God hold her in hell, nobody measures up, that's why I lost it; anyhow, I won't be calling any old snack a meal. Who would you pick out for the culprit? The Apache smiled, his eyes shone. If it's a question of picking there are two or three, but it's a bitch to know if they're the ones. You wouldn't put your hands in the fire for them? Not even if I was nuts, and a pyromaniac I'm not. I hope the mirror perks up and gives us something to go on. I don't think it will, it knows little of the world and even less about deaths they call natural because some bigwig is involved; listen, aren't you going to ask about Roxana? Mendieta smiled. Fucking Apache, you know everything. Was I or was I not a trusted informer for Sánchez? Out with it, then. In truth, I know nothing, lately she'd go out with very powerful people, they'd park their Suburbans and Cheyennes over there. Narcos? Curiously, no, people with money, only with money could you get close to the queen. What about Richie Bernal? He's a puppy and the Valdés aren't going to let him far off the leash, that is, if they haven't declared him worthless already. There's the Spaniard and Luis Ángel Meraz, what about them? Well, maybe the Spaniard thought she was La Malinche and knocked her off. And the other guy? Lots of times I saw him arriving to pick her up, always a big deal, cocky in his Cheyenne, so it's really easy, Lefty Mendieta: a guy who has everything might do anything. Someone bought cigarettes. Did you make a play for her? You think I wouldn't? that's why her death weighs on me so. You wouldn't be selling blotter acid, would you? What's with you, Lefty? the only things sold here are what you're looking at, if you need a hit you'll have to find it somewhere else; and if you want to know, for a little lie-down with her you have to sell nearly five tonnes of candy, that's a shitload and a half. Do you remember a big dark car, driven by a guy who was tall and heavyset, coming for Roxana? They all look alike, my man Lefty: the cars, the way they dress, their height; mostly they were older men, but it's hard to tell them apart, so you think it was somebody like that? He would be a perfect place to start, but you only talk about S.U.V.s and pickups. They came in cars too, dark and light. Did you see one on Friday or Sunday? Yes; what I did not see was her. Shouts made them turn their heads.

A man tossed out by Rivera and his helper rolled towards them on the ground. What you are doing to me is an injustice, he cried out, then as if to himself, I'm going to complain to Human Rights, and he began to cry. He was in love with Roxana, the Apache mumbled, since he got here he hasn't stopped feeling sorry for himself. Did Roxana play along with him? Why would she play along with him? that loser doesn't even have a place to fall down dead; he's Kid Yoreme, they say when he was a boxer he floored Julio César Chávez, but I'd bet it was the other way around and he never found his feet. Poor bum, Mendieta said, feeling like he was speaking to himself, and he went over to him. What's up, Yoreme? Ah, I had a little palm-leaf house, I let in the vixen, and once she was inside she said the two of us didn't fit and she threw me out. Let me buy you a beer. He helped him up. Thank God I've found a charitable soul. He's with me, Lefty said to Rivera when he tried to stop him. I'd rather he not go in, he's been causing a ruckus. I promise to keep him quiet. Will you vouch for him? The one I won't vouch for is you.

Yoreme followed him in, so woozy all he noticed was his urge to cry. Carvajal, who was speaking with Miroslava, came over to say hello to Lefty. The dancer gave a bored wave. Señor Mendieta, what a pleasure to have you here, how is the case of the girls coming? It's stuck, as if they died of old age. Whatever you need, I'm here to help. I'm aware of that, thank you. Excuse me. The manager went up to the Phantom, who immediately came over to Lefty. Anything special, detective? They say Meraz spent Sunday with Roxana. The bartender served a few beers and returned. What I know is he was in Mexico City. Find out for me, Lefty said, because Mexico City doesn't cover the whole world. He let Escamilla lead them to a table far from the catwalk. No-one will bother you here, you two are Roxana's widowers and I'm going to send you a drink, not on the house, but on me, your waiter, who would remind you that any nail will pull out a tack and that you have come to the right place, today the girls are horny and ready for anything, two hundred pesos for the private room and fuck whoever turns tail. Stop talking bullshit and bring us beer and tequila, ordered the detective, infected by the mood of his guest. Beer and peanuts, added Yoreme, who was definitely hungry. Is the Spaniard here? Not yet. Escamilla served them and they said, Your health. Chávez tells me you gave him quite a fright. Fright is what he gave me, every so often I still see stars winking from that passing cloud; what about you, what do you do? because I had a little palm-leaf house. Wrestling. You're pretty skinny, aren't you? Hey, I fought Santo, the man of the silver mask. Was he good? The best. How did it go? I came out alive. They fell silent. What am I doing here with you? Drinking beer, Kid. But I don't know you, you wouldn't be trying to drag me into some funny business, would you? Not at all. It's just that I promised, uh, did you know Roxana? Who? The love of my life, I promised her I would never hang around with strangers, I had a little palm-leaf house and I let in the vixen; so if you're planning to get me to help you with something bad, I will not accept; she's dead and I'm going to be good for the rest of my life. What did she die of? I don't know, but she died and I'm going to behave like decent people. Lucky you, you've got a project. Neither am I going back into the ring, so if you're Don King, José Sulaimán, or Bob Arum and you have a contract for a fight with Golden Boy, Manny Pacquiao, or Chávez himself, forget about it, I will not sign; I'm sick and tired of getting knocked around and sick and tired of the training; the weepy little rabbit left too. The waiter stood for a moment observing the pair, then shook his head sadly and went to the bartender, asked for something to cheer them up, and reluctantly placed the glasses on the table. The two of them didn't even notice the difference. The waiter served them again.

Two hours later: Do you know what my big dream is? the boxer's words were slurred, but his smile was broad. A rematch with Chávez, Mendieta guessed. Don't insult me, would you fight Santo again? Not even if I could live my life over, that night was the only time I wished I was dead. Silence. A fat tear rolled down Yoreme's cheek, even though up to then he had remained calm. That is the point, my esteemed, forgive me but I forget your name. Caveman Galindo. Well, that is the point, my man Cavey: death, I had a little palm-leaf house, Roxana is dead, they say she got killed in Mazatlán and I want to go see her. Mendieta felt bitter juices in his gut, Bardominos the priest crossed his mind like a dirty stain and he shook his head, hurried his drink, signalled Escamilla for another round, and gave his attention to the crying man in front of him. This bastard really did love her, he's made me sad, I can't deny it, but this bastard loved her and that's enough to earn anyone's respect; I'm so glad he doesn't know about the nipple. Suddenly he asked, Which days did you go to bed with her? Yoreme reacted. What's the matter with you, asshole? there are men like me who don't need to go to bed with a woman to love her for the rest of our lives; it's obvious you don't have a clue who Roxana was. A sob overtook him. I had a little palm-leaf house; if I catch the sleazebag who killed her, I'll cut him to pieces. Mendieta felt worse. I'm fucked, but I have to admit this imbecile is right. *Are you a policeman? You don't look like one. You're a lefty! Me too.* The waiter brought more drinks. Tell the manager to put it on my tab, Mendieta said. What about the tip? He pulled out a bill and handed it to him. And to carve my tab in ice.

Don't worry, Señor Carvajal will understand. Where's Miroslava? In a private room, with her best customer. What about Camila Naranjo? She called in sick, but Penelope's here, you want me to bring h er over? she's a Spaniard and her ass is ripe for juicing. No, tell the manager I'll talk with him later on. Very good, boss. Then he spoke to his companion: Kid Yoreme, let's go where they treat us like people.

They stumbled their way out.

They got into the Jetta. You know where I'm going to take you, you bastard? To a bar where they serve snacks. Wrong, fucking Yoreme, I'm taking you to Mazatlán. The boxer fell silent; drink tended to make him happy, but some powerful interior force was pushing him the other way. Fucking Caveman, he murmured, you are a real friend, bro, I want nothing more from life than to see Roxana, to be at her wake, to pray for her, to see her grave; you bastard, I never thought wrestlers were such nice guys, sorry, fucking Caveman, the weepy little rabbit left too; God willing when you die you'll go straight to heaven, if Roxana had met you she would have liked you. A tear rolled down Mendieta's cheek, he thought Yoreme must be affecting him, though he knew that was not the case.

He headed for the empty field where he had been before.

So you never slept with. That again? how could I take her to bed if she was always occupied, always in the arms of those lecherous pigs drooling all over her? it was her smile I loved, her coloured eyes, her aroma, I lived in a little palm-leaf house and one day the vixen came to visit; you fall in love without wanting to, one night you go out for a drink, you've convinced yourself there's no point in boxing, but you don't know what to do instead, you ask for a beer and you find yourself staring at a goddess suspended in the air, holding every fucking eye in the place; that's how it happened, I felt my heart explode; if you had met her, for sure you would have given up wrestling too, fucking Caveman; I thought if I marry her she won't want me boxing, so I should retire before she asks me to, I want her to think I'm intelligent, that at least I went to high school.

Mendieta stopped at an under-the-table liquor store, bought a six of Tecates and a Viva Villa tequila that tasted like rubbing alcohol. Yoreme, we are going to get drunk, buddy, that sorrow you're carrying around is so heavy it's contagious, in other words I'm fucked, fucking Yoreme. My man Cavey, you are a true friend, and what a shame you didn't tear Santo apart, I would have busted my hands applauding. And I would have done the same for you if you had knocked out Julio César. Is it true that's the name of the king of Scotland? Do you think? Better we say your health, is this Mazatlán or Culiacán? It's Guadalajara on the plains. They took Colegio Militar Highway to the wholesale market and from there the freeway that leads to the port. You're going really slow, fucking Caveman, give it the gas. Why are you always talking about a little palm-leaf house? Yoreme began to sob uncontrollably; after a while he said, If you are my friend, you won't ask me that ever again. Mendieta made a sign that so be it and he turned up the stereo: "Have You Ever Seen the Rain?" by Creedence. What awful music, fucking Cavey, don't you have Los Tucanes? Groups named for animals is something I can't stand. Why? Like you, don't ask me that. All friends have their mysteries, but you and I have too many, the more mysterious the more interesting, she liked to say. She had said the same thing to Mendieta, he remembered her incredibly arresting voice that turned the craziest thing into an indisputable fact. I can see you talked with her a lot. Yoreme drank, let his tears flow as if they were blood from war wounds, then spluttered: She didn't say that to me, the truth is I never spoke with her, I let in the vixen, she said it to one of the pigs she went out with, a lawyer rotting in bills. A politician? That night I followed them: them in a pickup, me on a bicycle; he didn't take her to a hotel, they went to a big fancy house right near the Alexa; a few minutes later he came out alone. In other words, he took her to someone else. That's what I thought too, but no, he came out for his cell phone and he made a call, and the weepy little rabbit left too. Did you hear who he was calling? How was I supposed to hear from twenty metres away? the house was white or blue, it was a huge mansion, yellow door, I'll never forget it. Your health, my friend. Your health, I don't know what would become of me without you, you're my brother, the only one who tells me what I should do with my life; you told me to stop boxing and I did, you told me to get a job and I'm hauling ass, you told me to stop doing drugs and I'm working on that, but you know it ain't easy. Good, pour me one, Yoreme, I'm drying out. You're going really slow, Cavey, floor this sucker or everything will turn to shit. Everything has turned to shit, my man Yoreme, just like you. And how do you know that? Because Julio César beat you. And Santo beat you. Because I gave him the chance, when I won the first fall with a knee to the balls and a stab in the eyes, he begged me not to beat him, he was pleading, swearing on the Virgin of Guadalupe; you're telling me I should have gone against the Virgin? That's a tough one. Exactly. Well, the same thing happened to me, I let in the vixen. Julio asked you to let him win? that I don't believe. On his knees. What! that's too fucking much, Yoreme. Why not? the guy wasn't Superman. He is the best boxer pound for pound in the history of Mexico, and that's not parakeet spit. My balls aren't either. But they're hanging pretty low. Yoreme began to sob again. Take it easy, fucking Yoreme, don't be a pussy. I just thought of her, bro, her fleshy lips, and the weepy little rabbit left too. Mendieta fell silent, thought about her lips, how when she grew serious they were Wonderland, Alice and all. You didn't get to see her tattoos, my man Cavey, she had a tattoo on her belly you couldn't take your eyes off, when she danced it'd spin and slide around her body, sometimes it didn't want to leave her ass; move, fucking tattoo, don't get stuck there, I had a little palm-leaf house. *You're impressed? It's a tattoo like any other. Isn't it?*

They reached the seed warehouse but Lefty pressed on. They passed the Cloverleaf and took the road to El Dorado. At a little rest stop, where two transport trucks were parked, they stopped to take a leak. They stood next to each other, pissing. In front of them a cornfield glowed in the moonlight. Cool air. Before going to Roxana's wake, Cavey, I'd like to see the place where she died, to put up a cross. Who told you they're holding a wake? They had swallowed four cans of beer and half a bottle of tequila. They aren't? aren't we going to the wake? All I asked was who told you. And if we aren't going to the wake, where the fuck are we going, Caveman? Don't get mad, fucking Yoreme, take it easy. Easy your whore of a mother, fucking Cavey. He put up his fists and let loose a right that made the detective wobble. Calm down. Lefty backed off, but Yoreme was on

127

him with a jab to the nose, a hook to the liver, and to top it off an uppercut to the jaw that sent him to the ground out cold. Fucking liar. He went through his pockets, pulled out his wallet, took the money, and threw the billfold away; the cell phone he flung into the cornfield and he roared away in the Jetta. The first thing he did was turn off the stereo, which was playing "In-A-Gadda-Da-Vida" by Iron Butterfly, and look for *norteño* tunes on the radio.

Seconds later, Mendieta woke up. Everything was spinning. He saw the wallet on the ground, patted himself, couldn't feel the cell. He swore at Yoreme and then at himself. The only reason I'm not any stupider is I'm not any older, what came over me to put myself through this little number? He looked over at the parked trucks, gathered his wits, and got to his feet. His pistol was safe and sound in the car's glove compartment.

If you were a trucker and some jerk turned up at 3.00 a.m. and woke you, a man dressed in black and bleeding from the nose, looking drunk and crazy, what would you say to him? A guy who is dirty and stinking, who is not going to tell you he is a policeman, and even if he showed an I.D. he has no gun, so would you believe his badge was real? Well, get ready, because you are the closest one to him and he is headed your way.

He knocked on the truck's door. No answer. He banged harder and could see a silhouette behind the glass asking with a movement of the head what he wanted. Open the window, the detective said. The trucker hesitated, but he lowered it. What's up? Uh, I just got mugged, they took everything. So what's that got to do with me? call the police. The trucker was not pleased to be awakened. I don't have

128

any way to do that and there's no pay phone in sight. So you couldn't find any other sucker to bother but me who's been hauling ass all the way from Hermosillo? Hey, I have a friend who's a trucker, I don't know if you know him, his name is Teófilo, but we call him Teo. The guy looked at Lefty. I've heard of him, where do you know him from? From the neighbourhood. What neighbourhood would that be? The Col Pop in Culiacán. Aha, and you see him and say hello. The fact is I don't really remember him. What do you mean you don't remember him? you said he was your friend. He's a friend of my brother's, he was his best buddy when they were kids. Who's your brother? Listen, I'm only asking for a favour, I got mugged, they took my car, my money, my cell phone. And you can't tell me who your brother is? His name is Enrique, but that bastard isn't going to come get me, he lives far away, and if you aren't going to give me a hand, well, fuck you. Listen to that, aren't you the touchy one. Have you never fallen in love? And how, he jerked his thumb towards the bunk. And later on the woman got snuffed? Such luck I haven't had. Well, are you going to help me or not? You're saying you fell in love and they killed your girl. More or less. And the guy that killed her also stole your car? You aren't going to help me, I'm going to try the other truck. Lefty moved off. What do you want me to do? He went back. Let me use your cell or take me to the tollbooth, there must be a telephone there. You're just as prickly as your bro. I won't let you insult my brother, you fucking numbskull. Look, I'm Teo and you must be the snot-nose. I was never a snot-nose. The little kid then, the youngster, the younger brother, I thought you were a lefty or at least that's what they called you. Are you Teo? What's left of him. Forgive me for what I said; in the neighbourhood people speak well of you. About a year ago I saw your bro in Las Vegas, he's getting fat; listen, in case you want to know, I was there the night your brother had to run away. Really? to this day I don't know why he left. Because he was an idiot, why else? listen, are you going to get in or are we going to continue talking long distance, here's my cell phone; I'll start this sucker, take a piss, and we'll be on our way. Lefty got in. Let me call, I bet they'll come get me. Don't look in the bunk because my girl gets embarrassed. You mean she can still blush? What kind of stupid question is that? just like I said, same as your fucking brother.

He called Ortega. No answer. Zelda picked up on the second ring. Do you know what time it is? Time for the cats to yowl, what are you doing up? Rodo just left. Everything alright? I don't know what you mean by "alright", because I think we ended up mad at each other. Bad scene, Agent Toledo, truly. Listen, here I am chatting about me, what's wrong? He told her. And he stole the Jetta? The money too, the cell phone, and all my desire to be nice. So, what's next? Call the Federal Highway Police, get them to stop him at the tollbooth or on the road, he's headed for Mazatlán and he hates speed limits, and if it isn't too much bother, come pick me up. He gave her his coordinates.

Yoreme stopped at the tollbooth and two highway patrolmen grabbed him. He offered them money. When they turned him down he let out a wail: I wish somebody understood me, I had a little palm-leaf house and I let in the vixen. The officers were touched and wanted to know what was wrong. They killed my girlfriend, and he continued sobbing. When? Yesterday, in Mazatlán. Was she the one that got strangled in the Golden Triangle? That's her, I'm on my way to put a cross on her tomb. So why did they ask us to arrest you? Who? The State Ministerial Police. It must be a mistake, I've never committed any crime, a friend lent me his car and money so I could go to her wake. One of the officers opened the Jetta to look for the car's papers and found the pistol. What about this? Who knows? the car belongs to my friend. What does your friend do? He's a wrestler, he fought Santo, the man in the silver mask, and if the guy hadn't begged for a break my pal would have torn him apart. The officers exchanged glances, then cornered him and pulled out a set of hand-cuffs. Without a pause in his sobs, Yoreme knocked out the one closest with a left to the stomach and an uppercut to the jaw, then climbed into their patrol car and floored it heading back towards Culiacán. The other drew his gun, but did not fire. Far from pleased, Yoreme was bawling and doing one-ninety.

Teo and Mendieta were reminiscing about the old neighbourhood, with the subject of Susana Luján taking up at least a quarter of an hour. You earn good money, right? You have no idea how much. Then, why are so many badges poor as church mice, you included, from what I hear you go around in a Jetta from the year of the Flood. It's because we're saving up for our retirement at the beach, cottage, palm trees, all that; listen, what was it my bro did that he had to run to the other side for good? You look into it, aren't you a detective? Is it true the two of you were guerrillas? Sure, I trained Subcommander Marcos. No wonder. No wonder what? No wonder he's so nice. Being nice is a form of struggle, don't you think? It must have been something really awful for that bastard not to come back to Culiacán even once. He came back once. When? When your mother died. Are you serious? why didn't I see him? Because he was in disguise and he didn't think it smart to let you in on it, there were people who didn't belong, flies in the milk. The fucking sonofabitch. You would know, you come from the same one. A few minutes passed, Mendieta replayed scenes from his mother's wake; nothing, no-one at all like him. How was he disguised? As a woman. What about you? Me, I was waiting in the car, I couldn't be seen either. Fucking pair of fruitcakes, you're off your rockers.

A patrolman parked about seven kilometres closer to the city was awakened by a call from his buddies; he got out his rifle and set himself up at the edge of the highway, taking cover behind his vehicle. Three minutes later a patrol car came flying towards him.

Mendieta and Teo lit up fresh cigarettes and followed the passing police car with their eyes. What are those assholes playing at? Exercises to keep from nodding off. See if they don't fuck themselves on the guardrail. Who cares if they do? another stripe on the tiger; so, you aren't going to tell me what my brother did? Do I look like a fucking stoolie, or what? It must have been something really serious. Well yeah, the bastard was such a homeboy and he hasn't been back for twenty-something years. I'm going to look into it and if there's anything illegal there, by God I swear I'll quit my job before I let them go after him. You mean you want to get to your beach house early, don't you, you chickenshit; and you can't think of a better excuse than your bro; what kind of a dolt are you? getting your family caught up in your bullshit. I'm going to throw both you bastards in the slammer. You sure turned out to be touchy, fucking

Lefty, you were just a little tyke when we were deep in that crazy shit; look, asshole, all the stuff about your brother you'd better keep under your hat, you don't want to be the one to give my buddy Quique a heart attack; besides, you're drunk, fucking Edgar, and I've never met a drunk who isn't a loudmouth; why don't you tell me about that little girl you lost? Pause. Not long ago I spent a few days in Mazatlán and I got to know her. Did you really, really get to know her or did you just fool around? And then a report came in about a dead woman, we went to see what was up, and it was her, fuck, I felt like shit; then I took a friend to see the place where we found her, just to pass the time, and he mugged me. I guess you're telling me he felt something for her too. Why would you think that? the dude came along out of solidarity. And then he mugged you, there's real solidarity for you; since you're such a prick, either you're a loser and you aren't worth my time, or you're hiding something from me. You're right, he was in love with her too. You don't say, and the two of you were going buddy-buddy to cry for your dear lover girl, what a couple of ball-busters, and the asshole left you eating dirt so you wouldn't see him cry; such a modern take on love, I don't get it. She was a dancer. Ah-ha, a late-night one? He nodded. You've complicated your life, Lefty my man, some bitches are just for ogling and at a distance. I don't think you know much about love, why don't we ask your girl? Sure, ask her, she must be awake. Mendieta turned towards the bunk behind him and called: Señorita, are you listening? Teo opened the curtain. Answer him, my love, he's a kid from the barrio, the brother of the bastard who bought you. Mendieta saw she was an inflatable doll and he smiled. Enrique bought her for you? He gave her to me when we saw each other in Las Vegas and she has never given me any guff, what's more she's from a good family. At that moment patrol car 161 from the State Ministerial Police pulled up and Zelda Toledo got out. If I ever find out you've done something to your girl I'll lock you away, fucking Teo, even if you are my bro's best buddy. That's what I said, a braggart just like your fucking brother; he turned the ignition. They said goodbye.

Nineteen

Midnight. The F.B.I.'s operations room in Los Angeles. On screen, the photographs of the four people implicated in the attack on Mister B. Highlighted alongside three of them were their details; the fourth photograph had nothing. The three were U.S. citizens of Latino origin: Mexican, Salvadoran, Colombian. The fourth is not in our files, Chief David Barrymore said. He's just as dead, an agent commented. Not at all, the official insisted, we can't leave any loose threads, who's to say he's not head of some clan? He looked at the image of the shooter on the screen and punched a number on his cell phone. Special Agent Ellroy, did you take the pictures with a cell? He listened. Well, one of them, the one they got in the chest, hasn't turned up in our files, he's white, round face, thin lips, short hair, features a bit refined, send us more pics; no? you don't have a damn camera? alright, you'll have to explain that one to your superiors, but what a blunder. He hung up. Impossible to get a picture with better resolution, the photographer got killed and the bodies were a mess so they put them in acid; send the finger-prints and the pic to the Mexican police to see if they have any-thing on him. You really think they might? With those guys you can never tell, but we'd better make sure; Agent Harrison, did you find anything? A woman about 170 centimetres tall, middle-aged, thin, stepped towards him, she was wearing loose jeans and a T-shirt: The three of them have records for activities against the United States and in favour of immigrants, especially since Washington announced the plan to build the wall and put troops along the border; Gómez the Mexican has been arrested five times for that, Castellanos the Central American twice, and Barriga the Colombian seven times; the last two lived in Los Angeles and Gómez in Gila Bend, Arizona. Nasty pieces of work. Precisely, sir, although all three fought in Iraq and won medals of honour. You can go, Harrison. Sir, the news on Donald Simak has been confirmed, they found his body in the Hotel San Luis in Culiacán, in northwest Mexico, near where the attack took place, he'd been dead for nine hours. What are you talking about, Harrison? to my knowledge no Donald Simak has ever been affiliated with the Bureau, and I do not need to remind you to keep your nose in your own business. Yes, sir. They exchanged glares that the rest noted, even though they kept their heads down.

A dry mouth makes silence more succulent.

Win Harrison went out to the small terrace where they allowed you to smoke. She thought about it. Her cold features showed no interest in the brightly lit city that extended before her eyes like a Trojan horse. She knew what they were doing to Simak could happen, but that did not make it fair. She also knew they all hated this man, the only man with whom she would have dared to have a child, because he loved to break the rules; only she was aware of his despair and the frequency with which he felt like a slot machine. He was a bastard, but she had spent the greatest nights of her life with him; he never learned how to cook or make cocktails or even look out the window; he was an artist of solitude and he was her friend. She never managed to get him to explain his obsession with immigrants or his recent plan to smuggle guns into the country next door. By the time she finished her cigarette she had reached a decision. She would take a few days off. Would L.H. still live in Tijuana?

Twenty

Nine in the morning. Mendieta was watching joggers and walkers near the Diego Valadés Parkway. Enrique said Jason is a champion miler, I don't want him to see me so out of shape, I've got to do something; damn, this hangover is embarrassing, fucking Yoreme, I'm going to string you up by the balls, asshole, then you'll get with the programme. He was sore from the punches, too. I'll ask Montaño to check me over, I don't want to end up with a heart attack from doing things I shouldn't. I won't tell him about getting beat up, I'd never hear the end of it and all he'd give me is cream for the aches. His eyes followed several lovely women, real tits and ass, but he was still lost in his thoughts. Maybe I'd better not, after all those courses on forensic medicine the only thing he knows about is corpses, and women of course, though I doubt he ever studied for that. He was behind the Forum, standing next to a path at the edge of the river, waiting for Luis Ángel Meraz. Am I doing this for Mayra or for society? For society, of course, that's who pays my salary, not to mention my bonuses. He smiled. Mayra is Mexican, why was she always slobbering in Portuguese? I've got to call her mother, she wrote her so many letters. From her advice and comments, you can tell they're responses to questions; what would Mayra have asked her? *If I write about these things some day, can I make you my character?* She was born in Guadalajara and her maternal last name is Palencia. What would that dude do with the nipple? You managed to suck it at last, you sonofabitch, it must have tasted great, you fucking murderer.

He continued mulling things over, not about to take a single step more than necessary, even kidding around; he had not slept a wink and his head was thick as a plank, though he was not sleepy. Briseño didn't want us bothering his friend, who could well become the next governor, but we should at least give the guy a reason to wield his power. Miroslava told me he's a kind soul: Richie Bernal might be the killer, he thinks he owns the world and everything in it, but the attorney? what a thought, such a well-behaved man with such a future. Fucking Parra, he must be bar-hopping with his buddy shrinks, the last thing he cares about is his patients. I was chatting with the dog again late last night and that bastard really understands me, he wags his tail and looks me right in the eye. What's up, beast? what are you going to do when the moon goes down, eh? when only a tiny moonbeam is left? Get in gear, you fucking hairy animal, don't you know you've got an astronaut cousin named Laika? instead of staring at the moon like you, she went out to meet it; you don't say, and how do you know she was the first animal to orbit the earth? did you go to college? No wonder you look at me that way. Parra's going to love you, what a couple of toughs you two are. Was the moon white or red? was it Mars? no, too far away.

He had been watching a documentary about soft rock when Zelda called on his replacement cell as it was charging. Did you manage to sleep, boss? Of course, Agent Toledo, what do you think decent people do at night? Sorry, I wanted to let you know that Meraz goes running every day by the Diego Valadés Parkway; I confirmed he got in last night, suppose we approach him there? you know Chief Briseño doesn't want us to bring him in to Headquarters. Who told you where he runs? A friend, don't forget I used to be a traffic cop and you see a lot of things doing that, among them, who goes by. I'll take care of it, you call Rodo and invite him to breakfast at Puro Natural, see if a lettuce salad and a Chakira smoothie bring him around. Guess what, he brought me a serenade last night, mariachis and all; while I was rescuing you, he was belting out "I sing beneath your window, so you'll know I love you so". Another reason for you to fix things up between you. Thank you, boss, I'll see you at Headquarters.

The goriest fights are between lovers, aren't they?

A couple came along, she was chatting about the shows coming up this year: And the December concert with Maestro Patrón, what do you think? Terrific. A lithe young woman ran by followed by a thickset man, and then an older woman with magnificent legs power-walking. Drowsiness set in. I need a cup of coffee, I'll go to the Lucerna. No chance, Meraz was approaching at an easy trot accompanied by a young woman the detective had seen in the newspaper speaking about violence against women. They were talking flirtatiously. When they reached Lefty: Attorney Meraz, might I have a word with you? The fellow stopped without losing his smile and shook Lefty's hand. How are you? forgive me, I don't recall who you are, but I'd be happy to talk, which media are you from? Detective Edgar Mendieta from the State Ministerial Police. Still nice as could be: What can I do for you, detective? He must have been about fifty, a pleasing face and incipient baldness, tall, more or less solid, running shoes maybe size twenty-nine-and-a-half. A few days ago a woman was found dead, Mayra Cabral de Melo, also known as Roxana, with whom you must have gone running more than once. Meraz smiled understandingly. Dayana, I'll catch up with you in a moment, my queen. The girl, who was wearing tight shorts and a red top, jogged ahead slowly. Omar Briseño told me about it, poor girl, it's upsetting, such a beautiful woman should have had a better fate; listen, detective, if you need anything, money to send the body home, since you know she was Brazilian, or paperwork expedited, I'd be happy to help. Where were you from eleven o'clock Sunday night until six o'clock Monday morning? Meraz looked him in the eye. Am I a suspect? I'm asking where you were at the time she was likely murdered. He turned to where Dayana was waiting for him. She can't compare to Roxana, but she is sensational. Have you got witnesses? She's standing right there, if you want, go ask her. Could I have your telephone number for whatever may turn up? Delighted, he handed him a card. And forgive me, attorney. No worries, carry on with the investigation. When was the last time you travelled to Mexico City? I got back day before yesterday, I was there for a week with Dayana. He turned again towards where she was waiting. It broke my heart, but I had to come back. A final question, one girl swears that on Sunday she saw you bring Roxana to the Alexa, that the two of you argued and then left again, together. I thought this was routine, detective, but I see that I really am a suspect and since we're into it, let me tell you that Briseño warned me about you, that for no good reason you might try to give me the acid test. He smiled and went on: Ever since Roxana got here, I've spent most Mondays with her, and if I didn't feel like seeing her last Monday it was because this little girl you are looking at is driving me wild, and I hope not to have to provide you with all the details. I can see you're not married. He smiled ironically, I'm not old enough, detective. Forgive me, I won't bother you any more. It's no bother, on the contrary, we have to catch the culprit, and I repeat, for whatever you might need I am here to help. They cut off a nipple, with a dull knife. No, how awful, poor Roxana. Did you know Yhajaira? Of course I knew her and what happened to her is sad too, is it a dancing-girl killer we're dealing with? We have no idea, they were both killed with a 9mm. I don't know anything about guns, but it sounds terrible. Thank you, attorney, you have been very helpful. At your service, detective. He caught up with the girl. Mendieta made his mind blank to keep from exploding, lit a cigarette right next to the people exercising, and walked over to the Jetta, which the highway police had brought back to him without any investigation, though they kept the Beretta, said they knew nothing about it. If this jerk gets to the governor's palace, for sure he'll turn it into a harem and guess which of my buddies will be his surgeon general?

While he listened to "Reflections of My Life" by Marmalade, he thought again about her eyes, her perfect face, her body. She told me she had read Jorge Amado, Nélida Piñón, Rubem Fonseca. One of those nights we went to Valentino's and she was surprised I didn't know how to dance. *What? The men from Sinaloa I know dance really well, they've got rhythm, and the girls are stupendous, one I know is enchanting.* I told her in high school I never dared, sometimes I'd almost get up the courage for a waltz, but I never took the first step. Why did I tell her that? In my entire life I never told anyone, and I said it to her with a passion I've almost never felt.

No, I was not falling in love, any more than I was in love with Susana, who before you know it is going to show up with her son. I also don't think I was born to be alone and certainly not to spend my nights conversing with my neighbour's dog, who as a matter of fact was terrific last night: he was up on his hind legs, howling at the moon, or was it at the spaceships Cervantes was talking about? I ought to find that bastard. His cell phone rang. Mendieta, he answered without looking to see who it was. Lefty, I'll expect you in one hour at the office of the D.A. It was the chief. Boss, how did it go with the Yanks last night? Briseño hung up.

Mendieta thought he should be smiling, but he couldn't move a muscle in his face. He headed towards his house and a cup of coffee. That guy Meraz is awful sure of himself, but he has that empty gaze that gives away what a sonofabitch he is; could so much sex be good for you? He called Ortega: Hello. What's up, fucking pansy, are you still menstruating? Now I'm bleeding a bit less. Take it easy, papa, the world wasn't built in a day. Listen, last night I messed up. When haven't you? He told him about his odyssey, but had a hard time describing Yoreme's face: You know what? let me call you back in a little while. Got it.

Trudis was sweeping out the garage and watering the potted plants. So, now you went to catch some early-rising rascal? No, I went for a stroll. With that face? It's the same as always, Trudis, just a little more ragged. Listen, where did you spend the night, the bed is just as I left it. I slept in the living room. You? let a girl who doesn't know you buy that line, you like comfort, a soft mattress, and if you were home you never would have slept on the sofa, why are you trying to fool me? How could you say such a thing, Trudis; I have to leave in half an hour. I made you eggs *montados* in *salsa roja* with beans. Nescafé is all I want. And leave without any breakfast? don't even think about it, Lefty, I repeat: you need your nourishment. Sure, but

143

I don't have time, the chief is expecting me. Get a move on and you can manage to eat something, your clothes are laid out on the bed and I'll serve you right this minute; and listen, for the glory of your mother, shave, how could you even consider going around with those whiskers? don't you know decent girls like their men clean-shaven? why do you think I didn't get involved with that guy Alex? just looking at the scrub brush on his chin gave me the willies. I'll bet what you were afraid of was Señora Chela. Nobody would want to mess with her, you're right, it was him who wanted to do it with me, but he's not the right flea for my bed mat. Whoa, Trudis, aren't you demanding. There is but one life, Lefty, and we've got to live it as God wills. Set the table then, I'll be with you in ten minutes; one thing, did you ever meet Teo, a friend of Enrique's? Of course, those young Turks were something else, they didn't fool around like the others. You mean they were brats? No way, they were just different, how can I put it, they talked about stuff no-one else did, they had their own thing. Did they go to parties with you and your friends? Teo was a good dancer, Enrique never tried, and they wouldn't always go. I saw Teo a little while ago, he's really in love. That is the best thing that can happen if you believe in love. You don't? Of course not, Lefty, if I believed, how could I go on living without feeling devastated? So, what makes you think I believe? Oh, Lefty, don't pretend, you dream about a stable love. Rather than reply, he went to get dressed and while he was at it he plugged in the cell phone to charge.

In the office of the Attorney General of the Republic.

You filed a report to your commander on the body of Peter

Connolly, the gringo who was killed in the Hotel San Luis. Felipe Montemayor liked to go right to the nub. Mendieta nodded. Briseño looked on eagerly. And you suggested he call the American consulate in Hermo- sillo and the D.A.'s office, why? The guy had two I.D.s, I thought he might be an undercover agent. Just the two I.D.s? He was a strong man with a small, neatly packed suitcase, he had an ordinary face and no-one noticed him, he registered as a make-up artist; I don't know, it made me wonder. Couldn't he have been some company rep looking for partners? Maybe, although his baggage didn't look like a negotiator's, he carried no cash, he was wearing an underarm holster without a weapon, and there was a map of the municipality of Culiacán open on the floor. Any markings on the map? None, and it was covered in fingerprints, including his own. Anything more on the case, Commander Briseño? Nothing, no-one knows who he is, just as Mendieta says, no-one saw him, a waiter recalls serving a few drinks to a sad-eyed gringo, but he's not sure it was him; we made a couple of calls and all his telephone numbers turned out to be false; the consulate doesn't have him registered. Case closed, then. Well, if they aren't interested in him, we certainly aren't.

He handed them a copy of the fax with the photograph of the guy shot down at El Continente. I need your help to identify this individual. Mendieta and Briseño looked blankly at the picture. The D.A.'s office and their requests, Lefty thought, I bet their computers are on the blink. Perhaps you have him in your files, he's not in ours. Where did he get killed? Very close to here, at El Continente hunting camp; some American connected to the U.S. president was there, no-one knows how word got out, but there was a protest by four people against that wall they want to build, they shot them all, the others turned out to be gringos; only this one hasn't been identified and they're asking for our cooperation. There was a silence during which Mendieta wanted a beer, Briseño a snack, and Montemayor for that pair of idiots to clear out of his office. Briseño took the fax. We'll see if we've got anything on him. I appreciate your cooperation, Mexico City needs to hear urgently.

Forty minutes later they were in Briseño's office. Those assholes want us to do their job. Well, you're in charge here. And you pay me no damn heed, do you? now Attorney Meraz tells me you've got him down as a suspect in the murder of that table dancer; Lefty, don't waste time on that, those girls float in and out, we have no reason to spend our limited resources on a case like that; close it, give Yolanda Estrada's body to her family, and the other one, bury it somewhere, and don't you dare bother Meraz, I told you he could be the next governor. Meraz said we could count on him for the cost of sending the body of Mayra Cabral de Melo to Brazil. He is a generous man, I don't know if he ought to spend his money on that. What I know is you shouldn't be so stingy with your budget; according to Camila Naranjo, one of the girls at the Alexa, Meraz took the dead woman out on the day she died, even though he claims he was in Mexico City. But that doesn't make him guilty. Nor does it clear him, just where was he? Let's not get drawn into trying to destroy his political career, Lefty; I order you to suspend the investigation and erase Attorney Meraz from everything. I couldn't care less about his ambitions, chief, if he's been stepping out of line he'll have to explain it. Forget about it, it's not in my best interests and I hope you understand that, what's up with the Spaniard? We requested information from Police and Civil Guard Headquarters in Madrid, we're waiting on that; we told him to stay put for a few days so he can lap up all the rum in the city. Watch out for Richie Bernal, Pineda says he's flipped and he's got something against you; I asked him to rein him in, let's hope he doesn't put a bullet in you. Lefty shook his head, fed up. Chief, you rub elbows with the cream of society, do you know who Anita Roy is? Briseño's expression hardened. I told you not to go there, are you stupid or what? He banged his fist on the desk, spilling a can of pencils and pens. Lefty stood up. The case of the girl with no tits had come knocking.

Twenty-One

Richie Bernal was behind the wheel. He and two of his sidekicks were parked near the entrance to Sinaloa State H.S. 25, *corridos* blaring on the radio, waiting for a babe they had spotted that morning. He wanted to declare his love for her, take her for a spin, and if she showed any openings let her tumble. What a lover-boy you turned out to be, you don't even leave one to be the godmother. The chick was cute, wasn't she? Being a bit older than Richie, the gunslingers did their best to follow his drift: She is whatever she may be, but the fact is the love of your life just died. Any nail will pull out a tack, my man Rafa, what can you do? and there are only two kinds of women: those that fuck and those that are dead. They smoked. From their spot on Los Alamos Boulevard they could see part of La Campiña Park and a few power-walkers sweating heavily. Other pickups and luxury cars were also waiting for the bell. Girls wearing short skirts began trickling out of the building and heading noisily off with their admirers. Hey, Grunt, are you sure she gets out at ten? That's what she said. You are such an idiot; Rafa, go see if it's true. It's five of, boss, don't you want to wait? No I don't, go in and tell her to give her teachers the finger, I'll do her homework for her; no, both you assholes go, see if the two of you together makes at least one, and do it right now, I'm telling you, then follow me in the other pickup and don't mess it up; if I take her to a hotel you wait outside, nothing's going to happen to me.

The bodyguards got out on the passenger side at the very

moment a Ford pulled up and three hitmen opened fire with their A.K.-47s. Rafa, in a macabre dance, fell face-first next to the heavy door, which he did not manage to close. The thirty holes in Grunt would stop spouting blood soon enough. Three students fell dead and two more girls were badly wounded. Everybody nearby swallowed hard. Richie's mother came to mind, and the river in his village, the thought that he was too young to. He felt like he was peeing, knew that nothing was as it should be, remembered he was a lousy shot. Meanwhile, more bullets shattered the half-inch windows and burrowed into the armour-plating. He turned the ignition, accelerated; the door swung wide and he drove off leaving behind screams of terror, wailing teenagers taking cover wherever they could, and the roar of the suitors' vehicles clearing out. The attackers drove calmly around the park, no-one paying them any attention. The walkers had vanished.

Richie headed towards Comercial Mexicana with his pistol in his lap. He saw they were not following, screeched to a stop, reached over, and shut the armoured door, then he turned off the stereo. He drove on. He called on his cell phone: Devil, where are you? In Colinas. They just peppered me in front of H.S. 25, they killed Rafa and Grunt. Who was it? No idea, send a few guys over to pick up the bodies and come get me. Where are you? I'll be in the Comercial Mexicana parking lot, next to Banamex; is La Jefa still there? Not that I know.

He parked. He saw his bodyguards' A.K.s on the floor, felt the wetness in his crotch, and was afraid, really afraid. He began to cry.

It's always good to know you aren't as tough a bastard as you think you are.

Twenty-Two

Zelda felt pretty low. Rodo had refused to meet for breakfast, he claimed he had a meeting with his boss. Let his mother believe that one. They had tacked the picture of the *Muro No* guy to the wall and were scrutinising it. The face was not familiar. I don't think he's Mexican. Neither do I, boss. What time does Ortega get in? He's out dealing with gangsta-wraps; what do you suppose he'll do with all those blankets? He's got experience looking at photographs. Back to Meraz, we ought to clip his wings, I don't buy his mister-nice-guy routine either. O.K., let's get him tonight. But I'm going with you. Are you sure? wouldn't it be better for you to fix things up with the tiger first? Don't mix things up, boss, and don't get me mixed up either, my work is my work and it is sacred. He smiled: Good, we'll penetrate his domain; so, what have we got? Zelda looked him in the eyes. Boss, would it be too much to ask you to tell me about it? there's an awful lot of talk going around linking you to Mayra Cabral de Melo; should I take that seriously or are you going to be straight with me? Lefty experienced a familiar discomfort, felt sheepish. She was his partner after all, he thought, she deserved his trust, and so he told her a few things, only what he considered necessary. Then they returned to the first question: what have we got? A body in an empty field, a nightclub manager who was surprised but not that surprised; a body in a living room, 9mm in both cases. You say the night watchman told you he was a tall, solid guy driving a big, dark car headed out of town? Oh, Zelda, get

Terminator to take someone out there to find the tyre marks, tell them to take pictures of all of them. In the second case the neighbours didn't hear or see a thing; I'd like to interrogate Elisa Calderón again with you there, I've got the impression there's something she could tell me, but I didn't know how to ask. We could bring in Miroslava and Camila Naranjo, too, she called in sick last night. She did? That's what they told me at the Alexa; what do we have on Escamilla? The usual, I guess, Rivera said he talked to you, did you speak with the Phantom? His story matched Escamilla's, plus he let on that he's Meraz's procurer. Neither of them is tall and heavyset. I told you about Cervantes, who's on the short side, and also about that confrontation with Richie Bernal; oh, and there's Kid Yoreme, did you find anything? Sorry, boss, I forgot, how's it going with the gringo? No-one wants to know anything about him, so we can take it easy, they're more interested in this one, he pointed to the photograph on the wall. Nobody's claimed the first body either, right? Not that I know of, and Ortega is running around like crazy with all the gangsta-wraps. Did he find any prints on Paty Olmedo's pistol that weren't hers? He hasn't said. So, where do we begin? At the beginning, Agent Toledo, because we're really lost. Silence. Boss, Mayra was so beautiful. Lefty looked at the ceiling: Did you see the photographs? Wow, how could I not, that tattoo on her pubis sure caught my eye. *Just to heighten the pleasure.* Look through the business cards, maybe someone has escaped our attention; oh, and get me an appointment with these guys; he handed her the two cards he had on him. Will they send her body to Brazil? Probably, her mother is in São Paulo, every time I think of calling her I can't face it. Doesn't she live in Guadalajara? She spends six months here and six there, maybe they'll bury her in Guadalajara. I think we should be looking for a man. Why? No woman would tear up the picture of the football team. Zelda, there's a Brazilian playing for Dorados, let's bring him in. Have you thought about her clients in Mazatlán? according to Elisa she went there all the time. Suddenly they felt better. You know what we forgot, boss? the tit, they cut off a nipple. Mendieta said nothing. I think it's an important clue. Angelita opened the door: Chief Mendieta, Commander Briseño requests your presence in his office right this minute. Angelita, please, what kind of manners is that? It's obvious you two don't watch soap operas. Of course we do, but we pretend not to. So, that girl on the wall, who is she? Mendieta and Zelda looked at each other, their mouths agape. Angelita, come on in, I'll go see the chief. Sure enough, the fine features in the picture of *Muro No* grew softer and the dim light gave her the definite aura of a young woman.

In the chief's office, Othoniel Ramírez was chatting animatedly with Briseño, who introduced Lefty and asked rather pompously, What do we have on the Alexa case? The detective, wondering what was up, spun out the story again. O.K., Briseño said, so everything is still fairly murky, a bit imprecise, let's see how things develop over the next few days. Speaking to Ramírez: Take good care of your table dancers, attorney, I've been told not all of them deserve to die. The profession has its risks, commander, what can you do? but I promise we will not give you any more trouble, we shall follow your recommendations and hand Yolanda's body over to her family; we'll give the Brazilian a Christian burial and that should wrap everything up; and allow me to insist, come over one night, you won't regret it, we always have surprises for our friends. Mendieta understood they had reached an agreement. Oh, and do have a little patience, I'll get my hands on what you need to prepare that dish, it is spectacular, but like I say, it has to be an olive ridley, other turtles just don't do it justice. Right, I'll follow your recipe to the letter. Give me two days to get you a good-sized one; the habanero chillies we can get in any supermarket. He stood up. Lefty gave his commander a penetrating look, which the man ignored.

Ramírez walked out smelling of cheap cologne.

I am not interested in your point of view, Briseño said before the detective could open his mouth; and I am going to insist, if you don't want the invitation from the F.B.I. for that course in Los Angeles, you should accept the one from the Spanish Police, they say Madrid is lovely this month. I would never go to a city that's lovely for a month. That's a manner of speaking, it must be lovely all the time, Madrid is famous for its low crime rate and its food; if I didn't have so much work I'd go myself just for the tapas and Iberian ham. Here they kill with bullets, over there with bombs, don't you remember March 11th? That terrorism business is no picnic. Between narcos and terrorists, which do you prefer? Neither. Mendieta spread the fingers of both hands. I met Mayra Cabral de Melo in Mazatlán and she was a nice woman, a dreamer, she was gorgeous; yesterday I spoke with Miroslava, a friend of hers and of Yolanda Estrada's. They were a couple of table dancers, Lefty, their death won't affect anyone, there's no reason to invest time and resources in that, it was one of the risks of their line of work; we have too much on our plate with all the gangsta-wraps and the narco-juniors, don't you realise we have to shut them down? how are we going to get that done? now the president has declared war on the narcos, they'll be sending instructions before long; Ramírez promised to take care of it, you heard him. What about my pea soup? Oh, so that's it. It's simple, chief, if they got killed it's because they did affect someone or their death stood to benefit somebody; they didn't die of natural causes. Even so, forget about it. Briseño fixed his gaze on the papers on his desk and Lefty stood up. Before you cook a dish with an endangered species, allow me to carry on with the investigation. Lefty, who do you think you are? you think you can do whatever the fuck you like? not with me in charge. Well, give me a few days without hearing your name on "Eyes on the Night" and maybe I'll get amnesia. But why? They were human beings, a couple of defenceless women. So what? since when are we sisters of charity? That's why we didn't investigate the case of Anita Roy either, right? Briseño opened his mouth, but not a word came out. You see? everyone has priorities, and I believe priorities ought to be respected.

He invited Zelda to the Miró. On their way out, Robles lent him a Walther P99 he had found for him. Does it work? No idea, but they tell me it's killed about a hundred. Lefty took out the magazine, opened it, looked down the bore of the barrel, pulled the trigger, put the magazine back in place, saw it was a perfect fit in his hand, put on the safety, and dropped it into his pocket. If I don't return it within a week, it'll be because I was worth shit.

As always, the place was packed with ladies planning parties or enjoying life in the fast lane. Chanel, Blue Code, Burberry, Blah-blah. Lefty ordered coffee; Zelda, *machaca* with eggs, cappuccino, and orange juice. On the way he had brought her up to date. You see, a table dancer isn't worth as much as a priest. Neither is a taxi-driver worth as much as a mathematician, boss, but when they're dead aren't they equal? all four of them are cold meat, yesterday's lunch, useless to society. So? Silence. You knew them when they were alive. Only Mayra, who was just a girl trying to find happiness. I remember you weren't exactly miserable when you came back from Mazatlán. What kind of comment is that, Agent Toledo? What's wrong with it? They fell silent. Briseño can't stop us, and there's something else, do you remember the girl with no tits? We aren't supposed to talk about her. Her name was Anita Roy, she was a friend of Mayra's, and they wouldn't let Mayra in to her wake. Zelda thought for a moment. You think she's part of the puzzle? When we interrogate their relatives we should test it out and we can't ignore the fact that both were mutilated.

On the way back to Headquarters, hemmed in by intense traffic, Mendieta changed the C.D.: "Conga" by Miami Sound Machine. Relaxing music, Zelda, so you'll feel like dancing. Boss, would you let me off the hook for tonight? my Rodo called and I'm going to have supper with him; we could meet up at the Alexa after that. He's a good man. If I get married I'm going to continue working. I don't see why not. Also when I'm pregnant. Have you seen *Fargo*? No. Rent it, you're going to like it. If Rodo comes to you, don't let him talk you into anything, my job is to work under your command. That's what we'll do, don't worry. He's got it into his head I should get a desk job. Don't let that even cross your mind, who does he think he is? you're not even married and he wants to give you orders. That's what I told him.

Cavalry charge. He looked at the incoming number: "private". And he let it ring.

He reflected: You were so sweet I can't believe you died like that, so mysteriously, and at the hands of a guy who left nothing to chance; well, he must have left something besides his tyre marks, we just haven't found it yet. I've got to speak with Dayana.

Zelda, before you meet Rodo, find a girl named Dayana, who made some statement to the press a few days ago about women's rights, she's going with Meraz. He dialled Angelita, who gave him the numbers for Paty Olmedo's landline and cell from the minimal file on her, which had not yet been thrown out.

He made a date with Paty for seven that evening at the Café Marimba.

After dropping Zelda at Headquarters, he headed home. The house was empty. He lay down and fell asleep. Thirty-two minutes later he woke up, showered, made a Nescafé, put on Brazilian music: "Onde anda você" by Vinicius de Moraes and Toquinho. And he sat quietly, as voices filtered in from the street.

How do you know I knew her? I dreamt it. Paty Olmedo was wearing a nearly see-through peach-coloured blouse and beige Bermudas. She was drinking beer and she had the kind of tan that will always be in style. Mendieta relaxed. You went to the wake and they didn't let you see the señora's face? No, they let me, it was a normal wake, I even went into the family room to see my friend, he's the señora's son; we went out for coffee. Did he tell you they mutilated her? Wait, how do you know that, did you dream that too? Don't be alarmed, it's a police thing. Hey, it's better than television, how awful. Could you introduce me to your friend? He's in Canada, he only came back for the wake, you know his parents are divorced? Since when? Since the señor found out his wife was cheating on

156

him. When was that? Two years ago maybe; my friend Marcos went to Toronto and they each went their own way; I heard the señora was a real party girl, she had lots of boyfriends, and they mutilated her for revenge; but she took good care of herself, she'd go to the gym and she studied dance. How old was she? Forty-three, but she looked like she was twenty. I bet she was good at folk dancing. I don't think so, she did jazz and I heard she was studying modern too, at a proper dance school, I don't know for sure.

She told him where the ex-husband lived.

Twenty-Three

How are you? One day at a time, what about you? Well, I'm in a bind, I've got you-know-who here, I told him we were expecting you to drop by and he's pleased. Don't bullshit me, fucking ass-co, I don't figure in his world. Listen, they nearly took him out last night. What? That's right, four guys in T-shirts that said *Muro No* welcomed him with a hail of bullets; but we sent them all packing. Who's we? There were about thirty agents spread across the property doing nothing, plus the escort helicopter; but the old guy, not even a scratch and hot to go hunting later on, so if you would like to make an appearance, it would be a pleasure. I'd rather not put you to the trouble. Are you hung over? What sort of vulgarity is that, Carrasco? dog-tired is what I am, which is not the same thing. The years take a toll, don't they, and even though you don't want to, you end up doing more stupid things than you can handle. That's what I tell my friends, including you; I called you earlier, are you returning my call? That's right, I couldn't before because I've been with my guest gunning down ducks; tell me, what's up? What's up is I can't wait any longer, the investor has plans for his money and he needs that million dollars. I've got no liquidity, Gandhi, not now; I invested it all in the hunting camp; it's a question of time, with Mister B. here the season is just starting. That's not my problem, Adán; when I lent it to you, two months and three days ago, I explained very clearly that the capital could be needed at any moment, and that moment is now; there's no way around it, we have five days to return it. Is that your last word? It isn't mine, are you nuts? but it is the last. O.K., Gandhi, see you later.

A few kingpins and minor drug lords kept their money with Gandhi Olmedo. He was honest, he never asked questions, and he was always happy with the cut they gave him. They let him make small investments and whenever they needed a vehicle they bought it from him.

After the meal with McGiver, Olmedo decided to get his life in order and as a man of action he set right to it. First off was to recover a series of loans that were out there dangling, and topping the list was the one to Adán Carrasco. No-one was asking for it, but that was a trick that never failed. Carrasco would find a way and in five days that money would be back with its owner; the modest amount of interest could wait.

He was in his living room with the lights on, listening to movie music, at that moment an instrumental version of "Everybody's Talkin'" from *Midnight Cowboy*. He contemplated the smashed guitars, paused on Jeff Beck's, at one end of the row, and recalled how the amplifier had malfunctioned and Beck hit it with his guitar, then he used the guitar to punish the floor until the instrument was good and ruined, and then he threw the pieces out to the audience. No doubt the scene was Antonioni's invention, but I loved it when I saw the movie; whatever happened to those Englishmen? Pieces of shit, they didn't even call. Then he felt his face go hard: Paty in his memory. Unbelievable, wanting to kill me, the bitch.

At that moment, McGiver was reaching an agreement with Dioni de la Vega on a tonne of pure cocaine sitting in Huatulco, Oaxaca. While she was driving him back to his hotel, Imelda, decked out in a sexy skirt, told him she owned a few bars and was about to close on the purchase of a halfway nice strip club her boss frequented. Would you have a drink with me, Imelda? You know, I don't think I could hold my tongue for that long. They smiled. Truly, you are very nice. I understand, but not tonight, another time. They said goodbye with smiles and one of those looks.

Twenty-Four

Heading back to the city at 205 kilometres an hour, Yoreme noticed a bus ahead of him and turned on the flashing lights and the siren. The bus pulled over, the boxer drove into a cornfield, jumped out of the patrol car, and ran towards it screaming: Open up. The door folded back on its squeaky hinges and he climbed aboard. Let's go, floor it, my man, the devil's on my tail, he said not pausing to wipe his tears; take me away from this awful place as fast as you can. The driver, thin with a moustache, wearing a vest and a bow tie, accelerated. What gives? if you aren't a policeman why were you in that patrol car? Well, I stole it, you see I had a little palm-leaf house and I let in the vixen. One of the passengers alerted the rest. Did you hear? that man stole a police car, there's a real bandit on board. Yoreme turned to face the dozen people watching him with ashen faces and wide eyes. Hi, good evening, I hope I'm not bothering you, I just want a lift to Culiacán. Culiacán? where's that? the nearest one asked. It's close, a little way up the road, we'll go by this cornfield, then a field of safflower, one of tomatoes, a dozen cheap motels, and we're there.

Yoreme realised that besides weeping he was sweating and a feeling like fear spread through him. He couldn't see his feet. Where the floor should have been there was a warm cloud that came up to his knees. Though he saw people moving their mouths, he heard only distant murmurs. He turned back to the driver, but the bus was driving itself. Where's the driver? has anyone seen the driver? The highway had disappeared too, the bus was off to the side and it was nothing but stinking scrap. He got off, found himself on a dirt path amid brambles. The day was dawning.

Cry? Trembling stifled his sobs. It began to rain.

The Federal Police put out an all-points bulletin and expected to catch him in a few hours. At that moment both the good and the bad were on his trail. The officers, suspecting he might be hiding in a farmer's field, asked for help from the cannabis growers. Later, the one who would help the most was the waiter who had served him on several occasions but had no idea where he lived or worked. Yeah, the dude would turn up, drink, and admire Roxana, he'd sigh and smile at her, but he never bought a private booth, what's more, I don't think he ever spoke to her; he'd look at her like she was the Virgin Mary, well, you never learn much about the customers. Escamilla shook his head. He reminded Mendieta that he had told him as much.

Yoreme ran a couple of kilometres through the countryside. On his left and right he heard applause, accusations, threats, advice, and to each he reacted in turn. He smiled, bowed, and raised his arms in triumph, his face turned to stone and his eyes gave off sparks, or he grew calm, his gaze peaceful. For periods he shadow-boxed as he trotted along, launching hooks to the liver and jabs to the body. He was wearing jeans and a dirty blue T-shirt soaked by the rain.

An hour later he hitched a ride with a milkman making a delivery to the city. Yoreme, riding in the back, saw the full bottles and realised how thirsty he was. He opened a twenty-litre jug and tipped it up. The driver saw him and pulled over. Hey, buddy, what's up? why are you drinking my milk? Uh, I had a little palm-leaf house, he said smiling. Don't do this to me, buddy, I need to deliver a full load. I let in the vixen and once she was inside. You know what? get out, I can't take you, you might drink all four hundred litres. The weepy little rabbit left too. I don't understand your babbling, buddy, and neither am I interested; either you get out or I drag you out. Don't do that, I'll pay for the milk, but don't leave me here. I'm glad you want to pay, but I can't let you drink it, I've promised to deliver the whole thing, come rain or thunder and lightning, it's what feeds me and my family. Look, I only drank two litres, I'll pay for the twenty, and before you make the delivery we'll top it up with water so you won't lose. The driver relaxed, I can see you used to be a milkman; come up front with me and tell me that story about the rabbit.

At 8.30 in the morning the milkman dropped Yoreme off at the church in Las Quintas. He paused before the statue of Padre Cuco and prayed that everything would turn out alright; he had no idea how it happened, but he was in a mess of trouble. Padre Cuco, I knew you, do you remember when you chased me out of the church because I was stealing from the collection plate? I'll forgive you if you make everything work out as it should; I know it isn't easy, but that's why you're here, did you think being a saint was going to be a piece of cake? no way, you have to lend a hand, you've got to help people who don't even have a place to drop dead; but nobody died here, come on, why are you giving me that idea? where are you trying to take me? I let in the vixen and the weepy little rabbit left too.

Little by little he remembered the events of the previous night. I went to see Roxana and I found out somebody got there first, like they say. I couldn't keep it together; I broke down, I lost it, then I went off with that wrestler, what was his name? Caveman Galindo, in the car I stole later on. Then the cops chased me. Then I found the milkman who brought me here. Fucking milkman, he smelled sweet. The police took away the car, so I didn't commit a crime; why did I run? Because I'm a jerk; let me calm down by shadow-boxing all the way home. I've fulfilled my duty to God and to society. I've gone to mass on Sunday and now I'm talking to you; you told me to look for a job and I found one, you asked me to get off drugs and I'm working on that, but it's hard, really hard, worse than facing Julio César Chávez.

On the Juárez Bridge he ran past Ortega, who was talking on the cell with Mendieta, but Ortega had no idea who he was. Mendieta was describing him as sullen, agile, quarrelsome. Ortega saw a guy throwing punches to the jaw and figured he was a boxer in training. He even returned his hello. I'll call you back in a little while, the detective said, once he realised he could not make an accurate description of his enemy. Fucking Yoreme.

The boxer continued to jog, peaceably enough, towards the Science Centre on the paved strip that runs alongside Carlos Murillo Depraect Botanical Gardens. I had a little palm-leaf house. What did Roxana die of? If somebody killed her I'll take him out, could it be the guy in the mansion with the yellow door?

He arrived home to an abandoned house in Villa Universidad where he made sure not to attract attention; he never played music or bothered the neighbours. He was a shadow. That way he managed to escape notice and anyone who spotted him thought he was the night watchman. With the help of a locksmith, he'd made a key for the service entrance and could come and go as the only inhabitant of the building, whose legitimate owners had packed up and taken off with the police on their heels.

Once inside, he lay on his cot and slept. He dreamt he was king and that his top minister had five hundred cakes brought in for him alone. When he woke up, he knew very well what had happened. Caveman must be looking for him like a rabid dog and, you know, a match between a wrestler and a boxer might be unusual, but it has potential. If they were going to fight, and no doubt they were, they should make the most of it, they could find a promoter and suggest a match. That might fill Revolution Arena or maybe even the stadium where Dorados plays. Who knows if Caveman would want to, I did just knock him out, so he might be afraid; besides I stole his car and his money and I threw his cell phone into the corn-field, maybe he'll be more angry than interested. Fucking Caveman, what a hard jaw you've got. The federal cops. They don't forgive. I tricked them but good. For sure, once I've knocked Caveman out, they'll turn up looking for trouble: You're under arrest, Yoreme, you may be champion of the world, but we're going to fuck you up. Every badge wants revenge, I haven't forgotten what happened when I knocked out Baldy Sopipas, that fucking uniform, every time I ran into him after that he practically had a heart attack, and I'd be like silk. I had a little palm-leaf house and I let in the vixen. So what if I took the patrol car, nothing happened to it, and who were those fucking weirdos who gave me a lift? The dudes had their old ladies, were they ever past their prime, they looked to be a hundred at least, and the driver, what a nut, he ran off and left us hanging like fools. But was it me who was crying? Why did I wake up in that wrecked bus? Why should I have to put up with so many fucking mysteries? and that milkman, what a good guy, he brought me to Las Quintas. The ones I've got to watch out for are the federal cops; Caveman, who cares? if he shows up I'll knock him flat a second time and that'll be that. You want more? you like hearing birds chirping? O.K., here you go. But not those assholes, no, they're heavies and they'll have their irons out from the get-go. The good thing is they're far away, as far away as she must be, the queen of all queens.

He let a few tears slide down his cheeks, blew his nose, pulled a litre of beer out of the little fridge that occupied a corner, and drank half of it. I should have been a milkman, those guys know how to live.

Twenty-Five

If you want to be one of my men, Leo McGiver, I'm going to lay down two conditions, a big one and a little one. Whatever you say, Señor de la Vega, good idea to settle everything at this meeting. They were drinking whisky with water in an empty bar. The big one: the day that I or my people find out, suspect, or are told that you've been seen with anybody else, you've run the red light, buddy, in other words you're dead meat; Dioni de la Vega's people are Dioni de la Vega's people, and don't you ever forget it; I can see you look pretty tough and, well, the Valdés family is right there and you've had dealings with them, which by the way you're going to drop this very minute. I owe them a shipment of weapons. You're forgetting already: Dioni de la Vega's people are Dioni de la Vega's people and nobody else's; look, you might die out there and there's no fixing that, nobody bargains with the Bony One and if she carries you off what can we do? There's the money, I'll have to return it. You've got two options: you can take it as a loss or you can promise to pay them later, in small monthly instalments, which is what I recommend. He smiled. McGiver looked at the table spotted with drops and he felt happy, too; they were the only ones drinking alcohol; a few metres away three bodyguards were having Cokes with lots of ice. The bartender was filling a refrigerator with beer. Music down low. Hey, de la Vega shouted, put on something better, something that gets me. The man changed the C.D. Let's see how you like this one, Señorita Imelda just brought it in. He turned it up a bit: Los Broncos de Reynosa playing "Ausencia Eterna". The smuggler tossed back his drink, the song made him sentimental. Now the little one, fucking McGiver, why did you kill Sergio? he was a promising kid, you should have understood that. Forgive me, Señor de la Vega. Just looking at him you could see the potential that boy had; Imelda told me the story, you stepped over the line, fucking McGiver, you really did, shooting a dude like that is hard to forgive. Absolve me this time, if you would, he looked so hot on the trigger I thought I was a goner. Don't let it happen again, open your fucking eyes and see what you've got in front of you, alright? Whatever you say. Find his parents, they live in Guasave, give them the body and some cash so they can give him a Christian burial. The police have the body. That's your problem, O.K.? Don't worry, I'll do it. But get on it right away, it's the least you can do. They drained their glasses. Another thing, a few minutes ago they made the transfer into your accounts, so you can get your people moving; two of today's gangsta-wraps were mine, understand? that's how bad things are, we have to defend ourselves. They agreed to meet later on.

McGiver walked towards the door. He stopped short to keep from knocking into Richie Bernal, who came barging in, rifle across his chest and consternation in his face. His four gunmen sat down with the others. Eh, Dioni, what's up, bro, how's the fuse? Burning on target, my man Richie, what a drag, I heard you were really hurting, what's the story? Nothing, they killed my babe, but I'm getting over it. Good for you, romances that kill aren't real romances, you sly bastard. It's true I went a little crazy, but that's all over, bro; sometimes you lose and sometimes you just stop winning. That's the way I like it, don't give in. Listen, could you do me a favour? What the fuck else are friends for? There's a badge, a guy named Mendieta, they call him Lefty. Hmm, can't place him. The dude pulled one on me and I can't take him out; La Jefa, she's protecting him. I understand, you can count on me; sit down, we haven't seen each other for ages. For at least eighty years. Anything new? Everything's fine, well, this morning they ambushed me. You bastard, was it that badge? no wonder you want to take him down. Whoever it was is not going to get away with it. And you say La Jefa is protecting him? McGiver stepped outside. It was a pickup with three guys shooting like crazy, they killed two of my men. But you escaped, fucking Richie, you are one tough bastard, let's drink to that. Cheers.

Twenty-Six

In the afternoon, the manager of the Alexa met with Zelda in the interrogation room. They waited a while for Attorney Ramírez, but he did not show and his cell phone went to voicemail. Is table dancing a good business, Señor Carvajal? More or less, we survive because people would rather indulge themselves than eat well or get an education, but with all due respect I would not like us to go any further without Attorney Ramírez. We've got two cadavers and a witness who says you let firearms into the club; from where I sit those are powerful reasons why it matters fuck-all if Attorney Ramírez is here or not. The case is closed, señorita, Ramírez spoke with your commander. Don't give me that shit, Carvajal, we'll let you know when it's closed, and then only if we feel like it. Well, I don't plan to say another word without Ramírez, who may well be out of town; I have the right. Do you really? you don't say. She stood up, opened the door: Camel, go get Gori. You can't beat me like your friend did the other day. Of course not, Hortigosa has a different approach; besides, you worked in the D.A.'s office during the last government, so you know we are a proper police force, respectful of citizens' rights even when they hide evidence and would rather cut a deal than help the cause of justice. They fell silent. Gori came in dressed in black, a cattle prod in his hand. He went straight to the manager, held him down, and zapped him in the crotch. The reaction was immediate. Alright, alright, ask whatever you like. Gori, I'm so sorry, with people like this your specialty is going to be an

170

endangered species. Don't put the hex on me, Zelda darling, what with all I've had to learn. He went out smiling. He is very convincing, said the manager, drenched in sweat. You have no idea how convincing he can be; how come the Alexa is owned by people in politics? During the last government, officials invested in two things: gas stations and nightclubs, this one is owned by a group represented by Othoniel Ramírez and, like I said last time, it's made up of Bernardo Almada, Luis Ángel Meraz, and Rodrigo Cabrera, who needs no introduction. I know, the former district attorney. You must also know he was the one who cut the crime rate in half. And you're not going to forget it, even though that was nothing but pap for the press releases; according to reports, you were in charge of purchasing for his office and José Rivera was his bodyguard; what made Meraz think of sending Mayra Cabral de Melo to Mazatlán? Carvajal, still sweating heavily, looked up at the ceiling. The invitation came from a friend of his, Joaquín Lizárraga, the mayor; Roxana was very discreet, the only thing she said afterwards is they paid her well and she wanted to keep going. How often would Yolanda Estrada go along? Never, and to be frank I don't understand why she was murdered, she was a normal girl, she didn't fight with anybody, and she was about to go back home. How often do the partners ask for girls? He fell silent again. That question I already answered. Tell me again. You are going to ruin me, señorita. Which one was the horniest? Attorney Meraz, three or four a week. What makes you think they were for him and not somebody else? Well, he takes great pleasure in women, if he shared them I really couldn't say. Yolanda Estrada must have been one of them. He never asked for her, Roxana was his favourite and Camila too, who dances like

Doris Day, and by the way she had a nervous breakdown and still isn't back to work. The others? In my fourteen months on the job, Cabrera six or seven times and Almada not at all, he lives on the other side, in California. What about you? Me, I get along with the girls, that's all. What about Miroslava? Well, a couple of times, no more. Never Mayra or Yolanda? No, it's not a good idea to wear out the goods. Why does your wife go to the Alexa so often? Carvajal took a while to respond, sitting in his sweat. She's jealous. Zelda looked him in the eyes. We think Roxana had other clients. Look, I'm not trying to impede your investigation, but I know nothing about those clients, only the ones I already named; if they fire me, tell your boss to give me a job here. You think this is a strip club? Not in the least, señorita. I'm guessing the one who takes the girls out the most is Othoniel Ramírez. Standing up, he went over to Zelda and whispered: That's a fact and most of the time I don't even find out. Is Camila really sick? Well, I don't think she'll be able to work for a few days. O.K., now scram, and tell Ramírez we want to ask him a couple of things.

In the office Angelita gave her a fax from the Boxing Commission showing Kid Yoreme's record. He knocked out Julio César, can you believe it? Chief Mendieta, too. What? Why would I lie? Listen, our boss is something else. That's for sure: something else. The photo of *Muro No* was still on the wall. Angelita, I'm leaving; if the boss comes in tell him I've gone to the scene of the crime. Zelda, you look really bushed, haven't you been sleeping? Maybe not, well, see you tomorrow.

*

In Esteban Aguirrebere's office, while the owner of San Esteban Farms handed out crates of vegetables to the girls, the detective listened. She was quite the woman, did you ever meet her? incredible, drove you out of your mind, you wanted to eat her alive; women from Sinaloa are really sexy, everybody knows that, but this one made every floor tile tremble; in truth I never did it with her, what a pity she died; it was obvious I wasn't going to get anywhere so I gave up, she liked the really big fish. On Sunday night he and his family had slept at the Hotel Meliá in Cabo San Lucas, his secretary brought in the receipt and it was genuine. What a pity, detective, truly. Cavalry charge. Mendieta saw the number and cut it off without answering, he stood up. Thank you, Señor Aguirrebere. Take these tomatoes, they're absolutely top quality. He handed him a box about the same dimensions as the outline on the carpet in Mayra's apartment. Hmm, is it the same size? we'll see. Now that the vegetable harvest in Florida has collapsed we're about to supply the White House itself. I'll make some *salsa mexicana*. However you eat them, you are going to love them, and don't forget that fried they're incredibly effective against prostate cancer.

Nothing there. Same story with the guy on the other business card, Canela, who got nervous and asked Lefty not to tell his wife, with whom he had spent the whole weekend at home. He was getting into the Jetta when his cell rang again, the same number. Mendieta. This is Rodo, detective. Hey, Rodo, what's up, what can I do for you? Well, I'm sorry to bother you, I don't know if you know, but Zelda and I had a fight. Really? you're such a colossal couple. It's something silly, she's mad because I haven't given her an engagement ring. Are you going to get married? Next year, but, well, that seems really far off, I'm focussed on saving up for a house. Congratulations, Rodo, she is a fine woman. But she's mad at me, last night I was with her until late and she wouldn't stop asking for that damn ring, the night before I took her a serenade with mariachis and she wouldn't even come outside, yesterday she asked me out to breakfast complaining that I never asked her and she raised a stink again; you can see I just don't know what to do. My man Rodo, to love is to offer dreams, show up at Headquarters with flowers and, give it up, get her the ring, there's no way around it; and hey, let's lay a little trap, we're on a case that has a connection in Mazatlán, I'm sending her there on Friday, why don't you ask for time off; if there's something to fix up, what better place than right there, facing the Pacific, I bet she won't be able to resist. Really, Lefty? Fuck whoever turns tail. Great.

In the Jetta he listened to Quiroz's update: "And the violence continues. Today two huge gunfights, one in Tierra Blanca on Universitarios Avenue, the other on Obregón near La Lomita. The body count: three in the first, two in the second, plus the four gangsta-wraps found by Commander Pineda in a canal on the outskirts of Costa Rica. Tonight, hear all the details on 'Eyes on the Night', hosted by Raúl Mercado."

He walked into El Quijote in search of himself. Hard to believe though it is, people who hang out in bars sometimes don't manage to keep their anxieties hidden. In his favourite corner he spotted Zelda talking with Curlygirl, who looked concerned. Lefty paused. A moment later the waiter saw him, waved him over, then headed for the bar. Zelda had not touched her food, but on the table sat seven half-litres of Pacífico, all empty. Well now, what are we celebrating, Agent Toledo? The end of the world, boss, the end of everything. Did we get a bulletin about it? Sent by me and received by me, she made a face. That *barbacoa* looks fabulous, why haven't you tasted it? To make Curlygirl mad, Zelda said in a stage whisper, he says there's none better. The waiter arrived with a beer for Lefty. Curlygirl, bring me an order of *barbacoa*, let's see if it really is the best in the world. Zelda didn't like it. You didn't like it, Agent Toledo? Zelda took a bite. It's delicious, Curlygirl, really, it's the best I've ever tasted. You see? O.K., bring an order for me and another beer; Lefty drained the bottle he had in one long guzzle. The place was packed with happy customers.

Agent Toledo, pull yourself together and request an advance because you're going to Mazatlán on Friday, I want you to interrogate Joaquín Lizárraga since everybody here is clean as a whistle. Did Meraz buy you off? No, but Briseño insists it was suicide, and now that he knows the former district attorney is a partner he'll never want us to dig any deeper; so drink up and go get some rest. What about one for the road? Let me have it for you. Cavalry charge. Boss, have you seen Zelda? Let me put her on. Angelita, what's up? Rodo came in with a bouquet of roses. If he's still there tell him to shove it up where the sun never shines. Oh, Zelda, he's already gone, he looked so sad. No no no no, he's not sad or any fucking thing else, he's a bastard through and through, a bullshitter just like every other man. They're beautiful and they smell wonderful. If they don't fit up there tell him to take them to his bitch of a mother. Oh, Zelda! you two make such a lovely couple, he said he keeps calling you, but your cell goes to voicemail. Tell him I lost the telephone, tell him not to fuck with me and I hope he rots. Zelda, this is awful, you sound horrible. I'll see you tomorrow, Angelita, and don't let any bastard like him pull the wool over your eyes, all men are revolting. She handed the cell phone back to Mendieta and started sobbing. Curlygirl brought her napkins to dry her eyes. Boss, forgive me, I love that asshole more than my own life. Of course, sweetie, the waiter said.

But you guys are men, men always do crazy shit, and we girls have to put up with it.

That night Lefty could not sleep. Who killed Anita Roy? Did Mayra know who the murderer was? In the silence not even the dog barked; he kept tossing and turning. Maybe the one who knew was Yolanda. By two a.m. he had had enough. I hope Mick Jagger is worse off than me, fucking loco, how did he manage to go so far? on his songs alone? That's why they killed her; if we knew what weapon they used on Anita, we could pin it down. He picked up the Ribeiro book: "Clearly, what counts, what really counts, is who the cock belongs to. A small cock doesn't disgust women, though they would still prefer it a bit longer; it's more satisfying that way for one reason or another." He slammed the book shut and remembered: *It's part of your body, you should feel proud. When it's at its maximum it conveys how vigorous you are and when I saw you peeing I knew you were a lefty, isn't that marvellous?* I'm going to get you, you pervert, there's no escape; if he still has the nipple, what will we do with it? Fucking Yoreme, let's see what your parents can tell me.

Twenty-Seven

The Valdés mansion was imposing: the high walls, the purple-and-yellow tiled cupolas softly lit, the pair of rubber trees, the garden filled with flowers.

It was 4.00 in the morning and no-one was moving.

The guards kept their vigil without a glance at their wristwatches. They knew any slip-up could cost them their lives long before the threat reached Marcelo Valdés, who was resting in the quiet of one of the bedrooms. They could not say which because none of them had ever crossed the threshold. Was he sleeping under an oxygen tent? That had been the rumour for years, but no matter how often it was said no-one could ever confirm it.

At 4.12 a heart-wrenching cry pierced the thick walls.

The godfather, Marcelo Valdés, who for supper had enjoyed a tasty grilled steak with guacamole, *salsa mexicana*, spring onions, and half a litre of beer, had died peacefully in his sleep.

In Mariana Kelly's apartment on Valadés Parkway, Samantha's cell phone rang. Thirty seconds later the lights came on. Brief sobs. Sounds of movement. Unease. Luigi, Mariana's dog, observed the women and did not wag his tail; he understood that something serious had occurred.

Twenty-five minutes later, two black pickups parked outside the apartment building started their engines. From the parking lot came the Cadillac Escalade E.X.T. with Guacho at the wheel and the two women in the back seat. Dark glasses, formal dress, light make-up. Only the morning before, Samantha's son had flown back to Vancouver, where he had been studying English since the previous summer.

One pickup in front of the Cadillac, the other behind.

Samantha, Marcelo's heir apparent, went over how she planned to handle the situation. She would hold an austere wake, no media and no fuss. In the afternoon they would take him to the family crypt, a live band would play just as he had suggested years ago when he thought he would never die, although lately he had not mentioned it. That over and back home, they would hold a meeting to take advantage of the presence of all the kingpins. The division of territory would be maintained as agreed, at least while they tested the waters. This business of the war might modify the borders of each gang's turf and it made sense to seize the moment. There was an American gang that would have to disappear, of that she was certain, the one that had killed her husband.

It's not that I miss the imbecile, it's the principle of authority. Her companion nodded. Samantha's sense of hierarchy frightened her a bit, but she was not about to say so.

Samantha found her mother in pieces. They hugged, wept. Mariana wrapped her arms around them both. What are we to do now, my daughter? the pillar of our house has fallen.

In the living room she met with Max Garcés, commander of the guards, and with Eloy Quintana, the most powerful drug lord in Sonora, well-respected because he kept a low profile and focussed on moving the merchandise. Garcés would have been about forty years old and Quintana seventy. Samantha confided her plans, asked Eloy to let everyone know, and ordered Garcés to take care of security so everything could go ahead without surprises.

The people from the funeral home carried the cadaver out. Minerva handed her daughter a box containing the jewellery he would wear.

Four black pickups joined the cortège to the funeral home.

The embalmers received the body, puffing on cigarettes and whispering among themselves. None of that in front of him, you sons of bitches, Samantha confronted them, do you know who he is? They straightened up and shook their heads. You have in your hands Marcelo Valdés, idiots, and you're going to treat him like what he is: a great man; only God would you treat better. She produced a fistful of dollars and put it in their hands. Then she showed them the box. His jewels, too bad for you if any of these goes missing; she opened it. Take a look. In glittering splendour lay an emerald rosary and rings and bracelets heavy with precious stones. The men stubbed out their cigarettes. Please forgive us, señorita, you have no need to worry, Don Marcelo is the greatest man this land has ever seen and we will do right by him. You'd better, assholes. She left the room. The first one she ran into was a docile Richie Bernal, her eyes drilled him. Get out of my sight, jackass, I have a few things to clear up with you later on. The little narco lowered his head and stepped aside. She stalked on. Max Garcés, who had been brought from Valdés' home village of Badiraguato, was her shadow.

At the first light of dawn, a dark car travelled slowly past the seed warehouse. It did not stop. Neither did its driver notice the longer-than-usual glow from a cigarette at the construction site next door.

Twenty-Eight

It was eight o'clock in the morning when he arrived at the house in Los Álamos, one of the city's most exclusive suburban developments. José Antonio Lagarde, who had been Anita Roy's husband, opened the door. The night before, Mendieta had stopped by the Alexa and spoken with Escamilla, who told him how Yoreme looked at Roxana like she was the Virgin Mary. Lefty asked him to let him know if either Yoreme or Miguel de Cervantes showed their faces and he asked the same of Rivera. The Apache encouraged him to look elsewhere: This city is small, Lefty Mendieta, he must be someplace.

Lagarde was the owner of an export company and he had no record. The man did not even offer him a glass of water, he wanted the meeting over fast. I'm so surprised you're investigating this, detective, I would never have imagined it. Mendieta decided to go right to the nub: If you didn't imagine it, then why did you block the authorities from carrying it out? The man went pale and winced. You must know we always follow up on such cases. I was thinking of my son, I didn't want him to know what they did to his mother, but it's also my right as a citizen, so I don't understand what you're after. The man who mutilated your ex understands it perfectly well; Mayra Cabral de Melo was murdered and mutilated in the same part of her body. He winced again, and this time his lips trembled. And you must know they knew each other. I never approved of that friendship, nor of many others, though by the end Anita had nothing to do with her. Why did you keep Mayra from seeing her at the funeral home? There is no way I would have allowed her in; picture it, the place full of relatives and friends and she shows up dressed for her dancing. Silence. Why do you think they killed your wife? His face flushed, he moved as if to stand, his lips quivering. We were divorced and she got killed because she was out of her mind, she was sleeping with just about anybody; you want it loud and clear? she was a whore. Silence, which Lefty respected. And so was that dancer. Lagarde got to his feet. He was tall and heavyset, Italian shoes. If they got killed, they certainly deserved it; Ana was a lost soul, she was sleeping with my friends, with the husbands of her friends, you have no idea how many marriages she upset. Mendieta remained seated. I have nothing else to say. The murder of Anita Roy was not investigated, do you know what weapon they used? How would I know? they found her in an apartment downtown, with a bullet in her head and her breasts lopped off. Give me the address. I don't know it, it belonged to that Brazilian slut who put the finishing touches on her ruin. Mendieta went still. He did not do jigsaw puzzles, but that was precisely what he had in front of him, and two pieces, maybe three, just fit together perfectly. Lagarde sat back down, a crushed look on his face, his eyes on the floor. Do you collect guns? No, I've never even used one. Same as Meraz and Cervantes, Lefty recalled. What about any people Anita Roy was involved with? He thought a moment. I don't know. I would like a list of those people. How could you ask me that? He left the room and returned thirty seconds later. The guards are coming for you and don't you dare bother me again, I don't want to know anything about that woman, get it? nothing. Lefty stood up. I'll find out in any case and you'd better get something straight yourself: the primary suspect in the murders of Anita Roy and Mayra Cabral de Melo is you. He winced again and his quivering lips picked up speed. Don't make me laugh, how are you going to prove that? With caresses, haven't your many powerful friends told you how the police work? Lefty went out to the Jetta as the guards drove up in a Jeep. Lagarde signalled to them that everything was O.K.

Mendieta turned the ignition and cranked up the stereo. He listened to Lobo's riff near the end of "I'd Love You to Want Me". Before they hit the final chord he switched to the radio. A station with sweet ballads, then one with *corridos*, another with ads, and on the next it was Quiroz going full throttle: "No news yet regarding the murdered women in our fair city, will it turn out like in Juárez, where mysterious criminals sacrifice beautiful young maidens? Let's hope not. Commander Omar Briseño declared yesterday afternoon that he cannot release more information so as not to impede the investigation; on another topic, since el Señor Presidente declared war on the narcos the number of gangsta-wraps has increased. Last night on Niños Héroes Parkway across from Constitution Park there was a shootout that lasted twelve minutes. We have no information on the number of victims. For 'Eyes on the Night', this is Daniel Quiroz reporting." Then a commercial from the Interior Ministry blabbing on about fighting organised crime. He switched it off, waited a few moments, and went back to the C.D. player: "Mi Corazón es un Gitano" by Nicola di Bari. He called Patricia Olmedo, but she did not answer. She must be sleeping, the bitch.

Dayana Ortiz welcomed him in a spacious office. She was a publicist. What I want to ask you about is rather delicate. He had turned up unannounced so she wouldn't be able to communicate with Meraz.

Luis Ángel told me you'd be coming, he said you were tenacious and that if I thought it wise I should exercise my right to remain silent. She smiled. Dressed in white, she was elegant and sexy. We are investigating the death of a girl who had a relationship with Attorney Meraz; we were told that he was seen with her on Sunday night. Impossible, he was with me in Mexico City. How long have you two had a relationship? Well, we met years ago, but last month we became partners in this agency and for two weeks now we've been seeing each other every day. Will you be the first lady? Wish me luck. Eyes shaped like olives. What kind of car does Meraz drive? He has two B.M.W.s and a pickup he adores. Which do you like more? The white B.M.W., it isn't the newest, but it's the most comfortable. Any other reason? I don't like dark cars. I don't like black either. This one isn't black, but it might as well be. Tension in the air. I know Meraz likes pretty behinds, pardon the question, does he have any obsession with breasts? Look, detective, I don't know where you are headed, but don't worry, Luis Ángel is an expert on erogenous zones and he is very instinctive, so he's interested in everything; go ahead and smile. He preferred to get going.

So he owns a dark B.M.W. that's not black; the nipple, why would he cut off the nipple? why one? why would he take her to that place? He must have threatened the girl so she'd only tell me what he wanted. What about Estrada? Who killed Yolanda Estrada?

This time Paty answered. On the heels of his hello he said, Paty, I've been wondering, can I ask a favour? Of course, Señor Mendieta, tell me. Call your friend Marcos and ask him if his father has any guns. Guns? Don José Antonio? gee, I don't think so. I don't either, he's such a decent guy. And very religious, Marcos always complained about having to go to Mass and confession; is he a suspect in something? Why would you think such a thing? no, we're collecting guns for a museum; you know what, Paty? you're right, that's not a good idea, when you call Marcos tell him he has the perfect father, nothing like yours; have you seen the friend who gave you the pistol? No, and I don't think I'd recognise him if I ever saw him again. Well, sorry to bother you. No bother, Señor Mendieta, call whenever you like, or whenever you suspect any of my friends. I'll do that, some days I'm a suspicion machine; do you know if your father ever went to a strip club? My father? I don't think so, he's pretty boring. Maybe he went with Lagarde. Impossible, they've never been friends. Ask Marcos about it, he just might know more than you.

I got to know at least three of Roxana's perfumes. He was mulling it over in the parking lot of the morgue, unable to decide whether to take a look at the young woman's body. What's wrong with me? am I a numbskull or what? why see her? do I want to find the murderer or don't I? was it the same one that killed Anita Roy? That scare I gave Lagarde was useless. What could seeing her possibly clear up? maybe Bigboy Rivera knows something. Zelda's right, only a man would rip up the picture of the Brazilian team, some asshole who used to spend the night at her place rolling in the sea she was, the guy who carried off a forty-by-forty centimetre box that left an imprint on the carpet. Plus he cut off her nipple. He called Headquarters. Angelita, is Zelda around? She hasn't come in yet. What? it's eleven o'clock. She called in earlier, I guess she had a few too many, she told me about the per diems for Mazatlán. Send Terminator and

Camel to my house for a box, Trudis will give it to them.

Did she let Anita Roy use her bed? It's possible, and maybe the owner of the box was a friend of Anita's? suppose it's the same guy? Aguirrebere or Canela, did they know Anita? Paty Olmedo showed me a photograph, she was a real beauty; how right she was to dump Lagarde, what a drip; if she'd been living a normal life before, how come she suddenly caught the fever? Maybe she was always that way; she must have known Yhajaira, of course, who had that birthday party with Bigboy; I've got to talk to him, he must know more than he lets on. What did he let on? nothing. Would Yolanda give me a lead?

Parked beside him was a hearse from San Chelín and two flashy cars. Leo McGiver came out of the morgue followed by a middle-aged couple, peasant farmers with long faces; they were Muerto's parents and the smuggler was keeping his promise. Mendieta was intrigued, saw the funeral home employees bringing out the body, and, fearing something was up, he got out to ask. Hang on, dudes, who have you got there? Without waiting for an answer he raised the sheet and saw a face he remembered; they showed him the death certificate and the authorisation to remove the body. The parents approached. Can we help you, señor? Edgar Mendieta of the State Ministerial Police; are you the parents of Sergio Carrillo? Yes, señor. What did your son do for a living? The couple exchanged glances and turned towards McGiver, who was waiting beside a grey B.M.W. They killed him, the woman said without drama, and he was such a good son. McGiver walked over. Any problem? We'll see, I'm asking about the young man's work. The señor is from the police, the father muttered. Ah, pleased to meet you, I'm Leo McGiver, the young man was an employee. Where? The smuggler realised he would not get off easily. Could I have a few words with you in private, señor . . .? Detective Mendieta. His parents are really hurting and there's no need to worry them. They stepped away. Needless to say, this ticked Lefty off. Why are you interested in the kid, Detective Mendieta? Because I found him dead in a room at the Hotel San Luis. McGiver looked him over and knew he had better get right to the point. He was one of Dioni de la Vega's men, he asked me to take care of the paperwork so the body could be handed over to the parents; it seems nobody's been charged and his family just want to give him a Christian burial. Are you a lawyer? Something like that. Then you must know we always follow up on such cases. McGiver made a face that said some things cannot be fixed. Do you know what the kid was doing in the hotel? No, I was not told and I did not ask. Where do the parents live? In Guasave and they want to bury him there. Did people call him Guasave? Hang on, I'll ask; he went over to the parents and returned. Lefty smelled something fishy, but couldn't put his finger on it. They don't know, but you know how people are. Have you got a card? Of course, are you by any chance from the Col Pop? Lefty saw Leo's smile and did not like it. He took the card carefully. No, are you? Let's just say I had a friend there whose last name was the same as yours. You don't say. And another of my friends knows you. Who's that? Fabián Olmedo. Ah. A call came in from Zelda. You can take him away, Lefty told McGiver, who signalled the funeral home employees and walked to his car. He stank of chloroform. Thank you, detective, he called out, by the way you'd better stay on your toes, dark days are coming.

Boss, I've got Marcelino Freire here at Headquarters. Weren't you on your deathbed? No way, right after I spoke with Angelita,

Rodo turned up with his bouquet and he took me out for seafood: an *aguachile* and a *campechana* and I feel like a new woman. Where did you go? To Puye's, have you been there? Next to Canasta, I think. Precisely; one question: can Rodo come with me to Mazatlán? What's with you, Agent Toledo? you're going there to work, not on vacation. Don't be mean, he's really excited about it; I promise to do everything I'm supposed to; do I have to get in touch with Noriega when I'm there? That'd make sense, and I don't think it's wise to take your boyfriend along, aren't you two fighting? Well, now we're making up and it would be great if we could go together. Zelda, I'm going to allow it this time, but don't let anyone know, it could come back to haunt us; so, what's Freire like? Really nice, do you want me to wait for you? Yes, I'm headed there now, and he thought: what's the point of seeing the body?

He called Noriega. Fucking Lefty, what a miracle! I'm only calling because I hear you're behaving yourself. How's my girlfriend? She's turned into quite the babe, flushed and aroused. Send her over, asshole, that woman ought to be happy, you only live once; there's nothing easy about our work and if we don't find ways to relax we'll all end up on the fucking couch for sure. That's why I'm calling, we've got a case of two murdered table dancers, one of them had clients in Mazatlán; the guy who hired her is the mayor, Joaquín Lizárraga, you must know his office near La Casa del Caracol bookstore. I know the bookstore, the owner is named Laura and she's not bad. Well, the point is to find out who Mayra Cabral de Melo was performing for; Zelda Toledo will be there tomorrow, I figure if you can get the names and interrogate those guys you'll have more time to take her around. I love the way your mind works; listen, this war thing is a bitch, eh? this morning they found seven cadavers on the road to the airport. Yeah, it's as if the ban was lifted.

The football player did not know Mayra was dead, but he knew her story: she was Mexican, her father is a Brazilian who hooked up with a woman from Guadalajara when he came for the '86 World Cup; but the girl grew up in São Paulo, where her mother runs a bar and grill selling Mexican food and beer; how sad. The young man was wearing sports clothes and he looked perfectly ordinary. When did you meet her? Maybe a month and a half ago. Before or after you missed the penalty? Freire gave them a look. Before. Did you go to the Alexa every night? Only when we had something to celebrate, but you can see the team isn't going anywhere. Of course, Lefty jumped in, because you'd see her at her house. That never happened, I always connected with her at the nightclub, through the lady in charge. What would make you tear up a photograph of your country's team? Me? that would never even cross my mind, the players who make the team are saints, it'd be sacrilege. They spoke for eighteen minutes without him showing any trace of guilt; they put the usual constraints on his movements, though they had to allow him a trip to León in Guanajuato for a match.

Before you go, boss, take a look at the file on Kid Yoreme. Mendieta wanted to penetrate Meraz's world, but he was curious about the boxer. We need to interrogate Othoniel Ramírez, the guy is evading us. You're right, Zelda, send a patrol car to pick him up before Briseño forbids it. We have the pictures of the tyre marks, what should we do with the box they brought from your house? Have them take it to Mayra's apartment, there's an outline on the carpet near the window, see if it has the same dimensions.

He opened the folder with Yoreme's file.

Name: José Ángel Camacho Arenas

Birthplace: Culiacán, Sinaloa

Three-round fight in the Revo. We were just kids. I'd already won twenty bouts, each of them in the first round thanks to my specialty, an uppercut to the jaw. Julio had won that many too with those exploding punches he could throw and we were both undefeated. The dude came in close and told it to me straight: Yoreme, I don't think I can beat you, bro, you hit like a mule-kick and I spent last night with a blonde like you wouldn't believe; I didn't sleep a wink, and the fact is I'm so out of it I'm barely here. Then he fell to his knees and keeled over on the canvas as if I'd knocked him out. He got up all woozy and kept talking. You know I want to be world champion, I've got the bloodline and I've got the ambition, tonight I'm in your hands. He kissed the tape on my wrist. Sheesh, I couldn't say a thing; he started sobbing and his manager jumped into the ring. What's going on? I told you this piece of trash ain't worth shit; get yourself to the dressing room. Dude, he was speaking to me now, you are going down, neither you nor Azabache Martínez can hold Julio back, so forget all this and get out of the way. Right. At first I was mad at myself for letting him go, and I cried about it. Then I realised the man was a true champion; even if I did have the blood-line, like he said, I didn't have the ambition; I followed his fights and his statements, I even went to see the Diego Luna movie. I'm in that, only you can't see me.

Once I boxed in Los Mochis, but it didn't go well, and after that I didn't want to travel anywhere. At the Revo I shined and at the Revo I fizzled, like a rocket before it hits the ground.

His parents lived in Colonia Libertad and Lefty went directly there.

An old man with dark leathery skin was drinking coffee in a rocking chair on the porch of a blue house. Good evening, that smells good. It's to help me sleep without nightmares; you aren't from around here, are you? And are you Don Miguel Camacho? At your service; old woman, bring some coffee for the señor; come on up, have a seat. He gestured towards a metal rocking chair. A woman who resembled Don Miguel came out with a mug, smiled shyly, and went back inside. Mendieta took a sip. From the corner of his eye, he observed the man, who likewise was taking in every detail of his movements. I'm surprised you were waiting for me, Lefty said with a smile. The old man's eyes were made of steel: You beget them and they go on to find their own demons, though that's not the case here, sometimes life gives you no choice. Do you know where he is? No, and I told the attorney as much the other day, it's been about three months; old woman! he yelled. The señora came out again. How long has it been since we've seen José Ángel? Three months and seven days. Alright. The woman went back inside. Mothers always keep count; I also told him I didn't know if he was dead or alive, and he said he was alive and kicking; I told him we didn't know he was still living around here, I thought he was up north; anyway, what did he do? not even when he was boxing did they come looking for him so often. Lefty took another sip while he thought it over. This coffee is marvellous. It's a pleasure to offer you some and if you would answer me I would appreciate it, the attorney said he didn't do a thing, so I don't understand why everyone is suddenly so interested. Well, I want to ask him about the fight when he knocked down Julio

César Chávez. What makes you think my son could have knocked down the champion? he was never any good; he was a fighter, it's true, but these local fights don't count for much; I don't understand who made that thing up. Did the attorney tell you why he wanted to see him? He said to give him a job, doing more drywalling at his business, one of those nightclubs where girls dance naked. Was the name of the club Alexa? That I couldn't say, but the attorney's name was Othoniel Ramírez, I remember because a *compadre* of mine has the same name. When did he come? Last week, on Friday. Thank you, Señor Camacho, I'm from the State Ministerial Police, but don't be alarmed, we have nothing against your son, we just want to ask him a couple of things.

You know what, it wouldn't be a bad idea to put him behind bars, that way at least we'll know where he is. Let's hope things don't go that far; I'll leave you my cell phone number; if he turns up, ask him to give me a call. Very good, did you really like the coffee? Yes, I loved it, I hope your son calls me soon so you can make me another cup. Come back whenever you like, it'll be a pleasure to have you. Lefty thought of his own mother. There are people who do not deserve the parents they get.

It was nine o'clock when he landed at Club Sinaloa. The parking lot was overflowing with dark cars. Never before had he crossed that threshold or laid eyes on those brightly lit gardens. He found it thrilling: the range of fragrances from the flowers and the sound of the fountains. Suddenly it struck him: McGiver had smelled funny, chloroform with, maybe, Hugo Boss: exactly how the room with the dead body smelled; does everybody use that cologne? At the door a man in a suit stopped him. He identified himself: Attorney Luis Ángel

Meraz asked us to stop by, he wants us to stay close to him. Hang on. He called on an internal telephone. You can go in, the boys wait for their bosses in the side room; only coffee and soft drinks allowed.

Through a half-open door he saw the edgy bodyguards suffering through the martyrdom of not smoking. He went to the next door and opened it just enough to see a room filled with big celebrities smoking, drinking, eating, talking. At a table near the door, having a grand time, were Meraz, former D.A. Cabrera, Fabián Olmedo, Federal Congressman Vinicio de La Vega, Dioni's brother, and Adán Carrasco, not that Lefty knew who Carrasco was.

He realised he had been so preoccupied he had neglected to bring either his pistol or his handcuffs, and now he felt very out of place: Who was he to march in and make a scene in front of the most powerful men in the state? Nothing but a jerk with a badge, actually I'm not even sure what I am. What gives a loser like me the right to interrupt such a fucking great party where everybody's laughing and having a good time? What have I done with my idiotic life? nothing but suck my thumb and bark at the moon. I'm a failure who doesn't even vote, doesn't ask for a raise, doesn't write letters, doesn't have an email address, hasn't travelled, doesn't believe in God or the Church, let's see, not even in the fucking U.F.O.s that make the moon turn red. A godforsaken fool who couldn't even recognise his only brother at his mother's wake, a bonehead with no girlfriend, who no doubt is losing his God-given ability to screw. Do I have the right to walk in there and tell Meraz: You are going to get fucked, you fucking faggot, you cocksucking murderer; and then bust his balls? Hmm, I don't think so. Next to those people I'm just a zero; I'll never laugh like them or see the world the way they do. A voice brought him back to earth: Detective, what are you doing here? Ah, Señor Aguirrebere, I wanted to thank you for the tomatoes, they were delicious. Would you like to come in? Thank you, I was just leaving; one question though: Did you ever meet Anita Roy? The man bent to his ear and whispered mischievously: She was dynamite. Then he pushed open the door and went in. Meraz's smile vanished when he spied Lefty; he stood and came over. Good evening, attorney. Don't tell me you're looking for me. The day I come for you, you won't see it coming, sir. Don't be a troublemaker, detective, and don't be a dummy either; how could you think I would murder Roxana when we were having such a good time? Why do you assume I'm here for you? Who else would you be after? as far as I know, none of these people was a steady customer of Roxana's. If the murderer is here, then I'm on his trail, but if he isn't then I must have come by mistake. Dayana told me about your meeting, would you like to have a drink with me? Very kind, but I must be going. Don't forget my offer to help, Roxana should be buried where she belongs, even the guys from Mazatlán sent a contribution. That's very generous of them, Lefty said, thinking: This asshole wants to tie me up in a bow, but he's the one who's going to get his finger caught in the ribbon. Nevertheless, still feeling unsure of himself, he turned and headed for the exit.

He dropped by the Alexa to say hello to the Apache. My man Lefty, I don't understand the mirror, there's a fucking revolution going on that looks like it's going to smash it to bits. If it's no good, then let it break; we'll ask them to put in one that gives messages you can understand. Now you're acting like the boss of the club, Lefty Mendieta; and speaking of Sunday, he glanced down at something written on his left arm, I spoke with a girl, Doris, and she told me she saw the guy you named come drop off the queen, but I don't buy it; the pickup was the same colour, white, the same model, but it was different and it didn't have Sinaloa plates. She got out, right? But he didn't, then Roxana got back in and they left. About what time? He had it on his arm. At eleven, more or less. Why didn't you tell me this before? My man Lefty, I get blank spots, I remembered and I wrote it down here. O.K., how many times did that pickup come for her? Let's see . . . all I know is the guy who brought her on Sunday changed his mind. How was Roxana dressed? Very sexy, a little blouse down to here and a miniskirt; Lefty my man, leave me be. The Apache put all of his attention on the one-way mirror, his mouth clamped shut and his eyes squinting: There she is, that fucking bitch, you shitty whore, I can't forget you. Lefty couldn't see any change in the glass and he walked away.

That sounds like what she was wearing when she was killed, so when was it she changed cars? did she change men too? if it wasn't Meraz, who brought her? whose car was it? what does Miguel de Cervantes get around in? Escamilla told him the Spaniard had not returned; Kid Yoreme came around asking for you, but he left after two beers. Strange that he's looking for me, where's Bigboy? He's not in yet, I called his house a while ago and his wife says he's been gone since morning. You know, I have the feeling something's not right with him, where does he get the money for such expensive cologne? The waiter shrugged: Like I told you, I don't hear, I don't see. O.K., be thankful I'm not in Narcotics; do you remember the Spaniard's address? That's easy. He gave him the street and number. It's a white house with little windows in the front. How come you know it? One day I took Roxana there. Who set that up, Elisa or Roxana? Roxana did, not that it matters now, but don't tell Elisa, she can get nasty; it was spur-of-the-moment, a day she didn't want to go with either Meraz or Richie. They came at the same time? Can you believe it? and she wanted to go out with a third guy who wasn't even there; fucking women, they're so strange.

No lights on. He rang the bell. Nothing. He tried the doorknob, same result. Garage empty. He remembered the detail about the gardener and the terrace where the guy watched the football match. He went around to the back and found a private little patio with two comfy leather easy chairs facing a big television screen. On a small table between the chairs sat the remote, an empty bottle of brandy, and an empty glass. He sniffed the glass, but detected no smell. Beyond lay a floodlit motorcycle track, where a four-wheeler with three girls aboard was roaring along; and in the distance Lefty could make out a canal without much water. He tried the glass door: locked. From his wallet he pulled out Cervantes' card, dialled but heard no sound. Maybe I won't be able to find my way in here either, maybe this occupational therapy won't solve anything, maybe I'm just acting out; well, yeah, I'm a fool like my ancestors, people give me beads; but my ancestors were nice people and I'm a jerk, and Parra's nowhere to be found.

He saw the gardener hooking up a hose to a sprinkler, then turning it on. Got a cigarette? No, I gave that up years ago. Listen, I'm looking for the buddy who lives here, have you seen him? Monday night he was here watching football. Have you seen him since? The gardener eyed him closely. Don't worry, I got in yesterday from Madrid and I have a message from his wife. It's just the way things are, you never know; are you Spanish? Mexican. No, I haven't seen him since then. What about before? Are you sure you aren't a badge? Don't insult me, I hate the badges. Me too, years ago they arrested my son and I never saw him again. A good boy, no doubt. He was a student leader, I never understood what he did wrong, all he did was dream. My older brother had to flee the country and to this day he can't come back. Was he a leader too? A guerrilla. If you really need a cigarette, my friend smokes, we just have to find him in San Agustín, that neighbourhood over there. Don't bother, the man I was looking for isn't in, you last saw him on Monday, I'll let his wife know. I saw him on Sunday too; he really likes football, never misses a match; he was singing in a really strange language. Maybe it was the same match I saw, at ten-thirty. That's it, about that time he had the television on. That match ended really late because there was a fight in the stadium and they had to wait until people calmed down, about one in the morning more or less. I didn't see him again; I'm also the night watchman and I go by here about that time. Probably he went to bed because of the fight. Who knows, he doesn't sleep much and when he can't sleep he walks around the motorcycle track, sometimes talking on his cell phone. Besides giving him the message, I'd like to see his car, I think he wants to sell it. It's a good-looking one. Dark, right? It looks that way at night, but in the daylight it's light green.

Lefty thanked the man and departed. You sure did remember her nipples, asshole, and for sure you sliced one off; sooner or later I am going to fuck you but good.

Twenty-Nine

Win Harrison called L.H. from an ordinary cell phone; it was tapped, but there was so much static the technicians ended up turning down the volume and never even reported the call. It was midnight and at that hour they only keep routine tabs on the agents anyway, nothing excessive. What a surprise. How are you? Never better. Listen, I fell in love with Edgar Mendieta, but he doesn't want to come to Los Angeles. What? why would you fall for that imbecile when you've got me, so handsome, available, and nearby? Such are God's inscrutable ways. Now do you see why women can't be trusted? they never learn to fall in love with the right guys. Neither do men and Edgar's such a scaredy-cat he's afraid of meeting me, will you tell him I'm on my way? How dare you ask me to call that idiot, I can't stand him and I won't do it. He hung up. Win smiled, slipped on loose clothing, put her landline and cell phone side by side, and plugged them into an answering machine with several different answer messages. She made sure her laptop had the photograph of the people implicated in the attack, which, by the way, would not come out in the media, and then made a ham-and-cheese sandwich with mayonnaise and pickles. She took enough money and a pack of business cards in the name of Jean Pynchon and left by the fire escape. Maybe she would learn why Donald Simak hated Mexico, even though it's such a pretty country and so mysterious. At least she thought it was, she who had got lost twice in the desert of Sonora and once in Mexico City. But Simak was implacable: I can't

stand it, it's full of corrupt, lazy, lying, and pretentious people, ruth-
less go-getters. What place isn't? If they killed him she would never
forgive them, but she doubted they had; anyway, the point wasn't to
find the murderer, she wanted to get to the heart of the whole mess,
something the F.B.I. never could, since it had erased all evidence of
its relationship with the agent. Why did they do that? It happens,
but never so fast, and she did not think it was Barrymore's doing.
Walking with her knapsack over her shoulder, she realised that this
mission was personal and a shiver ran through her. Hailing a taxi,
she took it to the bus terminal. She had time, the next morning in
Tijuana she would take a plane to Culiacán. She did not know Lefty,
but besides being L.H.'s friend, his file seemed to indicate she might
be able to trust him.

Thirty

At seven in the morning he called Zelda, who was about to leave for Mazatlán. No response yesterday, boss. Fucking Spaniards, they must be watching football. The address where I sent the request is on my desk. O.K., I'll try sending it again; have a good trip and take care. Thank you, boss, Rodo's here. He finished his Nescafé and left for Headquarters, where he re-sent the cell phone picture to the Central Command of the Spanish Police, Ministry of the Interior, requesting information on Miguel de Cervantes, a suspect in the murder of two women. Urgent. Right then it occurred to him to thank them for the invitation to the course they were giving and ask for more information: I am very interested.

Fucking Dwarf, are you behaving yourself? Who's that? Mendieta, asshole. Ah, Lefty, how's it going? Like in the cartoons. So, Devil told me you took on a really nasty scene. You know how it is, someone has to defend the citizenry from the crooks. This war thing stinks, doesn't it? those people in government have no idea what a fucking scorpion's nest they stomped on. What's wrong with you, Shorty? don't speak badly of our dear Señor Presidente. That guy? haven't you heard him? all he does is pick fights, you can see nobody busted his chops when he was little. Señor Abitia, if you continue offending the highest authority of this country, I'm going to have to lock you away in the Big House. You're right, I'd be smarter to shut my fucking trap. Listen, Shorty, I need to ask you a favour, do you remember Kid Yoreme? Of course, he fought some great bouts at the Revo, but then he started doing drugs. I need to know where he lives and where he works. Last I heard he was working in construction, but listen, my man Lefty, I don't know anything about that stuff any more. What? don't you still sell urine by the highway? That's all over, Lefty my man, and just in time, I was getting sick; Devil and Begoña saved me from that life and if you're looking for me we don't live in Lombardo any more, we moved to Las Quintas, we've got a huge house. Fucking Shorty, you always were worth shit. People get ahead, my man Lefty, that's the law of life, isn't it? but don't worry, I'll find that guy for you, I still have my connections.

So, call me.

He dialled Noriega. What's up? I spoke with Lizárraga, he said Roxana was a beauty and the fiesta at the businessman's club was a big success; one of the guys, Juan Osuna Roth, fell hard for her, but he told me he stopped seeing her a month ago, the reason being something I understand: he likes to suck tit and she never let him, she always said no. The jerk got weaned too soon. He's a tough dude, that Osuna, he's got a modelling agency, so you can imagine. Mayra kept going to Mazatlán, it seems she had work there this week. Lizárraga thinks after the first time she set things up on her own; listen, when is my babe due in? She's on her way, she's going to call you. Has she ever told you which brand of condoms she likes? She doesn't like them, she says sex with a condom is like sucking candy with the wrapper on. You don't say, what about disease, including the nine-month one? She had her tubes tied to avoid problems. How modern. You are going to have one hell of a great time, fucking Noriega, they say she humps like a dog in heat and has multiple orgasms. Pal, are we going to be milk brothers? She never wanted to do it with me, she says I'm not her type. I want her here already. Listen, find out who's friends with Luis Ángel Meraz. Is he our man? In Havana.

I love Mazatlán, this is the second time I've come in two weeks and . . . That afternoon was nothing but her and her smiling eyes, laughing about bicolour having nothing to do with bipolar, or does it? He relived those prolonged, sweet, all-encompassing, saliva-free kisses. *I love it that you don't stick in your tongue;* he wanted to say all women say the same thing and what he wanted to stick in was something else, but all he did was smile; he was only then surfacing after a tremendous obsession with a woman and still had no idea how to behave.

He called Foreman Castelo and his wife put him on. What do you want, fucking nuisance. What's up, my buddy Foreman, how's business? Better every day, listen you sonofabitch, what religion are you that you like to be fucking with me so early in the day? You know my only important friend is you. Well, damn the fucking day I met you, asshole, now what do you want? Leo McGiver, he says he's one of Dioni de la Vega's men. Is he a gringo? No, I don't think so, he's white, but he talks without an accent. It's not a name I recognise. That's what I figured, you're so dumb you're going deaf, but you have friends. You can fuck yourself, I'm not going to bother my friends for you. Well, even so, you've got your homework. He hung up.

As soon as he turned it on, the cell phone rang; it was L.H. in Tijuana. L.H., I'm at the Apostolis, looking at a steak with house sauce and roasted asparagus, I've already had the eel carpaccio on pumpernickel with olive oil and balsamic vinegar, and I've drunk my way through half a bottle of Pasión de San Rafael. Well, I'm starting in on a filet mignon with fine herbs and flour tortillas, and they just brought me a second bottle of Vino de Piedra, a '96. Nice, what's that economic crisis people talk about? It's the rich that suffer the crisis, Lefty my little buddy, you and I will be the same *in saecula saeculorum*. Where we are about to overtake you is in the number of bodies. That'd be an impressive stat, but I doubt it's true, here blood is flowing like an open faucet. You don't think it is here? it's like they were waiting for the starting bell. They heard your cell phone, that's all, does it still ring like a racetrack? It's the best ringtone, it really gets me. Listen, a gringa from the F.B.I. is heading your way, she's a friend and I'd like you to lend her a hand. Where? Wherever she lets you. They smiled at either end of the line. You should know by now, L.H., your girlfriends are my girlfriends. But don't step over the line, eh? Let me see her first, when does she get in? It won't be long, she'll be there today, she'll give you a call. O.K., later.

Again, he opened the folder that held Kid Yoreme's file.

Name: José Ángel Camacho Arenas

Birthplace: Culiacán, Sinaloa

Hands behind his back, handcuffed. I met her when I went to do the drywalling on the private rooms, she bowled me over. You look terrible when you're crying, Yoreme, you look like a pansy. Don't interrupt me, fucking Caveman, I had a little palm-leaf house and. My name is Mendieta, asshole, and this is the last time I'll tell you. So why did you say you were Caveman Galindo? That's none of your business. Well, let me call you Caveman, I was introduced to you as Caveman and I'm going to keep calling you Caveman, so what if you don't like it, and I let in the vixen; I was thinking a fight between you and me could make a good show: wrestler against boxer, doesn't that sound good? and the little weepy rabbit left too. Shut your trap, Yoreme, that's enough, I'm a badge, asshole, get it? and before you touch me I'll bust your ass, you fucking fag, did you meet Mayra Cabral de Melo, alias Roxana, the day you went to work on the private rooms at the Alexa or when you went there for a beer?

Yoreme sobbed. I had a little palm-leaf house and I let in the vixen. Mendieta took him by the neck and squeezed. You're going to calm down and stop crying, asshole, don't make me return the punch you gave me.

Ortega was snowed under when Lefty walked in. What's up, faggot, did you get over it? More or less, I've got an erection that won't calm down; have you got anything? She was an orderly girl, everything tidy, clothes hung up in her closet, make-up in its place, we found several unopened jars of Estée Lauder, her bank accounts up to date with an exorbitant amount for her profession and age, forty-nine letters sent by Elena Palencia Cabral de Melo from São Paulo; we read a few and they seem to indicate she's her mother, she gives her good advice: don't get involved, be careful with your customers, don't let them fall in love; besides that, we have nothing. Fishing his cigarettes from the papers and objects covering his desk, Ortega lit one. Does the mother mention any names? None. Finger-prints? It's Jack the Ripper everywhere; about the other girl, her room was the usual mess, including the closet, we found an electric bill and one from Telcel, but no cell phone; as you can see, nothing much. Which is what happens when you're useless. What do you expect? you want me to solve the case for you? go jerk yourself off, papa. Is it true you're going to open a store with all these blankets?

Look how bad it's got, at this rate we're going to end up with enough to fill a warehouse; it's as if they'd sworn an oath, right? now they're even leaving messages on some of the bodies. He opened a folder. Look at this: "Gonna choke trash you betrey you pay"; where's your partner? In Mazatlán, Cabral had clients there and she went to find some answers; yesterday they handed over the body of the kid from the San Luis to this guy, I'd like you to see if he has a record. Lefty handed him the card: The telephones don't exist. You want this now? Mendieta was not planning to insist, but he ran with the thought: I've got a hunch. Listen, you bastard, don't push your luck, we're working flat out, you think all this dead meat is a game? the uniforms that walk in that door couldn't care less, they're like cattle the way they destroy evidence, the more the better, I'm fed up with those jerks; besides, in the San Luis we only found Jack's prints. He opened a folder and showed him: I guess a few from the telephone are clear, but there's no record of them, not of the dead guy's either. Well, compare them with the ones on the card, what can you lose? and you know, it's been too long since we had a few cold ones, how about we follow our instincts? Pal, I'm wasted, I can't, I'm just hoping I don't get a fucking heart attack. Have a snort, yesterday I fucked two lines. No, I want to steer clear of that too, it was really a bitch to get off it and I don't want to get hooked again. Then shut your trap and get to work on that mother, fucking Ortega, you would have been done by now. Which, Leo McGiver? Thirteen minutes later Lefty went back. He's clean. Don't fuck with me, how did you find out so fast? You aren't going to believe this, but the prints on the card match the ones on the telephone in the room at the San Luis where the kid was killed. No shit, in other words . . . But they're not in our files. Listen, when you have a minute take a peek in our cave, we've got a picture of a babe you're going to love. Is she naked? As God brought her into the world.

He went back to his office. Let's see, the dude was with the kid, he handed him over to his parents, and he was also at the scene of the crime; did he kill him? why not? But, what about the motive? The buddy looks tough and he works for Dioni de la Vega, the card has no address; so, we're fucked. Cavalry charge. It was Noriega. Lefty, you can go fuck your mother, you fucking fag. What's up, you bastard, what's wrong? You didn't tell me the babe was going to be wearing a pendant. What? Just like you hear it, she brought her boyfriend, a fatso with a face like my balls. No kidding, fucking dame, that's against regulations. And the worst of it is I've got to take them out to lunch, the buddy wants a *levantamuertos*. Ah, so you've become friends. Come on, how could we be friends; what would you do? no way can I toss the jerk in the slammer. It's a bitch, listen, so who are Meraz's friends? Everybody, that guy knows everyone in the port. All that flies, swims, crawls, walks, or jumps? And no-one thinks he's a bad guy. Noriega confessed that Zelda looked prettier than ever and he went on lamenting for a few minutes more: What do I do with the condoms? She doesn't like them, I told you. Still, I bought several. Well, give them to the buddy, better they get used than go to waste. Fucking Lefty, did you ever let me down, but ugly. He hung up.

He asked me if I was from the Col Pop, said he had a friend there named Mendieta, could it be Enrique? are there other Mendietas in the Col Pop? Fucking Mendietas, they're even in the United States. He dialled his brother but got no answer.

Angelita opened the door. You've got a visitor. What?

Win Harrison entered the room. Hi. She introduced herself, spent a few seconds looking at the picture of *Muro No* and sat on Zelda's desk. Angelita gave him a fax. Boss, from Spain. At least two dozen pages. Briseño came in and said to Win: Would you mind giving us a minute, please? Certainly. She went out with the secretary.

Edgar, I clearly forbade you to investigate the case of Anita Roy, in what language do I have to tell you? What a fucking gossip, that dude, Lefty thought. Why did you tell José Antonio Lagarde he was a suspect? To mess with him. How could you accuse an upstanding citizen that way? Like I said, he tried my patience and he was a bundle of nerves. Well, you've really done it this time, the man fled to Canada. Lefty remembered that his son was studying there but did not mention it. If he isn't guilty, then why did he run? You scared him. Well, he sure can't take much. The fact is he is guilty; Briseño glanced at *Muro No* and continued: He killed his ex in a fit of jealousy, he never managed to get over her, and her conduct got to him. Eyes wide, Mendieta studied Briseño. He came here and told me everything, he was ground to a powder. Lefty lit a cigarette: Why did he cut off her tits? Briseño made a gesture as if he wasn't going to answer, but then he did. They were really sensitive, he told me that just touching them would drive her wild; the thought of other hands caressing them pushed him over the edge. Mendieta blew a smoke ring: Is he a friend of yours? We go back twenty-two years, he's helped me and my family more than you could imagine; and by the way, if he had anything to do with the death of your friend he would have confessed it; he told me you also blamed him for

206

that; look, Mendieta, Mayra wasn't just a table dancer. He sensed his commander softening. Did he tell you how and where he killed Anita? A bullet to the head in the house where you went to see him. What weapon did he use? It doesn't matter, Lefty, what I'm telling you is to go in one ear and out the other. Tell me if it was a 9mm. Of course not. They looked at each other for a few seconds. Then you agree I should carry on. Until the final consequences; listen, who's the white chick? Somebody I'm going to ask out to a movie. Congratulations, she looks just your type; well, keep me posted. He turned and headed for the door. Chief, why did you tell me? To help solve the case. He opened the door and was gone. Lefty knew he was lying, was it to keep Meraz safe and sound? It would have been easier to blame Lagarde for everything.

Win came back in. L.H. sent me to you, you don't mind if I dispense with formalities, do you? Why would I? Lefty looked carefully at the thin, short-haired blonde with hard features and he could see she had a dagger stuck in her. Is this the fearsome F.B.I.? what a let-down. She was wearing a blue blouse and traditional-cut jeans. I know you were on the team that found the body of Peter Connolly and I want to talk to you about that. Ah, my chief called the U.S. consulate and they told us they'd never heard of him, they couldn't care less, and we should call his family; we did, but all his telephone numbers were false; they might have already sent the body to the common grave. So soon? Right now we have more bodies than we can store, let's call the morgue to make sure. Do you have any suspects? It was suicide. A bullet in the forehead? Why not? we've had them with two in the back of the head. They smiled. You're better than in the reports. You, in contrast, come practically unannounced, would you let me read this fax? Go right ahead. So Lagarde killed his wife; could the chief really not have asked about the weapon? pretty strange.

Mendieta's interest in the fax dissolved in one minute. What idiots. He tore up the pages and threw them in the wastebasket, then turned back to Win. We have a Spanish suspect who calls himself Miguel de Cervantes, I ask Madrid for information and they send me everything on the author of *Don Quixote*, you know who Don Quixote is, right? A contemporary of Hamlet's, did you only send them the name? And a photograph taken with a cell phone. Maybe it didn't arrive or the quality was awful, for example the picture of this man was taken with a cell and you can't see much, they both turned towards *Muro No*; so, do you have anything on him? No, except he's a woman. Win stood and went over to the printout. How interesting, nice one, Mendieta. You can thank Angelita, she saw it. Angelita is your partner, I know you have one. No, she's our secretary, you already met. God, that woman has good instincts; let's do a test, lend me your cell with the picture. Lefty handed it over. Win sent the photograph of Cervantes to her iPod. Look, perfect, maybe it didn't show up in Spain like that; try again and call them too; nobody gives up information if they aren't sure what you want it for; our Spanish colleagues are cautious, it's normal. You're right, why would they give me what I ask for? He dialled a number, but no-one answered.

Thirty-One

Silence reigned at the Valdés family home. Few suspected a wake was under way for one of the country's most powerful drug lords. Just past noon the final narco arrived from Ciudad Juárez. He came in an armoured car because Samantha insisted she would have no helicopters in the garden or near the residence. Let's not draw any attention to ourselves or cause alarm.

Among the few who guessed something was up was Daniel Quiroz; he drove by the mansion several times without daring to approach the gate. His instincts told him to stick around, despite the warnings from his colleagues from other outlets, including the Mexico City television people, who had spent a couple of hours circling the place. When he saw the Hummer with Chihuahua plates go in, he screwed up his courage. Quiroz, from "Eyes on the Night", he managed to blurt out to the hitman who opened the gate. Stop driving by, my friend, if I see you one more time I'll fill you full of lead. He closed the gate. A feeling of powerlessness, coupled with fear, took hold of the journalist and he moved off. He dialled Mendieta, but got no answer. Some fucking friends I have.

Inside, things were going as planned. Samantha Valdés and Minerva were receiving condolences. The open casket was on display in the centre of the living room. There were extra easy chairs and sofas, where the guests sat drinking and munching on hors d'oeuvres while they chatted in low voices: The coffin is made of silver, he had it done up special in Taxco. He's taking like five million dollars' worth of jewels with him. I saw him wearing that suit once when he came to Ojinaga. Samantha's a tough cookie, isn't she? You expected her to be any different? At one in the afternoon they were served *menudo* and *pozole* stews at tables set up in the garden. Whisky, beer, and bottled water were never lacking.

In his perfect make-up and sparkling jewels, Marcelo Valdés was saying a dignified adios to the world. At 4.00, an aged priest from Badiraguato said the funeral Mass using a portable altar the Valdés kept on hand, and at 5.00 the cortège left for Humaya Gardens. The stream of luxury cars and pickups with tinted windows passed by the Hotel San Luis as Mendieta was leaving it with Win. The display of power caused a twinge in his guts.

The reporter was nowhere to be seen.

At 5.38 they entered the cemetery. Besides the leaders of the Pacific Cartel, among those attending were two army generals from the Presidential Guard, one naval officer, and a representative of the Attorney General. In civilian dress, they offered their condolences with maximum discretion. Samantha was pleased, though it occurred to her that if anybody threw a bomb it would wipe out the entire cartel. She was aware of a tightness in the pit of her stomach. The band played one traditional tune from the region after another.

The Valdés mausoleum, eight by eight metres, was painted light blue and had a glass door featuring an image of Jesus Christ in bas-relief, plus marble columns and a cupola made of gold-leaf tiles. It was by far the tallest and most spacious in the cemetery. A pair of helicopters hovered overhead.

The coffin was opened for the final goodbye. Samantha hugged her mother, who trembled as tears coursed down her cheeks. Then the coffin was lowered into its niche and covered with a cascade of roses. The many floral arrangements were placed against the walls, several layers deep.

Auburn late-afternoon light, humid.

Then they returned to the house. The meeting would last only an hour to allow everyone to disperse as soon as possible. The new boss understood precisely where she had to squeeze and she would do so quickly.

The Pacific Cartel was made up of eleven drug lords: six Mexicans, one Colombian, and four Americans. They sat in the room overlooking the garden, drinking coffee and whisky straight up and listening to Samantha Valdés, their new leader. The following day, when they left the state, four of them would lose their lives, but only Max Garcés and La Jefa, as they all called her now, knew that. The rest were loyal to her.

We shall maintain the division set up by my father and respect one another's territories; any attacks will be answered by all of us together; we must be especially mindful of our connections in government now that the president has declared war on us and called us ridiculous minorities; we'll be the ones to deal with him and we may increase the regular payments, same story regarding the Mexico City people; you, she pointed at one of the Americans, take care of the D.E.A.; each of us must maintain control in his state and adhere to the agreements we've signed; let's do our best to limit the impact on regular folk, for sure there's going to be a wave of robberies, kidnappings, and innocent people getting killed, let's try to keep that from happening in the territories we control; we know how difficult that will be, for example in Ciudad Juárez, but we must make the effort; we're going to set up a special force, we've already ordered sufficient weaponry and it should arrive next week; I thank each of you for your presence, especially Gaviria, who came all the way from Miami, and Eloy Quintana for his stupendous work in the desert.

She stood up then and so did the rest of them. They embraced her, told her they were with her, that they would all grow together, and they took their leave happily, even those who were going to get whacked.

Thirty-Two

They went to El Farallón in a brand new black Cheyenne. They ordered *filete culichi*, fresh shrimp, and beer. Win wanted to visit the crime scene. Would you like to know who he was? Tell me only what suits you; he carried a double I.D., so if you like you could start with his name, it's always better to look into someone who really exists. Like Miguel de Cervantes? she took a sarcastic swig; I mean, I never would have looked for Don Quixote, well, or Hamlet either. She was thinking that if Donald does not exist in this country, she could get away with revealing his name to a stranger, even though it was against regulations: Donald Simak, and he was an agent doing advance work for the White House. What was an advance man for the U.S. government doing in Culiacán? The father of the president has been duck hunting near here for the past few days, Donald was among the agents sent to size up the situation and report back. The father of the U.S. president is hunting here? That's what I said. Harrison, intense black eyes, skin whiter than white, brought a shrimp to her mouth. So, it's no mystery, anyone could have killed him. But it wasn't anyone. Oh, I get it, terrorists. Win looked him in the eye: I've got no time for satire, Mendieta, I'm not playing around; since there is no way you could know, I'll let you in on it: the father of the president was attacked when he landed at the camp where he goes hunting; he wasn't hurt and his attackers were all killed, among them the woman you have up on your office wall; we need to clarify the connection between the two events and that's why I'm here; and

213

you might as well know this too: you are not liked at the F.B.I. What a shame, because I'm dying to make a good impression so I can work with you people. They glared at each other. I know what you think of us and I don't give a damn; I want to know who gave the order to kill Simak, the rest can't be fixed. Hey, don't get testy, you're the buddy of one of my best friends and I'll do whatever you ask.

Thank you, if all goes well, in twenty-four hours each of us will be back to his own work.

They had guava pie for dessert, with coffee.

In the room at the San Luis, Mendieta learned she had come in search of something else, maybe some toehold for fulfilling a last wish, of the love of her life? Why not? Is there anyone in this world who doesn't have one great love? Only him, and he wasn't really sure. He took advantage to check the place out once more. She was trembling and her eyes took on a glassy shine, maybe the shine of someone wanting vengeance. I'd like to see his suitcase, his clothes, and his pistol. Mendieta called Ortega, who first said it was evidence and then that he would send it all to her in a box. There was no pistol, Lefty said, we found a map of Culiacán, open but no markings, do you have any idea what he was looking for? He must have learned the attack was coming. But they didn't pay any attention, typical. O.K., let's go to the morgue. As they left the hotel, they ran into the caravan accompanying Marcelo Valdés. What's this? Beats me, judging by the cars he must have had powerful friends. The brand new black pickup bringing up the rear was Richie Bernal's, but Lefty didn't even know he had been ambushed at the high school. Are we going to the hunting camp? You are, I need you to do a couple of things and that's one of them. Alright. At the

214

morgue it did not take long: she saw the body, read the forensic and ballistics reports, and said fine. Mendieta had several questions, but did not ask them; he did not want to get involved. Neither did he dare take a peek at Mayra.

Win located El Continente on the Cheyenne's G.P.S. It occurred to Mendieta that he ought to be looking for Yoreme, but he resigned himself and headed off; he could do that when he got back. Besides, Shorty Abitia hadn't got back to him yet. Who was McGiver? what was he doing in the room where that kid died? did he know Enrique? what had he meant when he said, You'd better stay on your toes, dark days are coming? Just how big and strong is the murderer? is he from Mazatlán? He would have to call Foreman again. No wonder Lagarde got so nervous, why would he say Anita was killed at Mayra's house? Fucking Yoreme.

Name: José Ángel Camacho Arenas
Birthplace: Culiacán, Sinaloa

I couldn't work, fucking Caveman, I was paralysed, I let in the vixen; I don't know how I managed to finish the job; and from then on I haven't missed a day at the Alexa; sometimes she wouldn't show, but I was always there, my eyes wide open, watching for the moment when she'd smile like she was about to connect with an uppercut; she put a hex on me, Caveman, I had a little palm-leaf house, she made me hers without laying a finger on me, isn't that fucking amazing? it didn't take much, I watched her for maybe a minute, only it was really late for me and really early for her; I'm short of money, my man Cavey, and though you haven't said, you must be in the same boat, I can see it in your face, we losers never have what

215

counts, we've got that mark in our eyes that not even death will wipe away, stupidity you can disguise and you get by, but not the sign of the loser, they pay us any old thing just to keep us from dying of hunger; so let's make that fight happen, if you want you can put on a mask and it'll be mask against mane, we'll make a bundle and then we can sit back and reminisce about the queen; what do you say? too bad you never met her.

What's wrong with you? Lefty asked himself, aren't you a tough bastard? don't you eat girls alive? what a limp-wrist you turned out to be. *I don't believe you're a badge, you're too tender, upstanding, cultured; you know who Vinicius de Moraes is, you want to go to Rio to see the girls from Ipanema; policemen don't think like that; are you corrupt? you're not really, why?* Her caramel voice in his mind. Now you want to cry? Don't be ridiculous. A dude who has cried for so many other things can't cry about this. Why can't I? Because I can't, love is a poison that makes you stronger, don't use that strength to cry. Good thing I'm not with Trudis. Countryside. So Mister B. likes to hunt around here, who could be the owner of that camp? Cavalry charge. Boss, I'm calling to report in. Where are you staying? At Las Flores, suite 602, with a view of three islands, incredible; now we're going out to eat with Noriega, you should see how well he's getting along with Rodo, I can hardly believe it. Careful, God just might put those two together. I'll keep that in mind; listen, I interrogated Lizárraga and he claims to know nothing about what happened after the first contact with Mayra. One guy, Juan Osuna Roth, admitted to having relations with her, but he hasn't seen her in a month. I put the squeeze on him and he suggested we speak with Fermín de Lima.

*

The white building was bright in the sunshine. On the ground floor, down an outdoor passageway lined with rose bushes, they found the tycoon's office. We'll wait for you over here, Noriega piped up, and he dragged Rodo off to follow a blonde in a black bikini who was on her way to the pool. Toledo understood that her host did not want to be directly involved, and although she did not agree she decided to let it go.

I want to speak with Señor de Lima. Who is it who wishes to see him? Zelda Toledo, State Ministerial Police. You? Me what? Zelda smouldered. A few moments ago we were speaking with your boss. Chief Mendieta didn't mention it. Mendieta? wasn't his name Miranda? Oh, no, Miranda is the chief in Mazatlán, I'm from Culi-acán. Allow me a moment, please have a seat. She watched her place a call, smile, and then beckon her to her desk with a finger. He'll see you in five minutes, would you like some coffee? Do you have Diet Coke? The woman stood up and watching her step away Zelda had a single thought: Powerful men would not be powerful if their secretaries were ugly or badly dressed.

In five minutes she was shown in. The way things are, with Carlos Slim losing money if he stops to bend down and pick up a hundred-dollar bill, everybody is in a lather, so to the point, señorita. You sent a donation for the transfer of the body of Mayra Cabral de Melo. Oh, that was nothing compared to what that woman deserved; look, I did it on behalf of several friends for whom she put on a few shows, anything else? Who got turned on the most by her dancing? We all did, some might have shouted louder than others, but as far as being turned on goes, I'd say it was a draw. And who would drive her here from Culiacán? Hmm, I'm not sure, but I think it was a big guy;

yes, he brought her a few times, but usually she came with Attorney Ramírez. She was killed by a bullet to the head and the murderer cut off one of her nipples. The businessman said nothing for a few seconds. You think someone from here is rocking the cradle? Tell me who introduced you to her. The mayor called one day to invite me to a private show with a Brazilian dancer, but I don't know how they came up with her; I figured through some agency, that's usually how you find performers; and don't get angry, but that was a while back. We are looking for a tall, heavyset man. So, it's not me. But you got a good look. De Lima made a gesture to say he did not understand.

Boss, he promised to expand on things tonight.

Call me tomorrow.

"Oh, your lips of rubies, red as sunset seas." Sincerely, Sandro de América.

At the entrance to the camp Mendieta was stopped.

How's Mister B. doing? The uniformed man in charge of the gate looked at him suspiciously. That's none of your business, identify yourself. He showed his badge. You can't come in, you have no jurisdiction here. No? maybe the one who has no jurisdiction is you, tell me who you are that you can obstruct the work of the state police. Clear out or you're under arrest, the guard raised his voice. Hang on, Adán Carrasco left the side of Mister B. and walked towards them. The detective remembered seeing him once before. Right then they were getting ready to leave for the lakes. Can I help you? Edgar Mendieta, from the State Ministerial Police, we were called about an attack. Behind Carrasco he could see a parking lot filled with

Jeeps and luxury cars. Who called you? All I want to know is what happened. Who did they say the attack was on? The father of the president of the United States. False, the man is relaxed as could be and hunting as God wills. Was that him with you over there? So you can see I'm not lying, the gentleman is in perfect health. What happened that night? Nothing, if you like I can call the district attorney right this minute, he's a friend of mine and he comes here every weekend to go hunting. Mendieta's discomfort was evident. Here he was, surrounded by Americans in uniform, their weapons in view, and he felt out of his element. No need to worry, Agent Mendieta, you can go; there's no crime to investigate, and when you want to come out for a little hunting, I can guarantee you a wonderful time. Mendieta was about to respond, but like everyone else he was thrown to the ground, when the Cheyenne he'd come in exploded and rapidly burned to bits.

Thirty-Three

A fight's come my way, Don Silvio, and I want you to train me. The man, eighty years old, with a storied past in the city's boxing world, listened impassively; it was not the first time the Kid had approached him, but Yoreme didn't know which way was up and had no business entering the ring. He remembered when the Kid first walked in at the age of fourteen, he put him in the ring and told him to start moving; he looked good, like Cuyo Hernández used to say, If you've got legs you'll make it, and the boy had them, plus a nasty uppercut that could rescue him from poverty if he worked on it. But he lost. It wasn't his opponents who put him on the ropes, it was cocaine, that garbage that flooded the city from who knows where. Who are you going to fight, Kid Yoreme? A wrestler, it's to make a little money, you know how bad things are; I'll talk to the people at the Revo and suggest we split fifty-fifty, I let in the vixen. That vixen again, thought Silvio García, he turned up one day spouting that drivel and he hasn't been able to stop. Who is it? He calls himself Caveman, he almost beat Santo, the man of the silver mask. Another one just like him, he thought; he knew Yoreme was anxious for an answer and even though there was no way he would train him, he decided to do him a good turn. Alright, Kid, but you better not leave me in the lurch, eh? Yoreme's face lit up. No, sir, how could you think such a thing? I had a little palm-leaf house, I need your guidance and your wisdom in my corner; remember Don Silvio? Do it, Kid, give him the uppercut, the uppercut is your punch, and they fell like a tonne of bricks, I let in the vixen. O.K., you're going to have to study your opponent carefully. I already beat him once. Yoreme was ecstatic. But first, you've got to get in shape, a boxer needs to be incredibly strong and at weight; so starting tomorrow, you're going to run three kilometres. I've been shadow-boxing and jogging a bit along the river. Three kilometres tomorrow, four the next day, then five, and when you've run five for a week, come and see me, when is the fight? We have time. O.K., then start jogging, don't drink any beer or snort any garbage. I'm giving all that up, Don Silvio, the weepy little rabbit left too, for her, I'm doing it for her, up in heaven. The old man did not want to know who he was referring to. Start running, Kid Yoreme, your opponents are right there taunting you.

Thirty-Four

Two uniformed officers hoisted Mendieta up from Carrasco's boots while two others took aim at his head. A rattled Lefty cursed the day he got roped into this mess, who was Win Harrison? the fucking terrorist, did she ever fool me; damn L.H., I will never forgive him for that blunder. The others were getting up, among them Carrasco, who was collecting his hat. Who the hell are you? he said to Lefty, his eyes murderous. Somewhat recovered, Mendieta decided to draw on his own hatred of so many things. I'm Edgar Mendieta from the State Ministerial Police, and who the fuck are you, Carrasco, to get attacked twice in a few days? what is going on? They watched Mister B. saunter over, hunting rifle in hand, utterly unperturbed, as if he were in his bedroom; agents surrounded him immediately. As of then the camp was on a war footing. The manager came running: A pickup exploded, Mister B., nothing serious. Step aside, the old man ordered. He reached the place where everyone was standing. Who are you? he said to Lefty, who by then was hand-cuffed. I was the driver and I was saved by a miracle. Carrasco, let's go do our thing and leave this to the experts. Sir, William Ellroy had arrived in a hurry, are you alright? What do you think, are you blind? The guard who had stopped Lefty at the camp gate spoke up: Special Agent Ellroy, this man is the driver of the pickup that exploded. Mister B. looked at him calmly: You do your work and we'll do ours. He took Carrasco by the arm and they walked to the vehicle that would take them to the ducks.

Mendieta was led to the small room at the back of the house Ellroy was using as an office.

A few hours ago, somebody who did not want to identify himself called to tell us about a gunfight here a few nights ago and I was assigned to investigate, have you had any problems? because I just saw Mister B. relaxed as could be and the attack was supposedly on him. If we had any problems, the last police force in the world we would turn to would be Mexico's. Ellroy came close and gave Lefty a punch in the mouth that knocked him flat. Answer properly, you idiot, who gave you the order to kill Mister B.? Mendieta spat. Fuck your mother, he thundered, you little shit of a sentry, go hit your fucking whore of a mother; I'm a detective with the Mexican police, not an undocumented immigrant, and I'm in my own country. He spat again. The bloody wad landed on Ellroy's shoe. Take off the cuffs if you're such a tough bastard, you fucking pansy. Ellroy cleaned the wad of spit with Mendieta's pants and gave him a kick that Lefty tried to return. He won't crush me, he thought, he might kill me, but he won't humiliate me, he's nothing but an insecure jerk with a badge, a knucklehead with power who's afraid of me, who thinks he can scare me with insults and punches; some gringos have class, but not him; the one who will never hear the end of this is Win Harrison, that fucking horrible old bag, look what she got me into, and that imbecile L.H., how could he trust her? Ellroy sat in his chair, two agents sat Mendieta in another, he was bleeding, but his glare was homicidal: there is nothing this asshole can do to me, he roused himself, this pansy can suck my dick. Who told you about the other attack? Your fucking mother called me on the telephone. Ellroy's eyes were like two glowing coals. The truck, is it yours? Of course, can't you see? it was a present from Santa Claus. Because it has no registration or plates or anything. The first attack was carried out by four individuals, we are in the process of identifying one of them, the photograph is terrible; I don't know why, but I have the feeling you took it. Who are you? So I came to find out if the camp is the way it looks in the pictures. I can see you like to deal with the specialists, great, they'll have fun pulling your balls off. You and your specialists can suck my dick, I've got one who could give all of you lessons. Ellroy signalled to one of the uniformed officers, who opened the door and stepped out to get the experts. Win Harrison pushed him back inside. She showed Ellroy her I.D.: This man is mine. She took Mendieta by the arm and stood him up. The agents pointed their weapons. You can't take him, he just attacked the father of the president, he blew up the truck he came in, and he's got a lot of explaining to do. He can explain it to us, and when you take pictures of perpetrators use a damn camera, the terrorist we couldn't identify turned out to be a woman, and the one who figured it out was this man you were just beating up; if the pickup exploded it's obvious that someone wants to stop us, and don't you dare obstruct an investigation by the F.B.I., Special Agent William Ellroy. She shoved the uniforms aside and they went out. They climbed into a Jeep and drove off. Several agents were inspecting the smoking ruins of the Cheyenne.

Would you like to tell me what all this is about? and take these fucking handcuffs off me before I bust your fucking chops. Would you hit a woman? Lefty was furious. They stopped. Harrison used a laser to free him. Are you trying to kill me? we've barely met. They're trying to throw us off and it wasn't the people from Tuesday's attack, who are all dead; somebody else, we'll have to do some work to figure out who's behind it all. That explosion was aimed at you. It could be, you're a good detective so you know we can't be sure without investigating. And who do you think is going to investigate this? We are. He breathed, the highway calmed him down a bit. Where did you get that pickup? I called from Tijuana to rent it, I already reported what happened and we're waiting for an answer; in the office where they gave me the key, they can't remember who brought it in. Did you look at the papers? You know this doesn't usually happen. Silence. What about this Jeep? They lent it to me. Lefty opened the glove compartment. He expected to find a registration in the name of Fabián Olmedo, but no, it was from a rental company. If this wasn't an impossible case, it sure looked like one, and somebody was going to have to pay him for the broken dishes. On the way by, he eyed the seed warehouse, where everything looked normal.

I'll see you in two hours at Café Miró, according to the reports it's your favourite. You said you wanted my help on a couple of things; there's one left and we've got about twenty hours to do it in, he warned, while he got out of the Jeep at Headquarters.

My God, Lefty, what happened to you? did they jump you from behind? His face was swollen, his lip split. The war on crime is no piece of cake, Trudis. Let me clean you up, I was headed home early, good thing I didn't, is your tetanus vaccine up to date? because it looks like you got kicked by a mule. She cleansed his face with alcohol. They say plain soap is better, but I put my faith in alcohol; don't squirm, Lefty, you aren't a child. Ow. Do you have to go out? because you should ice it for a while, your mouth is really swollen and your gum is split too; I'm going to get you some Isodine so you can swish it around, or better yet, gargle with lime juice and salt, it's more effective. I might as well do it with tacks. Those are for something else, let me see. Ow. Don't be a coward, what, aren't you a badge? look at how they left you, I'm going to lay out clean clothes so you can make yourself handsome; who do you think just called? No, Trudis, I already told you to tell him I'm away on a trip. Oh, Lefty, I hope God doesn't punish you, the poor boy, it's not his fault. They fell silent. But it wasn't him, it was Zelda, as soon as you can you're to get in touch with her or turn on your cell. It had shut down with all the hullabaloo at the hunting camp and he had not noticed.

He changed his clothes and dialled.

Boss, Lizárraga's a slime-bag. Why do you want to see me again, Agent Toledo? Señor Fermín de Lima told me he went to a private party where Mayra Cabral de Melo danced, and he said the invitation came from you. Don't believe him, besides being a rich man, de Lima's a liar, it's another of his tricks, Lizárraga smiled broadly. Who was at that party besides Fermín de Lima? Is this a tough broad I'm facing? how could it be, señorita? with that lovely face of yours I don't believe it. Señor Mayor, please answer my questions. The privileges of my office don't matter? Of course they matter, that's why I said please. The politician's smile went from entertained to tense. I don't feel like answering and you can make do with that. Noriega tried to stop Zelda from throwing her glass of water, but he was too late, the man's face and shirt were drenched. You are never going to help the cause of justice, señorita; the mayor was red with fury as he got to his feet. And you won't be able to govern as long as that clique has you by the throat, because frankly I don't think you have any balls; you said de Lima's a liar and you may be right, but he was not mistaken when he said, clear as could be, that you would try to stonewall. You must have a superior. And you must too, so start telling me who was at that fucking party and what happened that made them so damn happy; Mayra's dead now, the least she deserves is some clarification. Noriega was speechless. You are going to regret this, Agent Toledo, no policeman or woman makes me look ridiculous, especially in my own office, but he sat down. Who brought the girl from Culiacán? Bigboy Rivera. We know that, and you were the contact for Attorney Luis Ángel Meraz to bring her here. It was a thank-you for the people with money who always give us their selfless support; I don't know if you're familiar with what Meraz has in mind. Not really, but I know he's ambitious; Meraz told us you picked out the place for the party, chose the guests, took care of everything: drinks, food, and nice surroundings, so all the powerful people of the port could spend an evening letting loose. But that was three months ago and the table dancer just got killed, I had barely been sworn in then. I want to see if your guest list coincides with de Lima's. The man fished in a drawer, pulled out a folder from which he handed her a sheet; at the bottom, in ink, was de Lima's name. Toledo put it in her bag.

One more thing, Señor Mayor, Mayra Cabral de Melo continued coming to Mazatlán, who brought her? You don't know, señorita? you aren't as tough as I thought. I was hoping maybe you wouldn't notice. Excuse me, but you are a bitch. And you are a bastard. They smiled. If Attorney Meraz does not become governor, you people are going to pay for this.

What do you think, boss? Hmm, Meraz again, sounds like we have the key to the whole mess, so now get some sun, you deserve it. Don't do anything until I'm back in town. What's that about, Agent Toledo, are you planning to disobey orders? have a good time and don't look for five legs on a cat. He hung up.

Cavalry charge. Detective Mendieta? It was Angelita. Patricia Olmedo's here, she wants to speak with you. About what? She says she'll only tell you. Put her on. Before I do, the chief asked for you twice and Quiroz called too, he wants to know what you're up to, he heard it was something heavy. I'll call him later, put Olmedo on. Hi, colonel. I am not a colonel, what can I do for you? Well, I want to talk with you about my father, yesterday he spoke to me so sweetly and I'm really worried. What does that have to do with us? Well, I'm afraid he might do something, something to get revenge. You did try to kill him, how did you expect him to take it? But he's not like that, he's a hard man, a lynx who does business with people from all over the world. With the gringos? Mostly with them; oh, and I spoke to Marcos, his father is over there now with him and he never saw a gun in his house. Lefty pondered a moment, for someone who lives alone it's not a bad idea every so often to get close to a perfect body, even with clothes on: Let's meet at nine at the Marimba, if I'm not there by quarter past then I won't be coming, and it'll be tomorrow morning at eight at the Miró instead. Do I have to be there that early? He hung up.

In the kitchen Trudis was humming "Say You Say Me" by Lionel Ritchie, not a bad voice.

*

Mendieta waited five minutes at the table next to the coffee mill, his favourite spot. Rudy was not in, so he ordered a guava juice and a double espresso. Despite it being early evening, the temperature must have been 42°C. Harrison had changed her blouse, she sat down without offering any greeting. Around them the voices in the café sounded like an excited flock of birds. She asked for a Coca-Cola and a Black Forest on baguette. We gringos eat supper early, she said. Mendieta sipped his coffee. I looked at Simak's things and there's nothing there, did you go through them? No, who was he exactly? A special agent who worked on just about anything; they killed him early in the day and he was dressed to go out: that's what I can't understand, he was extremely suspicious. Did he use a cell phone? The most technically sophisticated you can get. Well, we didn't find one and his wallet had no cash. Impossible, he was incredibly careful and he knew you can't always pay with plastic, for sure he was robbed. Maybe, but if he was who you say he was, they didn't go there to mug him, they went to kill him, why? That's what I've been asking myself; three months ago he was put in charge of designing an anti-narcotics strategy for the president of Mexico, according to my reports he was on that mission. You don't say, the president just declared war on the narcos. I don't know if it was part of an overall plan, but he had certain defined responsibilities and one of them was to supply the Mexican army with guns. Under the table? Only enough to ensure expedited delivery. Lefty half smiled. The food arrived. He reflected: Who would kill a gringo special agent, who's a gunrunner and also happens to be putting together a campaign against drug trafficking? did the narcos know about this? why not? they have spies everywhere, why wouldn't they have them for this too? another gunrunner? that's likely. The other thing I want you to do for me is get me an interview with Marcelo Valdés. Mendieta was annoyed and did not try to hide it: Are you nuts? Harrison gave him an astonished look. I have absolutely no relationship with that guy, I've never even met him. Maybe so, but we know you're the only policeman he respects, the others he has in his pocket. Lefty felt flattered, there is nothing like having your enemy's respect. You want to get me in another mess? the Cheyenne wasn't enough for you? That was no problem for you, detective, or you'd be dead. His eyes turned hard: Who put the explosives in the Cheyenne? Who do you like: the narcos, the gunrunners, the army, the protesters against the wall, somebody else? Why don't you leave all this to the D.E.A.? Impossible, this is our business. What do you mean "our"? I'll explain later on, I need to speak with Valdés before it's too late. Are you expecting me to go and ask him why he killed Simak? They glowered at each other. This time I'll go, just get him to see me. How can anybody live in this city? thought Lefty, if the people here don't do you in, some visitor will. I have no idea why you want to see that man, but, whatever the reason, may God bless you. This sandwich is good, it's really tasty. Mexican kitchens are run either by saints or by witches, and the result is the same. They went to Mariana Kelly's house. She's not in, the bodyguard who met them did not give an inch. Do you know when she'll be back? No. Has it been a while since they moved Devil Urquídez from here? Yup. The guy was tall with an icy stare, and Lefty decided to try elsewhere.

Thirty-Five

McGiver and a representative of the Armed Forces were having a relaxed breakfast in one corner of the Mezzosole restaurant in the Hotel Lucerna. Since it was Saturday, the place was packed, though no-one would have known them. The smuggler had found a new customer, a thin, pale man with a feverish expression, now eating a plate of non-acidic fruit with toast. Good thing you didn't put down the deposit, Señor Andrade. I would have been ruined; fortunately Congressman Vinicio de la Vega learned what happened to the other supplier, knew of you, and could recommend you; also you called me in time. You can trust in us. The other fellow was very strange, we went out to eat and he didn't even look at the menu. The Lord's vineyard is made up of all kinds. The man savoured a slice of custard apple: Señor McGiver, if everything goes well, you will be in charge of supplying all fronts. That's my business, Señor Andrade, and don't forget that you, to put it quite simply, will be my only partner. Thank you, whenever I come to Sinaloa I love to eat the fruit, it's so fresh and tasty. The gunrunner, who was having *machaca* with onions and green chillies and corn tortillas for breakfast, nodded with a smile and recalled that rarely had he touched a piece of fruit in his life. Like my grandfather used to say, not even if I were sick.

Half an hour later, back in his room, he called Danilo Twain and gave him the quantities he had just negotiated. Green Arrow, that bit about the advertising worries me, White Arrow doesn't think it's enough. Look, the girl is pretty and unless she gets some publicity she won't do the deal. I hope you're not wrong, what about the rest? It's summer and the weathermen are predicting a big storm, we'd better wait. We'll be ready and on alert. Click.

He dialled Dulce Arredondo. Any news? They don't want to do it, they say it isn't simple, and until they see the money they won't lift a finger. What's with those bastards? why do they make you beg? They're the best, what's the big hurry? It's a present for a lady who just discovered Frida Kahlo. Does it have to be that one? It's the one she likes, she said so clearly. I'll see if I can convince them, and if I can't? No getting around it, pay them; by the way, tomorrow you'll get your cut for finding Andrade. Pretty eerie, eh? He doesn't sell his mother because he doesn't have one. Have you had breakfast? Yeah, I'll call you later on. From the window of his room with a river view he observed a spectacle that roused the boxing gene of his youth from its hibernation.

Yoreme was jogging along the bank of the Tamazula, shadowboxing. He was hearing Sony Alarcón narrating his fight. Left hook from Yoreme, now right, he dances away, feints, a jab to the face, he lands a blow near the liver, Caveman Galindo absorbs the punishment, lashes out with a pair of flying kicks but fails to touch the idol of Culiacán, the Kid moves in close and lets loose a flurry of hooks, Caveman doesn't feel the punches, he's choking, his nose is blocked, he's gasping though his mouth, Yoreme goes after him, gets set for his lethal weapon: the uppercut; at ringside his fans are cheering him on, I can see the great Efrén "the Scorpion" Torres, Huitlachoche José Medel, Barbed Wire Olivares, Butter Nápoles, Julio César Chávez, Finito López, Chiquita González, Salvador Sánchez, Morales the Terrible, Julio Cortázar. Yoreme pauses, acknowledges the cheers, but who is that there? ladies and gentlemen, it's the gorgeous dancer Roxana, carrying the crown she will place on the head of the champion, Kid Yoreme, the idol who had a little palm-leaf house and let in the vixen.

Across from the Hotel Lucerna, beside the bicycle path in Las Riberas Park, Yoreme suddenly froze. The crowd of walkers and joggers around him registered. He watched Dayana and Luis Ángel coming towards him, smiling. The recollection hit him like an earthquake: the night he followed Meraz and Roxana to that big house near the Alexa, where they went in and then the guy came out for his cell phone; he remembered the infinity of times Meraz had taken her out while he could only look. He remembered.

You killed her, you bastard, I saw you! Startled, Meraz stopped short; he was accustomed to the worst, but Yoreme's threatening gesture was impressive. He stood in front of the boxer. Young man, what are you talking about? You killed Roxana, asshole. He leapt on him. You killed her in the house with the yellow door. Double hook to the abdomen, uppercut to the jaw. Meraz dropped, out cold. Dayana screamed, everyone else was petrified, and the boxer raged on. He picked up the unconscious body and without anyone making a move to stop him, plunged into the river with it and held it under until it lay still.

Two policemen who happened to be nearby came running and pulled them out.

Thirty-Six

My man Lefty, I've lost my touch, Shorty Abitia said, you know what this business is like, you step away from the job for a minute and your contacts vanish, none of the people I saw knows anything about Kid Yoreme; listen, you're in the thick of things, is it true somebody killed Luis Ángel Meraz? Who told you that? Begoña, she says she heard it on the radio; listen, the one that didn't make it was Marcelo Valdés, eh? that's had Devil so busy we haven't heard a thing from him since. Mendieta did not want to reveal his ignorance: Well, he was getting on in years. Yeah, but did that old guy ever get things done. He killed a shitload of people. Well sure, but he also helped entire towns and you know what people say, if he hadn't put money into this city it'd still be a cow pasture. You sure are on top of things, fucking Shorty. I live up to the minute, my man Lefty, as you know. O.K., see you later. Don't forget my daughter's wedding. I'll be at that wedding if it's the last thing I do. He hung up, turned on the radio and there was Quiroz: "This morning, according to eyewitnesses, while he was jogging in Las Riberas Park, the much-lauded politician and former federal congressman Luis Ángel Meraz was attacked by a crazed pedestrian and dragged into the current of the Tamazula, where he was cunningly drowned before anyone could come to his aid. Two policemen walking their beat managed to capture the culprit, who is being interrogated in a holding cell at State Ministerial Police Headquarters. Rumour has it Meraz aspired to an important elective office, which has given those in the little world of politics reason to view his death with great suspicion. This is Daniel Quiroz reporting."

He dialled Ortega. No answer. With friends like these, who needs enemies? Eh, Montaño, what's up, are you scratching your itch? And how, after such a busy morning I deserve it, as a matter of fact I didn't see you there, Briseño kept asking for you. Are you talking about Meraz? Yup, they drowned him, it must be on the national news by now. Well, I'll leave you there in heaven. He hung up.

Though he was near Headquarters, he pulled over and parked. He lit a cigarette. The empty feeling was coming on strong and there was nothing he could do to stop it. Parra would not be back until Tuesday and now he didn't even have a suspect, was that why he felt suddenly lost? Luis Ángel Meraz, he muttered, how I would have liked to see you take the acid test, as you put it, the one everyone has to pass to prove they are what they claim to be; yes, you had the perfect alibi; and if it wasn't you, then who killed Mayra Cabral de Melo? He finished his cigarette. And who killed Yolanda?

Angelita greeted him excitedly: Boss, where were you? everybody here is going nuts. About Meraz? They're saying Marcelo Valdés died too. Who says? The police, right here. Pineda must be crying. You think? Not only because the guy died, but because a big mess is going to land in his lap, whenever there's a succession something happens; but we don't need to worry about Pineda, he'll probably do even better, he'll get extra commissions for keeping his mouth shut.

Shorty Abitia is looking for you. I already talked to him. Commander Briseño wants you to stay put until he gets back. From where? He's with the people interrogating the guy who murdered

Attorney Meraz. Is Gori with them? Yes, I think so, that's what I heard, people from the D.A.'s office came. I'll go see what's up.

I had a little palm-leaf house, I let in the vixen and once she was inside she told me this house is too small for the two of us and she threw me out; a rooster who felt sorry for me said, don't worry little rabbit, I'll chase that awful brute out of your house; so they went to his house and the rooster, cock-a-doodle-doo, crowed with all his might, he tried again and again, but the vixen paid no attention; the rooster knew he could do no more: I'm sorry, little rabbit, I can do no more, he's a fearsome beast, and he left, and the weepy little rabbit left too.

Yoreme's voice came out a bit distorted, but probably because of what he said Lefty recognised it and let out a sigh. Fucking Yoreme, no doubt about it, you are tougher than you are pretty. Terminator, who was watching through the one-way mirror, turned to Mendieta. This asshole is crazier than a fucking goat, for two hours he's been saying the same thing. He saw Briseño was there with two people from the D.A.'s office and Gori Hortigosa, who looked mystified. Yoreme was in a chair, staring at nothing, repeating his story.

The police stood up and went out. Briseño fixed him with a glare: Detective Mendieta, what have you been up to? Up to you know what. We caught the guy who killed Meraz, we've got no record on him, and he hasn't even wanted to tell us his name; it's worse, all he'll say is that insufferable drivel about a rabbit and a vixen; these people are from the D.A.'s office, they want to know if it has some political connection, they nodded, but the idiot can't even remember his own name and not even Gori has been able to get anything out of him; let's go eat, want to? Look, if you don't need me,

I'd rather stay here. When the superiors began to drift away, everybody else felt hungry too. Well, my man Lefty, I'm going to put away a few tacos, so let's send this buddy to his suite. Leave him, my man Termi, let me see if I can loosen his tongue. Aren't you afraid he'll give you a knuckle sandwich? No way, don't worry about me. Do you want me to stay? Take a break, Gori, go have lunch with the rest, they might need you.

Fucking Yoreme, you really did it this time, you bastard. My buddy Caveman, what's happening, bro? He stood up, then sat down and lowered his head. Are you still mad about what I did to you? you know I met a milkman and he took me to see Padre Cuco, I had a little house, then I saw a driver who, listen, I let in the vixen, the feds have your car, I have an idea for a fight at the Revo, I'm training. Yoreme, shut your trap, asshole, why did you kill Meraz? Who's Meraz? The politician. I had a little palm-leaf house. He grabbed him by the hair. Shut up, don't give me that bullshit. I won't hit you again, Cavey, I promise. O.K., asshole, now tell me why you drowned Meraz. Cavey, what are we doing here? weren't you going to take me to see Roxana? Sure, I'll take you, Yoreme, I'll take you, but tell me why you gave the ring-around-the-rosey to the buddy who used to take out the queen. He let out a sob: He killed her, Cavey, he killed her. Did you see him? Yoreme sobbed harder. Where did he kill her? How would I know, but he killed her, he only wanted her for himself, he lorded it over everybody every time he took her out. Mendieta understood, gave the boxer a few pats on the back. Crying a bit less, Yoreme reminded him: So, when are we going to rumble? mask against mane, that's something Culiacán's never seen. Lefty said nothing and walked out. In the hall, Gori Hortigosa approached him. My respects, Lefty my man. My friend Gori, when the chief comes back, tell him I put the file on this dude on his desk. Terminator touched his arm: Before I forget, Lefty, that box didn't fit the mark on the carpet.

He felt bad. He called Angelita to tell her to give the file to Briseño, took two tranquillisers, and left the building. If there's a place for me in this world, I don't think I'll have time to find it.

Cavalry charge. Boss, where are you? Where I deserve to be. I heard about Meraz and I'm wondering. Don't even think about coming back, if I see you in Culiacán before Monday I'll toss you in the slammer. Well, you better hurry because I'm walking into Headquarters. What about Rodo? He's great, last night he gave me a lovely ring and I think I'm going to be very happy with him. I'm pleased, but watch your temper, Agent Toledo, what was that all about anyway? Boss, that has never happened to me before, it's true I was having my period, but, I don't know, I felt like a zero without the ring. Listen, come over to El Quijote.

Let's see, boss, Meraz is dead, but we aren't sure he was Mayra's killer, the guys from Mazatlán obviously don't fit the profile, and it isn't Kid Yoreme or Aguirrebere or Canela either. I don't think it's the manager and Ramírez is evading us. The interrogation made Camila Naranjo ill, Elisa Calderón is a tough cookie, but that's all; Yolanda Estrada is like a shadow, it's as if she hadn't died, what did you make of Miroslava? Nothing there; you know what I think, Zelda? there's a piece of the puzzle we're leaving out; you said you wanted to ask Calderón a few more questions and the Apache says Mayra would go out with powerful people who weren't narcos or the Alexa's usual clientele; she danced at Club Sinaloa, we've got to pick up the thread there. Boss, remember the footprints? What footprints? The ones at the crime scene, they were work boots, army-style, or a mountaineer's. Olmedo might use those, right? Others could too, is there anything on the girl with no tits? Case closed, the murderer is her ex and he's a good friend of the chief's, and before you ask he confessed his crime and said he had nothing to do with killing Mayra; this morning I had breakfast with Paty Olmedo, she told me her father came to see her, they cried together and reconciled, and he told her to get ready because she was going to be his only heir; she was a little frightened and she asked him not to rush things, not to think about retiring; she even said: Papa, why don't you find a woman, one your age or younger? you're at your peak, not that you should let it go to your head, but my girl-friends tell me you're still attractive. Forget it, daughter, young women are a disaster; I had a girlfriend, a beauty, last night I found out they killed her. Oh, Papa, what bad luck. I'll say. Could you tell me who she was? Anita Roy's dance teacher, we had dinner several times. Was she really beautiful? One eye was green and the other the colour of honey, tanned, Brazilian. I'm so sorry, Papa, how sad.

They fell silent.

Boss, I'll ask them to bring in Elisa Calderón and Ramírez, how's that sound?

Mendieta told her about Win and that he was expecting a call from Devil Urquídez, who right then was getting him a new appoint-ment with Samantha Valdés, because the previous had to be post-poned due to an emergency.

I'll go see Olmedo; when you have those two, call me.

*

He received him in the room with the guitars, wearing a pair of filthy boots. Music: "La Mer" by Charles Trenet.

Señor Olmedo, I have several questions I hope you will answer without obliging me to allude to money laundering or other crimes in which your name has been mentioned. Olmedo listened indifferently and waved his hand as if to say nothing mattered. I know you were friends with Mayra Cabral de Melo, Roxana, who was murdered on Sunday night, when did you last see her? That very day, I took her home about midnight. Silence. Did you accompany her to the door? No, I left her in the street, she never allowed me near her house; I found out yesterday when I went to see her, the Phantom told me. Is he your contact? He nodded. So what happened? you left her near her door and? he noticed the boots. Right, I dropped her off on the corner of Carrasco, she walked to her building, and I drove on to the parkway. Did you see anything in the street? people? cars? A big dark car, I even saw a guy get out and say hello to her; that's all. Lefty took out the photographs of the tyre marks. Señor Olmedo, we found tracks made by a car like the one you describe, did you notice anything particular? something that might help in the investigation? She had plenty of clients, it wasn't the first time I dropped her off and someone was waiting. We believe these tyre marks are from the murderer's car, they go deeper because the car is armoured. Olmedo studied the photographs. They're the latest Goodyears, you can't get these yet in Mexico, and yes, they're made for big cars, for city driving and they're very durable on country roads. Has anyone bought a car like that from you, one that might use these tyres? Well, I'll take a look, but don't get your hopes up; call me in two hours. He returned the photographs. Where and when did you pick her up? Near her house at about four, we were going to eat in Altata, but she changed her mind, I went with her to pay her electric and telephone bills, we bought a couple of sandwiches, fruit, water, and we sat on the riverbank; she didn't like to drink, he looked at Mendieta, who was listening calmly; as a matter of fact, she got bitten by ants, on her arms; at ten o'clock she asked me to drive her to the Alexa, she said she had taken two days off; when I dropped her there we argued a little, I told her our relationship scared me, she got back in and we went to talk until I left her at her house. You were driving a brand-new white pickup with Sonora plates. Olmedo smiled: I can see you aren't really, he said. What do you mean? Well, I always thought the police were a bunch of dummies. I understand; one more thing: I met a man who told me you were his friend; he's tall, heavyset, white. Leo McGiver. Where does he live? That I don't know, but not in Culiacán. He led me to understand he was a lawyer, but I don't believe it. Gandhi looked up at Jeff Beck's guitar. He got me that piece. Lefty turned to the wall, then back to Olmedo. But his real business is guns, he added, while Claude Bolling began to sing "Borsalino". He insinuated that he worked for Dioni de la Vega. I know nothing about that, not long ago he told me he knows a brother of yours, I don't recall the name. That's amazing. What? Nothing, I was thinking out loud, were you friends with Luis Ángel Meraz? We maintained good relations, so sad what happened to him. He was also a friend of Mayra's. He was the one who introduced me to her, at Club Sinaloa. Who else from the club was her client? Easier to say who wasn't, but the one who really got stuck on her was me, I'd go see her two or three times a week. I suppose most of them drive big cars. And they buy them at my shop, you'll see the list soon enough. We found footprints at the crime scene that look like your boots. We all wear these, but if you want to analyse them, go ahead and take them. That won't be necessary, your daughter already made me change my mind about you. Cavalry charge. Mendieta, Lefty answered thinking it would be Zelda, but no, it was Devil Urquídez: My man Lefty, I'll see you at the Apostolis in three hours.

The men looked at each other. Did you know her, detective? More or less, did you have any contact with Yolanda Estrada? No, but Roxana spoke of her with great affection. Did she tell you about anything else, any threats or difficult clients? She never mentioned it. Silence. Have you been to Meraz's house, the one with a yellow door, near the Alexa? No, my dealings with him were at the club; find the culprit, detective, in fact, if you get him, I'll trade you a new car for your old one, you can pick out any one you like. Lefty smiled. It's a deal, Gandhi exclaimed, and they shook hands.

Thirty-Seven

Richie Bernal's new black pickup was wrapped around the fence outside the Culiacán Institute of Technology, leaking fluids and giving off smoke. Inside, the body of the young man held more than fifty bullets, same story for each of his four bodyguards, who ended their careers then and there. "El Hijo Desobediente" by Los Tigres del Norte was playing at full volume. The curious kept their distance, as the savagery was such that for once no-one dared go any closer. Two patrol cars of transit police pulled up, their occupants showing little inclination to take charge.

The killers had been waiting for him near the mansion and caught up to him on Obregón Avenue across from San Miguel Mall. They knew Richie was restless, bold, and that he would go back to roaming the streets. Ideal for sending a message to Samantha. When he reached the fork across from the Tech they went at him. A pickup pulled up on either side and the five hitmen in each let loose with their A.K.-47s. Bernal's people responded, but it was useless. His pickup was brand new and with all the hurry to get things ready for the funeral it had not been armoured.

Richie had been wandering sadly around the house. He was a nephew of La Jefa, but that would not save him from being rep-rimanded. He had crossed a line, he knew it, and she would never forgive him for the deaths of Rafa and Grunt. After the meeting of the kingpins, which he helped guard, he stayed on in the resi-dence in case the call came, but no, the honchos were too busy. So he suggested to his men that they all go eat hamburgers before he got chewed out and maybe sent back to his hut in the mountains of Badiraguato. Boss, wouldn't you rather have tacos? there's a place I know on Patria where they're delicious. I want burgers and that's what we'll eat, got it? Near La Lomita there's a place where they say they're pretty good. Let's go, he turned up the volume on the stereo and stepped on the gas.

Thirty-Eight

Following Zelda's recommendation, Lefty went to Puye's to eat a dozen clams with lime and chillies, and half a dozen oysters on the shell.

Perhaps you are a person of few friends and you see them mostly through your work, or maybe they live far away. One night you run into one of them by some miracle and then you see him again several times over the following days, even though you're not looking for him. That happens all over, and here you are watching the bastard walk in wearing a black T-shirt and a tired expression; he's a badge and the brother of one of your best friends. Fucking Lefty, I'm glad you turned up. Mendieta spied Teo's big smile and sat down with him. It's your turn to pick up the tab. Only yours? Like I said, as stuck-up as your brother. The food came and Lefty gulped the first spicy raw clam. How's things, on your way back home? What's this all about? why so much aphrodisiac? Just in case. Well, just in case, my babe has a sister who's younger and even better looking. I'll pass. They were drinking beer. What's the story on your friend, did you catch him? The bum is behind bars. You must have given him twenty years for insulting the authorities. Twenty-five. I don't doubt it, badges are a sadistic bunch; so, any news on Susy? did she drop by with the son you gave her? Not yet. Who would have thought that you, the fucking snot-nose, would pull that one on her. Take note, where I put my eye I plug the target. What needs a plug are your batteries, according to your bro the dude is about to start college and Susy can't manage that on her own. She should just tell me how much, all she has to do is ask. You're willing to miss a few payments on the beach house in Altata? For my son, I would do anything at all. Now there's a real man, not a little fucker. Listen, Teo, do you remember a tall, white guy from the Col Pop, he's kind of hefty now, whose name is, or at least he calls himself, Leo McGiver? Teo studied him. What about him? He's a suspect in a murder and I can see you do know him. Was he the one who offed your girl? Lefty considered for a moment. It could be, all I'm sure of is he took down a dude in the Hotel San Luis. They lit up and inhaled. I know him, or better put I used to know him, he was quite the tough guy; I remember he used to smuggle Levis and soap from the United States. He took a drag, blew out the smoke, and continued. So Leo is still alive, are you going to put the squeeze on him? When I get him in my sights. The waiter brought over an ashtray, a couple of beers, and picked up the dishes. Enrique knew him too, knew him well. Lefty dialled his brother. What's up, bro? No, this is a miracle, I'm always the one who calls, I hope you aren't dying. That isn't the surprise I have for you. Don't get married, little brother, you're fine as you are. I'm not that brave. Nor that stupid, so what's the surprise? He handed the telephone to his companion. What's up, commander? Teo was smiling like a little kid. Let him tell you the story, I've already told him several times how he's just as annoying as you. Teo listened for a few minutes. She turned out really good, she keeps me warm as can be at night; listen to me, you bastard, Leo McGiver's here, he killed a dude and your bro is about to lay his gloves on him, what do you think? He listened, then said O.K. He handed the cell phone to Lefty. What's up? Are you going to fuck with Leo? He killed a dude. Was the dude a good guy?

Well, I doubt it, he worked for one of the biggest narcos. In other words, a great scientist was not lost. I don't think so. Look, I owe Leo a favour, Teo will explain it; Susana and Jason are about to leave for Culiacán, I hope you can spend some time with the kid. I can't fool you, I'm anxious to meet him. I like that and I hope you aren't bullshitting me, you bastard. How could you think such a thing? Well, here's a big hug for you.

Teo took a swig and lit another cigarette. Lefty waited. Ever since we were little kids Leo was special, wild, crazy, at ease with everything; I don't think you ever met him because they left the Col Pop when you were small, but he was always our buddy; when we took up arms, he sold us the weapons. I gather he's a big-time gunrunner now. Your bro asked me to talk to you about the favour he owes him; before I say anything, you should know he wants me to tell you so you won't throw Leo in the clink; if you can't promise that, we'd better leave things as they are. Enrique, who's been out of the country for so many years, owes McGiver a favour? nobody could refuse to go along with that, much less Lefty Mendieta: The jerk walks, none of my people will touch him. That's the way I like it, be a man, he took a drag; so, Enrique killed a guy; that's right; I went with him, he told me he had an outstanding account and the time had come to settle it; we went to a house, and since the dude did not want me to go to the door with him, I thought it was about money; not at all; I saw him knock, a man I knew opened up, and Enrique put a bullet in his forehead; the guy went down just like that; your bro came trotting back. What's the story, fucking Quique? what the hell was that about? That was something I owed him. But he was a priest, you bastard, a priest. Yeah, but the faggot was a child molester and now he's fucked.

Lefty dropped his cigarette. Teo was so caught up in the recollection he did not notice how pale his companion's face had turned or that his breath had grown short. Everything got complicated; since I was really nervous I nearly crashed into a fucking patrol car, they pulled us over, took us out, frisked us, then beat the shit out of us; we were so freaked out we didn't even feel the blows, your fucking brother didn't kill any old Christian, he offed a priest.

That's when McGiver showed up; he was a buddy of the badges, he greased their palms and they let us go; he gave them the heaters and the car, which we had liberated anyhow.

We were at his house when some bigwig from the D.A.'s office came to the door; if he didn't turn Enrique in, they would come and take him; the dude faced the music and he didn't flinch; that very night was the first time your bro dressed up as a woman, same as me; we left for Los Mochis wearing miniskirts and we holed up for three days in the house of some guy named Poncho, until McGiver took us to San Luis Río Colorado in a small aeroplane that he filled with pistols and rifles later on; then he got your bro across to the other side with a false passport and put him in a safe-house. Silence. Did Enrique ever tell you why he owed the priest a bullet? Never, and I never asked him. He stubbed out the cigarette. It's your turn to pay, fucking little Lefty. They stood up. We'll be keeping an eye out for each other. And they left the place.

In the Jetta, he broke down and wept.

He didn't stop to think how long it had been since he last cried or any of that shit. He just cried like an idiot. When he calmed down he called his brother. So? Thank you, bro. Silence. Well, get to work, it'll keep you in shape. Yeah, and away from temptations, his voice broke. Forget it, you bastard, forget it; we'll talk later. Click.

Is there anything better than a brother? Don't give me that shit, faggots, of course there isn't.

Well, maybe a sister.

He picked up Win Harrison, who was dressed the same as the day before. She asked what time they were going to see Marcelo Valdés. I think that one is going to stay on your wish-list, remember the long line of cars we saw yesterday when we left the San Luis? well, they were taking him to the cemetery. Then let's see his daughter. Samantha? aren't you stepping beyond your turf? No, all I can tell you is she is the next stop on the road to finding Simak's murderer. You don't get it, she and I have a relationship of intense loathing. Well, a little love wouldn't hurt either of you. That's something you won't ever see in your life, she is a difficult woman. Is there another kind? Lefty smiled. Besides, we've been working for like twenty-five hours, your time is up. I meant total working hours. Win understood Mexicans, their strange and at times ingenuous sense of humour. So, on another topic I asked a trusted colleague what we had on Miguel de Cervantes, besides being a novelist; this is what we found:

Name: Ander Aramendi, thirty-four years old. One of the most dangerous members of the E.T.A. Birthplace unknown, but he grew up in Biarritz and Valencia. In the organisation for at least fifteen years and suspected of acting on his own for the last three. Spotted in Spain, France, Mexico, Venezuela, and the United States, where he probably worked as a hitman for murders and acts of terrorism. His aliases are writers and artists of the sixteenth and seventeenth centuries: Miguel de Cervantes, Francisco de Quevedo, Pedro Calderón, and Diego Velázquez.

How do you like that? you had an international fugitive in your grasp. Could someone like that really live in Mexico? Well, you saw him, you talked to him, and you took his picture. Mendieta remained silent, then said: Of course, he could easily have killed the girl. The girl, you, and everyone else in that bar. And Simak too? It's a possibility, but not the most likely, know anything about a gunrunner named Leo McGiver? Tell me. Simak was also into smuggling and he was supposed to meet McGiver, who has some sort of exclusive arrangement for this country; before he turned up dead Simak signed an agreement to supply the Mexican army, which was then cancelled and now McGiver and his group will benefit; I know he's with the Valdés family now, which is why I really need to see Samantha; from what I've been told she'll become head of the cartel. Actually, we have a date with her in thirty minutes. Oh, by the way you can throw away the photograph you have in your office, the lady has been identified. Who is she? That is something I am not authorised to tell you. What jerks.

He turned down the volume on the stereo, which was playing "Reach Out, I'll Be There" by the Four Tops. Do me a favour. A big one? A friend of my chief's killed his wife and he's in Canada, from the glove compartment he pulled out a napkin, this is the address of his son in Toronto, I want to know what weapon he used and if he also killed Mayra Cabral de Melo. He had been planning to break into his house in Los Álamos that night, but thought he might as well set things in motion. Win looked at him. You want the Bureau to work for you? He turned the music back up. A hit from 1966. Win looked out at the Tamazula River as they headed across it, pulled out her cell phone, and punched in a number.

Thirty-Nine

When they entered the restaurant several of the tables were occupied by bodyguards drinking soft drinks. Devil Urquídez welcomed them. What's up, Lefty my friend? everything O.K.? On target, my man Devil, what about you? Good, but what can you do? you know Richie got killed? What's wrong with me, Lefty wondered, lately I don't find out about anything. Guess I'd better send my condolences. Right, it'd be hypocritical, but Richie might appreciate the joke, after this we're having the body sent to his family; she won't be long, you can wait for her in here. He opened the door to a private room where a table with three high-backed chairs was set with an array of low-calorie snacks.

I don't intend to be part of this conversation, and since I have fulfilled my duty forgive me if I feel liberated; you can tell me later what comes of that favour, but first fill me in on El Continente. I went to see Adán Carrasco, the owner, this morning and everything is back to normal; he used to be one of ours and he still lives like an American: ham and eggs for breakfast with pancakes and bacon on the side, he eats his steaks with French fries, his car is big, and he bets on the Cowboys. Is Mister B. still hunting? I am not authorised to reveal anything regarding the president's family. Lefty smiled coldly. Samantha Valdés walked in dressed in black, red lips, decisive. Sit down, Lefty Mendieta, I don't eat people. I'd rather be on my way; they shook hands. No, no, you should stay, if I decided to waste my time it's not for her, it's for you, I need to speak with you. I'll send

251

Pineda over. I'm not interested in Pineda, the one I want to deal with is you. Listen, sorry to hear about Richie, and I really would prefer we speak another time, I'll give you a raincheck. Don't be a dunce, Mendieta, why spend your life vegetating like an idiot when you could be living like a tycoon? I'll hear you out, but not now. The women sat down and he went to find Urquídez. Devil, my buddy, I need to know the whereabouts of a man who does business with the señora, Leo McGiver. You're in luck, my man Lefty, he's waiting for her in the Hummer. Send a guy out with me so he'll open up, I need two words with him. I'd better ask the boss, hang on. He spoke with Max Garcés, who had been listening to their conversation, he nodded. Devil himself accompanied him to the vehicle with tinted windows and closed the car door behind him.

McGiver smiled. A pleasure to see you, detective, how goes the investigation? So what did you mean when you told me dark days were coming? Leo's gaze was a dagger. You have been sentenced, Mendieta. By whom? McGiver continued eyeing him, as was his habit. Outside, Devil and Guacho were standing guard. Are you sure you're not from the Col Pop? What I asked is who wants to kill me. The smuggler made a face. In front of me, Richie Bernal asked Dioni de la Vega to take you down, I warned you because something tells me you are from the Col Pop, a neighbourhood close to my heart; now Richie's dead and Dioni is getting stronger and more daring all the time, what are you going to do? Mendieta did not light a cigarette. There inside, an F.B.I. agent is asking Samantha Valdés for your head. McGiver's smile disappeared. Do you know why? You killed Sergio Carrillo in the Hotel San Luis, your prints were on the telephone, that's my business; then you took out Peter Connolly, an

F.B.I. agent, over an arms contract. McGiver's expression grew hard. They know all that? Lefty nodded. This comes with a grateful hello from Enrique Mendieta. McGiver scrutinised him once more before breaking into a smile. Who would have thunk it, eh? He tilted his head and nodded appreciatively. So how is he? He seems well, Teo too. McGiver thought for a moment. A couple of locos. Listen, I know you smuggle just about anything, did you bring in an armoured car with tyres like these? He glanced at the photographs. It's been years since I sold cars and when I did they were classics; you should ask Fabián Olmedo, he has all the contacts; listen, thank you and say hello to your brother. I'll do that.

We know Mayra Cabral de Melo had other clients besides the usual ones, the ones you mentioned; big shots who came to the Alexa to get her or picked her up at her house. She was a bitch, I told you that, and I don't know who she had dealings with, that's why I don't let them fool around on their own, they don't get it that this is a high-risk profession; I don't have any names, but I do know she went out with farm owners and politicians, a lot of them she met at Club Sinaloa, only Attorney Ramírez would know about that. Any army officers? No idea, but would you doubt it? They spoke for thirty minutes, until Zelda figured that was all she knew. You can go. Thank you and congratulations on the ring, now the thing is for real. Zelda smiled weakly, she was not so sure about that, but she was damn sure she would never again bare that side of her personality to a witness.

She was still going head-to-head with Ramírez when Lefty came in. Detective, what a pleasure to see you, would you please explain to the señorita that the case of Roxana and Yhajaira is closed? when I tried to speak with your chief I couldn't reach him. With the death of Meraz it reopened all on its own. He stopped smiling. Even if that's so this has nothing to do with me and I have more important things to do. He rose from his chair. Sit down, Ramírez; Lefty's eyes were giving off sparks. The lawyer obeyed. What I said is true, the dead girls are none of my business. I want to know who asked you to request a suspension of the investigation. Luis Ángel Meraz and now he's dead; we were about to close on the sale of the business and we didn't want the story in the news. Who was the buyer? Imelda Terán, she's fronting for Dioni de la Vega. What would a narco want with a second-rate strip club? Is that what you think of it? listen, it keeps food on the table for quite a few families and turns a sizeable profit for the owners. Has Dioni seen the place? No, but he met Roxana at the Sinaloa. Where you took her that last night? Ramírez lowered his head and considered. The Friday before she died, I left her at a residence Dioni keeps near the Alexa and the next I heard she was dead. Did Meraz know about that relationship? He nodded. And did you have anything going with Roxana? Well, I never slept with her; I saw her naked because I took a number of photographs of her, we wanted to make a brochure for the clients, she had them blown up and she hung them in her bedroom. Who did you distribute the brochure to? In the end we didn't do it, no-one liked that tattoo she has that practically kisses her labia; when you're locked and loaded who wants another penis along? she maintained it gave her twice the pleasure, but that didn't matter. The information you are providing is very useful, why didn't you show your face until now? I was out of town, I went to look at a group of girls in Guadalajara, as a matter of fact they're due to arrive tomorrow.

Ramírez led them to the house. Yellow door.

The watchman greeted them at the gate, told them Señor de la Vega had left the previous Sunday early in the morning and had not returned, neither had he called. The man was about seventy years old and did not look like a hired gun. How long have you been working for Señor de la Vega? Since I was a child, first for his father and for the past fifteen years for him. Did you meet Roxana? Of course, the prettiest woman I've ever seen. Did she come here with de la Vega? Sure, in fact they came on Friday night about ten o'clock and left Sunday morning, they looked happy; though it's none of my business, as far as I'm concerned those two really loved each other, I heard he was going to buy the bar where she worked and give it to her. You know the girl was murdered? One of Dioni's bodyguards told me that, what a shame. Does your boss own other vehicles or only cars? Come on, ever since he was a boy all he loved was trucks, his wife has a B.M.W. but I never saw him driving it. And has he always been so bullheaded? Absolutely, but now he won't go anywhere without his bodyguards. What colour is the señora's car? Sea blue.

Rodo came by Headquarters to pick up Zelda. Before he arrived, she and Lefty went over Olmedo's list of all the businessmen, politicians, narcos, and members of the city diocese who had bought luxury cars, without finding anyone worth pursuing. A car with gringo tyres, the detective thought aloud. Since her price was high, whoever was driving it has plenty of money and the time to wait around for her. Who would have spent a Sunday waiting for her?

Silence. Someone with no family, someone from out of town, or someone totally stuck on her. Lefty tried to picture it: Yolanda opened the door. Yhajaira, how are you? Fine, Roxana went out early. You aren't fooling me, are you? He pushed her aside and went to Mayra's room and then to hers. Yolanda stood still. The guy returned to the living room. I'm going to wait for her, understand? O.K., but not here, it's my birthday and I'm expecting someone. He blew up, yanked the picture of the football team off the wall, and threw it at. No, maybe Bigboy saw him when he came to the birthday party. A priest, said Zelda, interrupting his thoughts, and Lefty choked, those guys have no immediate family, at least not publicly. If it was somebody from out of town, we're fucked, Mendieta said to change the subject, have you noticed how many big, dark cars there are around here? And they continued speculating until Rodo arrived a few minutes later.

He went back to the house with the yellow door. I need to see your boss. I told him you'd come by and he wasn't happy, he said to tell you to go fuck your. Hang on, talk to him, tell him Lefty Mendieta wants to see him. The old man gave him the once-over and closed the door. Two minutes later he reappeared and handed him a cell phone: It's Señorita Imelda. Lefty introduced himself, I want to speak with Dioni de la Vega. What about? That's none of your business, tell him to stop acting like a fool and pick up the fucking telephone. The watchman's eyes opened wide. I don't like your style. I don't give a shit, señorita, tell that bastard if he has any balls he'll get on the line. Shut your trap, you fucking turd of a badge, I'm not Richie Bernal. I don't give a fuck about Richie, the one I'm calling about is Mayra Cabral de Melo, why did you cut off her nipple?

Silence. That shut you up, you fucking narco, too bad I don't have you in front of me so I could bust your face. You're barking up the wrong tree, copper, the wrong fucking forest, and you better not step out of line if you don't want to get snuffed; that the Valdés family protects you means shit to me, you're going to pay for pulling this stunt, and listen, I would never have killed Roxana, do you hear me? never, I'd cut off a ball first. Cut them both off while you're at it. I'm doing my own investigating and I'm closing in on the culprit; I'm not going to let this lie, copper, I'm going to make that bastard pay. Lefty wanted to tell him he was after the same thing but he held his tongue. I don't want you messing with this, not you or anybody else, and just so you know I'm not lying, I'm going to let you in on something: Richie Bernal asked me to take you down; don't worry, now that they took care of him, I'm not going to bother, but the bastard who fucked with my girl and defiled her is dead meat, and you better stay out of the way if you don't want to be worth shit, understand? or are you wanting to come over to me? if that's the case the first thing you need to understand is Dioni de la Vega's people are Dioni de la Vega's people and nobody else's. Where can I meet you? Imelda will pick you up, but not now, tomorrow or the next day, today is special, I've got something much better happening, and if I picked up the telephone it was only to stop you from making such a fucking pest of yourself. You know the buddy who killed her drives an armoured American car? I know, I also know he took the eighteen thousand dollars my girl had on her, and let me tell you again: you will not get that asshole, he's mine, you'll see what I do with him.

While he drove towards El Quijote he thought about the nipple, and if de la Vega wanted to settle this, let him, all in all, they're two peas in a pod. Oh, Mayra, my queen, you liked to walk between the horse's legs and in the mud. So, where do we badges walk? *I don't believe you're a badge, you've got that charm nice guys have that makes them look ridiculous.* Maybe it would be better to bark at the moon.

Forty

Castelo was nervous. He looked at his watch: 6.43 in the evening. What the fuck was he doing here when he should be at home drinking coffee and taking it easy, watching television, chatting with his wife? A favour. What's up, fucking Foreman? did you finally get over being a faggot? Hello, señor, not yet, it's not like the flu, you know. The previous afternoon he had received a call from the main fixer for the head of the Tijuana Cartel. Then a few hours later came another from a cousin of the top honcho in Nogales, Sonora, and in the morning a third from the captain of the guards of the godfather of Reynosa. They wanted to hold a meeting and needed his house in Altata, about sixty kilometres from Culiacán. They all asked if he could do them the favour of lending it to them. The meeting would take place at some point that very night. In advance, two men from each gang would come to inspect the place. The house was located at the edge of a mangrove that Castelo cared for with the fervour of an ecologist: when he was drunk he would pee in it, which was supposed to protect it from ants. On the other side lay the bay, always calm except in hurricane season; two hundred metres up the coast stood the white mansion of the closest neighbour, and beyond it the restaurants.

Foreman had done work for all three narcos and could not refuse. They had made it clear that the day he would not lend his friends a hand was the day his life would unravel. What good is a jerk like that?

The men who arrived at noon said nothing to him. They checked the bedrooms, the roof, the tanks of the toilets, the cistern. He realised the one giving the orders was the guy from Sonora. Then they unloaded a case of Chivas Regal 25, several boxes of shrimp, meat, chorizos, sausages, spices, gallons of purified water, and twenty cases of beer. I think I'll leave you now, Castelo said with a smile, make yourselves at home, this is the key for locking up and. You are not going anywhere, Don Foreman, warned the lieutenant of the Nogales kingpin, those are our orders, you can sleep, watch television, whatever you want, but you're staying here. Those assholes don't trust me, he thought. Do you know if they want me for anything? Why don't you cook supper? they're going to be hungry as beasts when they get here; for sure my boss is going to want shrimp *ceviche*. Bro, said the one from Tijuana, stop playing the dummy, cook something for us and make supper for the bosses. Mine will want shrimp in *salsa ranchera*, really hot, the Reynosa guy said. The one from Sonora said his boss would be happy with beef. Foreman smiled, sipped from his litre mug of coffee, then went into the kitchen. He understood this was an order. Sons of fucking bitches. He left his white panama hat on the table and put on an apron. His bald pate shone.

At 7.35 a roar of engines announced the approach of half a dozen pickups and S.U.V.s. Six A.K.-47s got the vehicles in their sights. Riding in the cargo beds were twelve gunslingers, their automatic rifles and a grenade launcher at the ready. See who it is, said the guy from Sonora. Castelo crossed the small garden to the entrance gate crowned by a flowering bougainvillaea, where the caravan had stopped. Fore-man, open this fucker, yelled the don of the Tijuana

Cartel, who was driving the lead vehicle, and hey, thanks for lending us your spot, we won't be too much bother. If you don't eat what I've cooked, don't invite me again. We're starving, the Nogales boss shouted, you wouldn't have any shrimp on hand there, would you? Wait until you try them, you won't want to share. Castelo walked along beside the rolling pickup. Put me on the list for the shrimp, too, hollered the one from Reynosa from the back seat of the dual-cabin, and fuck whoever turns tail, what about you, Quintana? Oh, I think we should eat like regular folk, Eloy said, while he shook Foreman's hand, what about you, Dioni, will you have the usual? I dance to whatever they're playing. So, let's eat, the one from Reynosa was still going on breakfast. Quintana ordered his lieutenant: Make sure the boys are well positioned outside and give them some feed. I'll take care of it, hesignalled two of his companions to follow him.

The narcos occupied a table that in a moment was filled with delicacies: shrimp *ceviche*, *aguachile*, grilled sausages, fried chorizo, *carne asada*, red snapper *zarandeado*. As soon as the man from Reynosa sat down he was served his *ranchera* shrimp. At a side table, a hitman opened beers and readied the whisky. Two salt shakers bearing Coca-Cola logos lent the table a sense of order. Each kept his gun at hand.

For more than an hour they ate and entertained themselves with happy memories: Do you remember when I was into killing young guys with white shirts? What a mess you got us into, we had to take down the commander of the federal police.

Then they moved on to the purpose of the meeting. The killer in charge of the drinks handed around glasses of whisky. Quintana took it straight. The salt shakers were down by half.

The one from Tijuana spoke up. This war is something new, they don't want to negotiate, it seems what they're hungering for now are bodies. If that's what they want, they won't be hard to beat, the trouble is our operations will get disrupted and the bros won't want to work. That's no problem, a shitload of people are unemployed. Like twenty million. Not all of them are any good. Out of twenty million some of them have to be. A lot, I'd say. The people in the mountains, how are they doing? They're all set, the weapons arrived last week and they're waiting for us to give the word. Mine are all lined up, too. But we should wait; let them throw the first fucking punch. They've already thrown a few in Michoacán. That must be their strategy. Where did Samantha get her guns? From a guy named McGiver, but he's small-time, we've got the good ones. McGiver's my guy too, but he still hasn't delivered. Don't forget they killed the gringo who was our contact. Who did him? Nobody knows. Until a new one turns up, McGiver will do. I'm not so sure, it looks like Samantha's got him in her net. What about our friends in government, what do they say? Nothing yet, they'll let us know what's what before long, but we can't rest easy. The point is that Samantha's idea of negotiating is fucking ridiculous, we need someone with balls in command and the one who has them is Eloy Quintana. I'm with you, Don Eloy. Me too. They all pledged to follow him. They would break with the cartel and form their own group, they would hire whatever gringos they needed and then put up a fight, in a few years they would be the ones on top. Quintana explained his plans and ambitions at some length: All of Sonora would be theirs, plus all the territories the others represented. They got to their feet and embraced. Dioni, now you'll be boss in Culiacán; who is this guy

McGiver? A smuggler, apparently he's from here. Well, we've got to put him down, he's in too far. I'll take care of it. Castelo, panama hat over his eyes, swirled his whisky in the bedroom next door without taking a sip. He was chain-smoking.

They said goodbye. Foreman, thanks, and don't forget, whatever you need, here you've got friends not fuckers. Ten minutes later, the only sound was the roar of vehicles fading into the distance. On the table sat a pile of dollars that Castelo did not touch. He turned out the lights and sat drinking coffee. He preferred it to whisky. He thought of his children, who were expecting babies. Can you guess when he would allow his descendants to get involved in shady business? Never.

Forty-One

Mendieta was chatting with the night watchman. Sitting on a couple of bags of cement, they were smoking, taking it easy. That's right, he came back at dawn; big dark-brown car; he went by at a crawl, looking over his shoulder; I thought he was going to get out, but no, he kept going, then he accelerated and disappeared towards the freeway to Mazatlán. Are you sure? Who was it said the devil knows more for being old than for being the devil and there is nothing stupid about me? White smoke drifted up. I couldn't see the driver clearly, but I saw the car. And you say it didn't look like a Mexican car. As far as I'm concerned it's a gringo car, a little jacked up, wide tyres. The city is full of those cars, the detective reflected, what would be easier to find, a car or a man? a man, of course, cars don't make mistakes. They lit up again and spent a few minutes in silence, watching the night. Why hasn't it rained? They say the climate is changing. On the day of San Juan a few drops fell, but that was it. Watch out, it might come flooding down all at once next month. This is the second time I've seen you here, I never thought the police really looked for culprits. Well, now you know. Was that girl something to you? Last puff. A friend; Lefty stood up, well, I'm going home, have a good night. You know something? the old fellow stood up as well, maybe the man you're looking for doesn't live here, because he went by heading that way, then he made a U-turn and drove by slowly on his way back. Was the car noisy? Not at all, it was like silk.

At home he went over Olmedo's list once more: no foreigners. If he's a gringo there's no reason his name would be on it.

For hours he ruminated on the case without reaching any conclusions. What about Rivera, where does he fit in? What can I say, another unsolved case.

Forty-Two

The convoy of drug lords took the highway to Culiacán. In the most protected position rode the Hummer belonging to Eloy Quintana, the region's new godfather. They were going pretty fast. At the fork for the New Altata development, they came face-to-face with the devil. Two vehicles fired bazookas at them head on, two more hit them from New Altata Road, plus another two from the rear. Quintana's men returned the fire, but it was too late. Fifty-four gunslingers armed with A.K.-47s and Barrett rifles came at them from the gas station on one side of the highway and the beer store on the other, running and shooting like crazy until nothing moved. Funereal scene. Futile fire. Max Garcés and his lieutenants leapt out from their hiding places to give each victim a *coup de grâce*. Zero losses. Samantha Valdés, dressed in black, hair pulled back, drove up in her dual-cabin pickup. Guacho opened the door of a Hummer and there was Quintana, wounded. He's mine, the woman said firmly. Quintana looked up. Garcés handed her a Smith & Wesson. You're just like your father. I don't think so, he was a nice guy; I don't have that luxury. She fired three times. Quintana crumpled. Samantha returned the weapon and, followed by Garcés and her driver, walked back to her vehicle. There's no way we can sidestep the confrontation within the government, she thought aloud. Garcés, I want you to take charge; make it absolutely clear who's boss here; tomorrow I'm meeting the Mexico City people in Los Angeles and I want them to know what I'm after. No need to worry, Jefa, rest assured.

Foreman Castelo was waiting nervously. He knew he had sold his soul to the devil and the first thing that would be affected was his reputation. He felt bad about that, he was a serious professional with a certain prestige, and that meeting had ruined his career. He heard the dual-cabin pickup stop at the gate of his Altata house, where Samantha had ordered him to remain. It was past midnight. He stepped outside, Guacho went to position the bodyguards who were travelling in the Hummer behind them. The woman lowered the armoured window. Foreman, ask for whatever you want, I know you like rocking and rolling, but you could also retire, everything that has anything to do with you will be on my tab. I'll think about that, I want you to know how much it pained me to learn of Don Marcelo's passing. I know, he told me once that if I ever had any clean-up problems you were the only sure thing, and did you ever demonstrate your loyalty today. Of all the messes I fell into, not once did your father fail to bail me out. He told me a few stories; though you know already I'm going to spell it out: Foreman, you can count on me exactly the way you counted on my father, let me know what you decide. Do you know who Leo McGiver is? Who wants to know? Lefty Mendieta. Are you still friends with that lowlife? Nobody's perfect. Leo's one of ours, he pretended to sign on with Dioni de la Vega and we learned a few things; plus he got us the weapons we used tonight, could you hear them? they were awesome; now go get some sleep, your wife must be worried. Thank you. Samantha disappeared behind the glass and the vehicle got in gear. I never thought I would retire so young, Foreman mused, I just turned fifty-six. He went inside, splashed gasoline in the corners, lit matches, grabbed the pile of dollars, and ran. He was sobbing.

He had no desire to watch flames consume the house he had built little by little.

What's the story, Adán? are you expecting me to come pick up the money, or what?

Gandhi, the truth is I don't have it, the business is barely taking off and if what happened to Mister B. gets around, I doubt we'll see the volume of customers we need; I know I owe you, but understand that you lent it to me to invest and that's what I did.

I happen to know you did not invest it all there, but that's no concern of mine.

I don't believe you don't understand, you're a businessman.

I am not prepared to get involved in problems, Adán, not yours or anyone else's.

Give me an extension, please.

That was not our deal and now the situation has become complicated, how much is your camp worth?

Don't think you can run me off for that amount, it's worth much more.

I already told you, it's not me. On Tuesday I'll drop by with a notary, just so we're prepared.

What kind of moneylender are you that you can't give me an extension with interest?

One who only lends his friends capital that does not belong to him; so I'll see you Tuesday.

What time?

In the afternoon; listen, are you going to Meraz's funeral?

Gandhi Olmedo heard the click. He smiled.

McGiver was waiting. Dulce Arredondo had at last got hold of "The Two Fridas" and he gave it as a present to Samantha, whom he had not fully convinced even after tipping her off to the conspiracy. He told her about Connolly and thanked her for her protection; however, he knew it was a haemorrhage that would continue to bleed. Twain had made that clear and asked him to back off until further notice, the contacts were already refusing to deal with him. Suddenly, his only option was the cartel.

Forty-Three

It was Sunday and Lefty, utterly exhausted, was lying down. On top of having barely slept, he felt profoundly useless and off his game, every line of investigation had led nowhere. Was Dioni de la Vega the murderer? Nothing pointed to that possibility and he didn't have the energy to confront him. He was drinking Nescafé when his telephone rang; he let it ring, as he had the previous night. Before he finished his coffee it started up again; this time he picked up. It was Win Harrison. Come to the Hotel Lucerna for breakfast, I'm paying. Did you call a few minutes ago? No, this is the first time.

The place was packed, so they sat at the bar. I didn't see you yesterday. I was busy with the investigation the whole time. Any progress? We're at a dead end. By the way, yesterday when I got back to the hotel a man approached me: Are you Jean Pynchon? And who are you? They call me Culichi, did you rent a Cheyenne? Why? The man smiled, I did too, unfortunately they switched them on us. Are you sure? Absolutely, so if it isn't too much trouble. When I told him it had blown up, the colour drained from his face and he gave me the keys to mine and took off. They were served fruit salad, quesadillas, eggs with bacon for Win, and coffee. I thought it would be something hotter, more exciting. Me too, who knows what that guy was up to, he probably wasn't a businessman. With Valdés dead lots of strange people will be coming around, how did it go with Samantha? That woman is stubborn, she refused to tell me anything about Leo McGiver, she's so clever I'm starting to think she really doesn't know anything. I warned you, what are you going to do? Would you like to help me for another twenty-four hours? If you help me. I'm already helping, yesterday a squad located your suspect in Toronto and he confessed: he killed his wife with a Ruger 9mm, he didn't kill Mayra Cabral de Melo, but he did do in Yolanda Estrada; he thought she knew about his crime and he freaked, so he went and got her; I'm told the guy is so overwrought he's sick and he's prepared to do his time here. How decent of him, what can I do for you? When McGiver turns up, let me know; I was going to ask you to take me to Dioni de la Vega, but they killed him last night. Where? You don't know? in Altata. All night the telephone was ringing, maybe that's why.

As soon as he turned on the cell phone, his boss called.

Where are you hiding, Lefty? Hard at work, chief, why? Last night there was a gunfight in Altata and I need you to give Pineda a hand. How many dead? Twenty-two, all members of the Valdés Cartel, which means this is going to turn ugly. Have they identified the bodies? All of them. Tell me who to report to. Pineda, and another thing: Lagarde called all upset, he wants to come back and go to prison, he says the F.B.I. interrogated him. Really? Just the way you're hearing it, he told them he killed his wife. Did he confess anything about Mayra Cabral de Melo? I don't know, the fact is he's about to have a heart attack and he doesn't want any part of Canada; Lefty, you and I had an agreement and I told you clearly that he had nothing to do with your table dancer. I remember. I ordered Lagarde to stay put and I want you on the case of the massacre; hand over the bodies to Ramírez tomorrow and that'll be the end of it. Wait, why are you blaming me for this? You contacted Madrid, Angelita told me, what assurance do I have you didn't do the same thing with the gringos? Chief, don't make stuff up, you know what the F.B.I. brings on in me. Where are you? not long ago I called your house and you didn't answer. I was out jogging, you know, a police officer should stay in shape. In any case, leave Lagarde alone; last night Zelda called Mayra's mother and she'll be here tomorrow, we'll give her the body in accordance with the wishes of Attorney Meraz, who we are going to bury today; oh, and stop by the storeroom for your bulletproof vest, you're going to like it, with all the shit flying we've got to take precautions; and if you don't have plans for lunch, I'm cooking green pea soup, in case you'd like some. Are you cooking olive ridley too? Briseño hung up.

Win and he said goodbye at the door of the Lucerna. Regarding McGiver, any sign of him, let me know; I'm going to track him down anyway, did you know he stayed here? Really? He left yesterday; thanks, Mendieta. Good luck. Would you like me to modify our file on you? If it's to make it worse, yes. Smiles.

At the Forum he looked over the list of movies. He couldn't decide between *16 Blocks* and *300*. He went to El Quijote instead, where he didn't enjoy himself either because it was his friend's day off.

Are you one of those people who thinks Sundays are awful? Well, Lefty is too.

At home he said hello to the dog and to its owners, who were on their way out to six o'clock Mass. Ring. He needed to speak with somebody so he picked up without looking: Fatso's place. Edgar? Fresh, unfamiliar voice. Who is this? Susana Luján, do you remember me? Hey, Susana, of course I do, how are you? I'm well, Edgar, thank God, Enrique told us you're a famous policeman now, he said you've put several drug traffickers in prison and they're even writing a *corrido* about you. Pondering "told us" not "told me", Mendieta decided to be prudent. Any success I've had is thanks to Enrique's advice. It's so nice to hear your voice, really; well, I know he told you about Jason and . . . Heavy silence. Are you there? Yes, I'm listening. Well, I'd like to talk to you about it. Tell me. Not on the telephone, in eleven days we'll be in Culiacán and he's really excited, Enrique told you he wants to meet you. Of course, Susana, it will be a pleasure to speak with you about this matter; yes, I'm excited too. Thank you, Edgar, so we'll see you then.

Christ.

After a horrible night, he answered a call at nearly eight in the morning from Robles. Boss, somebody's been gunned down at the edge of the Rosales Canal in Bacurimí. Call Pineda, that's his specialty. I can't, he's still on the Altata massacre; the chief is busy with that too, they say there are about thirty bodies. You see, all this talk of war was no joke, so there's no-one to go to Bacurimí? They found a voter's card on him in the name of José Rivera Güémez and another I.D. as an employee of the Alexa; it probably has something to do with the case you're investigating. I'm on my way.

I'm sorry for your mother, the detective muttered, you couldn't keep your promise to her. The eyes don't change, he closed them, where did I read that? Shit, in the end everything you manage to say is something you've read. Fucking Parra, he must be thrilled to be farting around with the gringos.

The vehicle's doors were open, he took a good look at the carpets that had been washed recently, the dashboard, the bloodstained seat, a bottle of water in the middle, behind the seat a black umbrella. Everything else spotless. Ready? a young technician had come, his cell phone's one of the good ones. Get me his calls and messages from the past few days. We'll have it all in two hours. Was it an A.K.? We counted thirty-two shells. And only one killed him? Two, in the head. The back window was shattered. They shot at him from behind and from the left.

At a prudent hour he dialled Zelda. Agent Toledo, be careful on the street, they gunned down Rivera in Bacurimí. Listen, boss, if Samantha Valdés becomes head of the cartel we'll have some clout, won't we? What makes you think that? You two know each other at least. They don't need us, Zelda, they have practically the entire Mexican police force and part of the D.E.A. on their side. I was just saying, in case sometime we need something, you remember we gave her a couple of culprits a while back. No-one remembers that, Zelda, are you at home? At the airport, I'm waiting for Mayra Cabral de Melo's mother; I called you on Saturday to let you know the chief gave me the order, but you were disconnected. He mentioned that yesterday, know who killed Yolanda Estrada? No. Lagarde; he confessed. Poor girl, there was nothing special about her, was there? He must have been the one who tore up the picture of the Brazilian team. That's possible, you know how we get when we're upset; listen, I'll take the señora to Headquarters and we can meet up there. Zelda, I don't want to know any more about this case, take her statement and hand over the body, I'm going to buy a bottle of Macallan and do I ever deserve it. Isn't it on the early side?

He was nearing the Col Pop when his cell phone rang. How are you this morning, nuisance? Living off the reputation of the

Mexican police. Bunch of fucking lazy bastards. Lazy your mother, asshole, half the force is working on a mass murder in Altata and I'm on my way back from the Rosales Canal where the sun rose on fourteen bodies. Altata, you say? don't fuck with me, I've got a little house there and I'm on my way there now. It's good of you to turn yourself in, eyewitnesses insist it was a pudgy bastard with an evil face. Your whore of a mother. Listen, the bit about the bodies is true and if you want my advice, don't go, who knows what's up. McGiver is a gunrunner working for the Valdés family. In other words, an upstanding citizen. Now give me my present, asshole, my birthday came and went and you just looked the other way. He hung up.

Trudis met him at the door. What's wrong with you, Lefty? your eyes look like they've seen the devil; have you been out drinking or could it be true that the war on crime is for real? We shall not stop until we have put an end to this terrible scourge of humanity. Bravo, my man Lefty for president, would you like some breakfast? since I didn't see you around, I didn't cook anything; I'll make you some red snapper *chicharrones* this very minute so you can start the day on the right foot. Just coffee, Trudis. There's no Nescafé, it must have run out yesterday, cough up some change so I can go to the Oxxo for a jar. Go to Hilda's, it's closer. I also need cheese, *machaca*, and soap. You can go to Ley later on, now bring me coffee. Before he went into the bathroom, he drank a long guzzle of whisky: Edgar, get in gear, act like you're dumb, don't lose your head, stay cool, if you want to make it to the end so you can scratch your belly at your beach house, you'd better behave like a real policeman. Passion makes you stupid, sadness wastes you away, so wise up. Who cares if there's one nipple less in the world? O.K., you find that intriguing, but don't get stuck, bro, don't get stuck or you'll get lost. In whooshed the image of Bardominos, the priest who abused him when he was eight. He recuperated with a double whisky. I need Parra.

He drank his Nescafé hot. Are you sure you don't want your *chicharrones*? You eat it, if there's any left leave it in the micro. What if the gringo calls? Tell him to call me on the cell phone. That's better, the poor kid, the way you act I can only imagine what happens when my kids call their fathers, it's horrible to think they might be like you. But he isn't my son. Well, he says he is. He told you that? And he told me a few things about his mother; I knew her, she was quite a babe, even I wanted to be pretty like her, she was the best-looking girl in the neighbourhood. Tell me about it later. He escaped. Getting into the Jetta parked in the street, he failed to notice the dog wagging his tail.

He drove about aimlessly, and the emptiness hit him. At last I understand the meaning of being a loser, of living a life without purpose, of practising a profession that has turned out to be useless for solving the case I care most about. Christ, and Jagger goes on as if time doesn't pass, collecting his fans' underwear. However, his mood soon lifted and he put all his attention on John Lennon's "Woman". Cavalry charge. He answered Zelda's call. Boss, forgive me for insisting.

Elena Palencia was dressed modestly. No make-up. She confirmed the football player's story. I want to give my daughter the funeral she deserves, she was such a good girl, obedient and always thinking about retiring; I put away enough money for her to live a good life. She sighed. I know she had a couple of accounts in

Mexican banks. The documents turned up and we'll make sure you get them. It's a huge loss, if you had only met her you would agree. What about her father? A poor fool the two of us pulled out of poverty; we have a business in São Paulo that he manages, but we can't leave him alone for long because his relatives will swindle him; my poor daughter, she wanted a career as an actress; she had the beauty and the talent, too bad you never met her. I did meet her, and as you say she was a wonderful person. Elena looked at Lefty. Are you the policeman from Mazatlán? How did you know? She told me about you, she told me everything, let me see. She opened a hand-bag filled with letters. It was about three months ago. Zelda looked on, amazed. Let's see, your name is, you're a lefty, aren't you? my daughter found that funny. She flipped through several letters and stopped on one. Let me look, she skimmed the page, here it is, hang on: Edgar, your name is Edgar. A smile crossed her lips. She loved to write letters, they were like her diary, her main pastime, and here I've got all of them from the past year. She handed the letter to Lefty, who saw his name. Elena, your daughter had beautiful penmanship, would you let us read a few? Of course, what about the papers, when do we begin? Right now.

Lefty asked Terminator to take Elena to the morgue with an order to hand over the body of Mayra Cabral de Melo. He returned to Zelda. Agent Toledo, if you'd like to glance over these letters, go ahead, I don't want to know anything about anything, all I desire is that bottle I told you about a little while ago. Angelita came in. Boss, Paty Olmedo insists on speaking with you. Tell her I'm not in. I'd hate to do that, she sounds so sad, she's whimpering on the telephone.

Gandhi Olmedo had hoped to meet up with his daughter on Sunday, but she was overcommitted with her friends, or so she said; they agreed to have breakfast on Monday. Paty was always late and this time too; mid-morning she called to apologise, but nobody answered. She went to the house, found the door unlocked and her father in his favourite chair with a bullet-hole in his forehead. Next to him, a bottle of whisky, two glasses, one untouched.

She keened, thinking: he really wasn't so bad, much better than Don José Antonio, who killed his ex and earned the eternal hatred of his son. Marcos had told her all about it. He wasn't ugly either; rough, disdainful, bossy, but not ugly; loyal to his collection of broken guitars. Not a hypocrite either, he told a lot of people the truth about themselves. She stood still a moment longer. And to top it off they killed the woman he liked, poor Papa.

The telephone rang: Yes? Is this the Olmedo family? Who's calling? A friend of Fabián Olmedo's, may I speak with him? He can't come to the telephone. Tell him that McGiver's calling, are you his secretary? I'm his daughter. Ah, how are you? your father told me how fabulous you are, you're his idol. Paty wailed. What's wrong? They killed him, señor, I just found him with a bullet in his head. No kidding, I brought him a piece of a guitar recently and he asked me to get him another, we've been friends since we were kids. Paty nodded, sobbing harder. Oh God, do I feel sad, señor . . . McGiver, Leo McGiver. It was only a few days ago when I realised how much I loved him, how special he was, I'm a mess. Let me tell you something, he built an empire for you, I advise you to seize the reins right now, don't hesitate. I'm not sure that's for me. Of course it is, he told me so not long ago, what's more, he was very troubled about what happened between you. He told you that? He believed in you and he told me as much, he said you were half-crazy, but in your hands his businesses would never fail, and I will be your first customer: I need twelve Hummers by tomorrow, if you've got them armoured all the better, I'll just have to get them checked over to make sure, I'll send for them before three o'clock; charge them all to the companies of the L.E.Q. group which you'll have in your records; since you'll be busy with the funeral, call the secretary and give her the order, and I'll take it up with the managers. She was not crying, she was listening with astonishment to something in her brain that settled comfortably around the smuggler's words. I'm small, she reflected, but the world of business is smaller still. I'll be in touch, he said. Will you stand by me? Listen, I'm about to leave the city, when I get back I'll look you up; what will you do with your father's collection? Continue it. I ask because he ordered a piece from me. Get it. I have something from Kiss in sight. Those faggots? don't even think about it. They said goodbye. Not only must the show go on, the business must too. Paty found herself once more beside the body and she sobbed, sat down, and dialled Mendieta.

Lefty and his team took possession of the place. The neighbours had not seen a thing, neither had they heard the shot. The technicians went over the cell phones and found that his last call had been the day before. Adán Carrasco answered, told them they were friends and it was about business. He was surprised to hear about it.

Cavalry charge. It was Zelda. Boss, you have to come.

Forty-Four

At this late date would they read a letter in which Mayra tells her mother about her fear of being murdered and by whom? Just as I thought, dear reader.

They were driving away from Headquarters listening to "Jumping Jack Flash" at full volume, when he received a call from Samantha Valdés. I need to speak with you, commander. I'm not one of your men, Samantha, I'm too stupid and still a bit honest. Precisely why I'm interested, Lefty Mendieta, you think we don't need honest men in our ranks? though you may not believe it or haven't even thought about it, this business doesn't work without a large dose of loyalty and honesty; internal divisions will wreck any group unless corrective measures are taken immediately. What happened in Altata was kind of vicious, wasn't it? It was necessary. What makes you think you can trust me? Lefty Mendieta, I know I can, or at least my intuition tells me that, and since you want to know, because of the respect my father had for you, even if he never said so, and well, I liked what McGiver told me; suppose we meet in an hour at the Miró. I wouldn't show, we just located the murderer of the girl from the Alexa and we're on our way to get him. Do you need support? He thought about it. It wouldn't be a bad idea, send over six men, the kind that shoot. Where? He gave her directions. Are you sure? Though you may not believe it, as you like to say. He was a friend of my father's. You figure out which side you're on. You are a tough cookie, Lefty Mendieta, they're on their way. Fucking Mick

Jagger, you're not the only one who does exciting things, faggot.

The trip was just long enough for him to recover his anger and run with its momentum.

They arrived at El Continente, which without the Yankee presence felt desolate. A few workers were going about their usual daily tasks. They stopped about twenty metres from the house. On a spot of wet ground, Lefty saw tyre marks he recognised. Zelda nodded when he pointed them out. Behind them, in their new vests, came Terminator, Camel, and two backups carrying A.R.-15s. Terminator waved the workers away, and they complied with a haste worthy of the movies. Adán Carrasco came out to meet them with a smile that hardened instantly. Behind him, his foreman, bristling with weaponry. What can I do for you, detective? he shouted, this time I see you've brought plenty of company. I've come for you, Adán Carrasco, you fucking criminal. What madness is this, detective? you know I'm a man of peace. A murderer is what you are and you're going to pay. I have dual nationality, detective, I fought in two wars and I am a friend of the father of the president of the most powerful country in the world. They each took a step forward. Tell the sap beside you to drop his guns and give yourself up; with all that pull they'll probably extradite you tomorrow. It was hot and humid. Carrasco drew his gun and pointed it at Mendieta, who did the same; the foreman pointed his weapons at the others, who reacted in kind. Before I do away with you, detective, how did you figure it out so fast? it's hard to believe. You left tracks you couldn't cover. Look, the guy made himself difficult, I owed him money and he didn't want to wait, I had to liquidate him, but I don't believe I left any tracks; if the Iraqis didn't break me, you fucking two-bit cops sure won't. He fired, as did the foreman, but they were nervous and the bullets only grazed their targets. Lefty and his people dropped to the ground shooting wildly, while Carrasco and his companion took cover behind the house. Then the police huddled between two parked hunting Jeeps.

A sudden blast from a bazooka made them retreat. Bullets from their A.R.-15s shattered windows and bounced off the wall without doing much damage; the detectives fired with the same result. A second blast from the bazooka set one Jeep aflame and the police froze. Seconds ticked by jaggedly. A third bazooka rocket, fired from the camp gate, hit the wall of the house, as did the fourth. The reinforcements sent by Samantha Valdés had arrived. They were very young. Lefty and Zelda slipped around to the back. Quiroz parked behind patrol car 161 and got out.

When they turned the corner they found themselves face-to-face with Carrasco and his foreman on their way to a dark brown car. The former sharpshooter pointed his gun at Lefty, who broke into a sweat and for the first time in many years was convinced that he did not want to die, he had survived so many things, and retirement was an option that intrigued him; he eyed the weapon directed at him from nine metres away, he saw the murderer move, and he felt dizzy; even so, he pointed the Walther at his opponent's head. Short hair, feral gaze. Zelda did the same. So you took out Fabián Olmedo too. No big deal given what a bastard he was. And who told you you could do that? No kidding, now you have to request authorisation to eliminate a dickhead? The foreman, utterly focussed with his A.K.-47, Carrasco with a 9mm Beretta. Beside them, the window of the room where Win had rescued Lefty. This is where it's all coming to an end, detective, it's a law of war. At that moment four police officers pointing their A.R.-15s joined them, along with a handful of narcos carrying A.K.s, the youngest of whom were carrying calibres that would soon become evident. Wherever you like, "Teddy Bear", you made yourself difficult for Roxana and then you killed her. The foreman prudently placed his Five-seven and his A.K. on the ground and raised his hands. A Barrett 50 punctured the water tank that bore the name of the camp and another shattered the windshield of the car with the wide tyres. Carrasco started shaking. Where did you get that idea, detective? From my balls, asshole. The circle around them tightened, the police looked pleased to have the narcos along. The murderer fell apart, I gave her more than three hundred thousand dollars and I could not win her. Zelda Toledo, alert to every movement, her gun trained on the criminal. So little? She was a bitch, a whore who could never get enough. According to what she wrote her mother, two months ago you adored her. She bewitched me with her body, her fucking dancing, and her unfaithfulness, even Mister B. tasted her pleasures. You mutilated her, why? She was your girlfriend, wasn't she? sure, I was wondering why a Mexican policeman would take such an interest, did she ask you for an engagement ring? Nope, nothing. He brought the pistol to his mouth. Bang. He fell back, work boots, familiar tread. Lefty recalled the explosion of the Cheyenne, when he fell on him he was wearing the same boots. The detectives, wrung out, lowered their weapons.

Just as they had arrived, the narcos vanished.

As in the legend of Benito Juárez untouched by the whirlwind, they were all unscathed.

*

"Dear Mama,

I hope you are well. In my last letter I told you I did not know what to do. Well, I do now. Even though I have the best clients in the world, I'm leaving. Teddy Bear Adán has been insufferable these days, threatening me. I already told you about that, that if I wouldn't go back to him he was going to kill me and who did I think I was. You can see how insulting he's become lately. I could ask my pimp to put him in his place, but I'm afraid. Remember how more than a month ago he forbade me to see Adán? If I let him know I disobeyed it could make things worse. I'll see him today to get money, which I'll send to you. So, the best option for me is to leave. Maybe the next letter I write will be from a different city. Regarding my dad"

In Carrasco's office they found this letter in her handbag. Of the money, no trace. The technicians arrived. Quiroz took several photographs before approaching the detective, who was leaving the building. My man Lefty, when are we going to have a few brews? Brews? a tequila is what I need. A moment later, Zelda Toledo handed him a bottle she pulled out of car 161. He guzzled a healthy dose. Walking towards the Jetta he felt his heart give a thud; he had a hunch, a suspicion, and he returned to Carrasco's body. A puddle of blood. He searched the pockets. Back with Zelda he heard her question, but he did not answer. In his fist he held a plastic bag wrapped in his handkerchief. Why would he have cut off the nipple? He got into the Jetta. Two things were imperative: restoring the integrity of Roxana's body and drinking whisky as God wills.

ÉLMER MENDOZA was born in Culiacán, México in 1949. He is a professor and author, widely regarded as the founder of "narco-lit", which explores drug trafficking and corruption in Latin America. He won the José Fuentes Mares National Literary Prize for *Janis Joplin's Lover*, and the Tusquets Prize for *Silver Bullets*.

MARK FRIED is a literary translator specialising in Latin American literature. He lives in Ottawa, Canada.